"MY GOD, EVERYBODY HEREABOUTS BELIEVES I AM THE MURDERER ROGER BEWLAY!"

"Well!" said Beryl. "Why don't you tell them you're not?"

Bruce studied his clenched fist.

"Angel-face, how many times must I repeat it? I can't! Maybe this morning I could have. I tell you straight, I was just about to call the whole thing off. But not now."

"Why not now?"

Bruce got to his feet. He stretched out his hand towards Beryl. Over his face, as though it were moulding itself there like moving wax, crept a smile. It was a smile of contrition, a smile of repentance, a smile that begged you to take no offence; and yet, at the same time, the smile of one who is deeply misunderstood.

"Well, you see," said Bruce, "there's a dead woman in my bedroom."

CARTER DICKSON

MY LATE WIVES

ZEBRA BOOKS
KENSINGTON PUBLISHING CORP.

ZEBRA BOOKS

are published by

Kensington Publishing Corp.
475 Park Avenue South
New York, NY 10016

First printing: June, 1988

Printed in the United States of America

1

The track of a great murderer, moving deviously from victim to victim, can never be followed step by step or set down as a connected story. How the police wish it could be!

Take, for instance, the matter of Roger Bewlay.

Along the sea-front promenade at Bournemouth, one fine September afternoon, strolled Miss Angela Phipps. Miss Phipps, in her middle thirties, was the daughter of a clergyman: both parents deceased. From an aunt she had recently inherited a small but comfortable legacy which enabled her to give up her work as governess and, as she put it, "look round a bit."

Miss Phipps was not at all bad-looking, to judge by the photographs we now possess. She is described as being brown-haired and blue-eyed, full of fun but very much a lady. And so, on a September afternoon, she strolled along the promenade at Bournemouth in the close-fitting hat and shapeless-waisted frock of that year 1930.

There she met Roger Bewlay.

It must not be considered surprising that this stranger, to put it bluntly, so easily picked up a parson's daughter of blameless life. On the contrary, it was almost too easy.

Like so many women of the so-called genteel class, painfully and rigorously brought up, Angela Phipps hid behind those calm eyes a hunger for romantic love and a capacity for physical passion which would have astounded her few friends. And in these matters—so Roger Bewlay might have informed you—everything depends on the approach. The chance of a rebuff lies not in your intentions, but in your manner of expressing those intentions.

And the quiet, courteous stranger, with his charming smile and his cultured voice, made no mistake.

In three days he had swept her into such an impassioned whirlpool of emotion that she could hardly write a coherent letter to her solicitor. They were married a fortnight later, at a registry office in London, and Mr. Bewlay took her away to an idyllic half-timbered cottage which he had rented furnished outside Crowborough in Sussex. A few neighbours saw her, flushed with happiness, during the month of the honeymoon. The paper-boy noticed her one afternoon in the twilight, sweeping dead leaves from the crazy-paved path, in that season of the yellowing leaves and the rising mists.

Nobody ever saw her again.

"My wife and I," the likable Mr. Bewlay told a sympathetic bank-manager, "must go back to London. I believe—let me see—we opened a joint account, in both our names, when we thought we might be staying on here?"

"That is correct, Mr. Bewlay."

"We will just close it up for cash, if you don't mind. My wife," he laughed, "talks of our going to America, and we may need funds quickly. This is my wife's signature, under mine."

All bills had been settled on the nail; the rent of the

cottage was paid. Mr. Bewlay left that night by car, apparently with his wife. No one wondered; no guilt cried to heaven; and (mark this) no trace of a body was ever found.

We next hear of Roger Bewlay, two years later, when he met Elizabeth Mosnar during a concert of the London Philharmonic at Queen's Hall.

Elizabeth was a thinnish, artistic, desperately sincere blonde of thirty-two. Like Angela Phipps, she had a little money which allowed her to dabble at piano-studies. Like Angela, she was alone in the world except for a brother who never bothered over her whereabouts anyway.

Elizabeth wept when she heard great music. She said she was spiritually lonely. We can imagine those two in the stalls at Queen's Hall—the fervour of music, strings and wood-winds rising to a triumphant cymbal-clash—while Elizabeth bent forward in absorption, and the stranger's hand slid tenderly over her own.

They were married in a tiny church in Bayswater, near Elizabeth's chaste lodgings, Mr. Bewlay using the name of Roger Bowdoin. In the drowsiness of summer they went down to a cottage which Mr. Bewlay had rented in the country between Denham and Gerrard's Cross.

He bought her a piano. Neighbours might have heard the sound of it, ecstatically; but not for long. Just before she disappeared from this world, Elizabeth made over her property to her husband.

"I don't understand business, my darling," she whispered. "*You'll* know how to take care of it."

The only things that remained of her, presently, were a few pitiful trinkets and a very bad water-colour sketch which she had been trying to make of her beloved husband. The next tenant of the cottage, unsuspicious, swept them all into the dustbin.

But the third victim?

We can understand the thrifty financial reasons which made Mr. Bewlay dispose of his first two wives. Andrée Cooper, the third victim, belongs to a different category.

Andrée had no money. She was only twenty. She worked—of all jobs—as a palmist's assistant in Oxford Street. She was a little Cockney, hardly of the intellect or education to appeal to Mr. Bewlay, though of considerable and flamboyant sex-appeal. Mr. Bewlay found her in a corner of the Bone Street Underground Station, crying because she thought she was going to get the sack.

"Poor little girl!" said Mr. Bewlay.

He comforted her. He bought her clothes—not many, because he was a thrifty man—and took her for a holiday. He did not trouble to marry her, perhaps considering this an excess of virtue. In the spring of 1933 he took her north, to a bosky cottage near Scarborough, where the whole gruesome business was repeated; and in some fashion *she* disappeared.

Andrée Cooper, be it repeated, had no money. There was no apparent reason for murdering her. Here enters the first hint of the abnormal, the underlying horror, which ran like a drum-beat beneath all these vanishings. And Roger Bewlay made his first bad mistake.

For Andrée had a boy-friend, who grew frantic and went to Scotland Yard.

"It ain't like 'er!" he kept insisting. "It ain't like 'er!"

Now the police are not deaf or blind. A bulletin, called the *Gazette*, circulates daily to every police-station in the United Kingdom. It puts each divisional inspector in closer touch with each other than you are with your next-door neighbour, and all information is pooled at C-One of the Metropolitan Police. Gradually there began to accumulate a collection of hints about a certain man—called variously Roger Bewlay, Roger Bowdoin, and Richard Barclay—which did not make pleasant reading.

It was our old friend Chief Inspector Masters, one summer day in 1934, who went with this file to the office of the Assistant Commissioner for the Criminal Investigation Department.

Masters, large and urbane, bland as a card-sharper, with his grizzled hair carefully brushed to hide the bald spot, put down the file on the Assistant Commissioner's desk.

"You sent for me, sir?"

The Assistant Commissioner, a mild-looking grey-haired little man who smoked a short pipe, nodded without taking the pipe out of his mouth.

"About Bewlay, sir?"

"Yes."

"Oh, ah!" breathed Masters, and his apoplectic colour came up in spite of himself. "This time, sir, we've found a proper swine and no mistake."

The Assistant Commissioner took the pipe out of his mouth and cleared his throat.

"We can't touch him," he said.

"Can't touch him, sir?"

"Not yet, anyway. If he killed these women—"

"*If!*" snorted Masters.

"Then what's he done with the bodies? Where's your evidence of death?"

There was a silence, while Masters stood at attention with his arms straight down at his sides. It was very hot in the office, with its overpowering odour of old stone. Even so, Masters thought his chief's face was looking a little strained and strange.

The Assistant Commissioner touched a note-pad on the desk.

"'The Laurels, Crowborough'," he read in his soft

9

voice. "'Fairway View, Denham. Deepdene, Scarborough'." He brushed his hand softly on the note-pad. "All cottages known to have been inhabited by Bewlay. For months our people have been digging and sounding and prying and searching. Nothing, Masters!"

"I know, sir! But . . ."

"Not so much as a tooth-stopping or a bloodstain or any presumptive evidence of death. It won't do."

The Assistant Commissioner raised his pale eyes.

"Suppose," he went on, "Bewlay maintains these women are still alive? That they left him of their own free will?"

"But if they don't come forward . . ."

"It isn't Bewlay's business to prove the women are still alive. It's our business to prove they're dead. If we can."

"He married 'em, sir. We could get him for bigamy."

"Five years? Two years, even, if the judge adds hard labour? No, Masters. That's not good enough for *this* gentleman."

"I'm bound to admit I agree with you, sir. All the same—"

"Where's Bewlay now? Have you traced him?"

This was the real reason of the weight on Masters's mind. It made him steam in his blue serge, and stand still straighter, and speak with powerful dignity to the sunlit windows behind his companion's head.

"No, sir, I have NOT traced him. And, if you don't mind my saying so, it's a hundred to one against tracing him if you want to keep this too much hush-hush and won't send out a general alarm."

"I wasn't blaming you, Chief Inspector. I was only . . ."

Masters ignored this with bursting dignity.

"'Tisn't," he pointed out, "as if the chap had ever done time, and we had a record of him. 'Tisn't as if I had a photograph, or even a decent description. Sir, I must have talked to two dozen people who met that chap, and not one of 'em is even sure what he looked like!"

"That's not unusual, Chief Inspector."

Though Masters knew this as well as the Assistant Commissioner, he was not prepared to concede the point.

"The men," Masters went on, "don't seem to have noticed him at all. The women—oh, ah! They all agree he was," Masters mimicked heavily, "'awfully attractive,' but they can't say what the attractiveness was."

"Ah!" said the Assistant Commissioner, putting the pipe back in his mouth.

"Tall or short? Oh, medium tall. Light or dark? Not sure. Colour of eyes? Not sure, but very nice eyes. Distinguishing marks or features? Can't remember. Lummy!" breathed Masters. "All I'm sure of about the chap," he wound up, "is that he's about thirty years old, he's got the manner of a gentleman; and—"

"And?" prompted the Assistant Commissioner.

"God help any woman he makes love to."

"Thank you. I can quite see that."

"So if you ask me whether I've traced him, sir, I can only reply that I have *not* traced him. If he calls himself Robinson, and lives at a quiet hotel and behaves himself, how in lum's name *can* I trace him? 'Tisn't as though we could tell what name he'd be using, or where he might be now . . ."

His companion held up a frail hand for silence.

"I think I know where he is now," said the Assistant Commissioner. "That's why I sent for you. I'm afraid he's done it again."

Silence.

"You mean he's—hurrum!—got rid of another one?"

"I'm afraid so. Yes."

11

Again for a moment there was no sound but Masters's noisy breathing.

"Oh, ah. I see. Where, sir?"

"Just outside Torquay. The Chief Constable phoned through not ten minutes ago. It's Bewlay, right enough. He's disposed of the body again."

And so unrolled the last move of the *danse macabre,* in which a certain gentleman's unshakable self-assurance once more carried him through.

Late in June, it developed, a Mr. and Mrs. R. Benedict had rented a furnished bungalow in the red hills behind the fashionable seaside resort of Torquay. They brought no servant, no car, and very little luggage. They appeared to be newlyweds, the bride-groom about thirty and the bride some half a dozen years older. Their behaviour was "very lover-like"; the girl remained aloof from company and all that could be noticed of her was that she seemed over-fond of wearing jewellery.

The police had no real reason for suspicion. This name R. Benedict was possibly, even probably, the merest of coincidences. Nevertheless the fact was noted by a constable, who passed it on to his sergeant, who passed it on to the inspector. The inspector began discreet inquiries, and set a night-watch on the bungalow.

Mrs. Benedict was last seen on the afternoon of July 6th, 1934, taking tea with her husband in a little garden shaded by apple-trees.

Early on the morning of July 7th, the front door of the bungalow opened. Roger Bewlay, alias R. Benedict, came out. Though the day was fine, Mr. Bewlay wore a hat and a raincoat. He walked straight up to police-constable Harris, lurking in the hedge after an all-night vigil, and wished the constable good morning.

"But the description, man!" Chief Inspector Masters

12

was later to rave, when he interviewed P.C. Harris at Torquay. "We wanted a full-face close-up description, and there was your chance!"

"I'll tell you God's truth," said the unfortunate constable. "I was so rattled, him coming up like that, that—well, I didn't get it."

"You were rattled," Masters said sourly. "Oh, ah! That was why he did it. Hasn't anybody in your ruddy district got a camera?"

"We were told, sir, not to get close enough to alarm him! Peterson did get one or two snapshots, but they're from a long distance off and he's wearing sun-glasses."

"All right! All right! Go on!"

Pleasantly informing P.C. Harris that he was walking the half-mile to the nearest shop for cigarettes and the morning paper, according to his custom, Mr. Bewlay set off down the road. He did not go to this shop. Instead he caught the nine-fifteen train for London, and faded away among crowds.

In the silent bungalow, two hours later, the police found a few odds and ends of clothing—his own as well as the woman's—which Mr. Bewlay had been compelled to leave behind. They found a few toilet articles, like other surfaces carefully cleansed of fingerprints.

But they did not find any jewellery. And they did not find the wife. It was several days before Chief Inspector Masters, digging into the evidence, unearthed a witness who for the first time could bring Roger Bewlay into the shadow of the gallows.

"We've got him!" exulted Masters. *"We've got him!"*

In Menzies Street, Torquay, was the small typewriting bureau of Miss Mildred Lyons, typist and notary public. On the morning of July 6th, Mr. Bewlay had telephoned from a public call-box, there being no phone at the bungalow, and asked whether she could come out there to do some letters.

13

Miss Lyons, a terrified freckled girl amid a ring of policemen, told her story in a dusty little office in Menzies Street.

"I w-went out on my bicycle, early in the afternoon," the witness said. "He dictated six letters, and I took them down straight to the typewriter. They were business letters. No, I didn't taken any note of the addresses."

"Don't you even remember what the letters were about?"

"No. They were just b-business letters."

"Go on, miss!"

"We were in the living-room. The window curtains were nearly closed, and he was sitting over in shadow. Mrs. Benedict kept running in and out of the room, to kiss him. It was terribly embarrassing. When I left he told me to leave the letters behind, open, for him to post himself."

Whereupon Roger Bewlay paid the typist's fee with a bad ten-shilling note.

He didn't do this deliberately, Masters decided. It was simply the unforeseen chance which inevitably, if the police can wait long enough, will trip up any murderer who ever lived. But its effect had been considerable on a freckled red-haired girl, now shivering beside a typewriter and plucking at its keys as though they gave her courage.

"I was *furious*," Miss Lyons declared, bobbing her head. "I didn't discover it until—well, until I went into the bar of the Esplanade at half-past nine that night; and then I was *f-furious*. Before I'd thought of what was decent or dignified, I got on my bike to go out there and tell him about it."

And then?

It was a warm night, she explained, with brilliant

14

moonlight over the deep leafy lanes. By the time she had cycled to the bungalow, Miss Lyons found her courage oozing away and her mind growing a little uneasy.

Any reason for that? No: no definite reason. It was only that it had gone ten o'clock; the house lay quiet and apparently unlighted; and her errand began to seem absurd. Then there was the effect of the night, and the glimmering apple-trees, and the utter loneliness. If she had known then that two police-constables— Harris and Peterson—were watching the bungalow, things might have been different.

As a sort of compromise she propped her bicycle softly against the gate-post, went softly up the path, and half-heartedly pressed the electric bell. There was no reply. That was not surprising, since the bell had never worked. But a spark of anger rose again in Miss Lyons when she saw a light, through imperfectly-drawn curtains, in a window immediately to the right of the door.

That light burned in the living-room. Moved both by wrath and the human curiosity we all feel, Mildred Lyons tiptoed over and peered in.

Then she stood paralysed. Her description, later, ran badly thus:

The room was lighted only by an oil lamp, in a yellow silk shade, hanging from the ceiling. The flame of the lamp had been turned low. And all human evil seemed to breathe out of that room.

On a couch against one wall lay the body of Mrs. Benedict: clothing disordered, stocking torn, one shoe fallen. Mrs. Benedict was dead. She had undoubtedly been strangled, since her swollen face was discoloured and there was a "bulgy kind of crease" round her neck. Roger Bewlay, breathing hard, stood in the middle of

15

the room lighting a cigarette.

Or, again, if Miss Lyons had screamed at that moment . . .

But she was incapable of it. What she could not forget was the dim, mean light; the dim, mean throttling; the murderer solacing himself with tobacco as soon as violent agitation had died away.

Miss Lyons turned round like a sleepwalker. She walked quietly down to the gate, and managed the bicycle without too much stumbling on the pedals. Only when she was well away from the bungalow did she begin to pedal like a madwoman. *She* wasn't going to say anything! *She* wasn't going to get dragged into the mess! She wouldn't have said anything, either—and be bothered to you!—if the watching police hadn't come round to enquire why she had gone to the bungalow at all.

After this confession, Mildred Lyons had hysterics. Chief Inspector Masters, though he patted her shoulder soothingly, reached with his other hand for the office telephone and put through a trunk-call to London.

"We've got him!" Masters said, to the Assistant Commissioner at the other end of the line. "This is good enough presumptive evidence of death. With that girl in the witness-box, we've got him!"

"Are you sure?" asked the Assistant Commissioner.

Masters stared at the telephone.

"For one thing," the Assistant Commissioner said, "we shall have to catch him first. You see no difficulties in that?"

"No, sir, I don't! All we've done so far is say in the Press we're 'anxious to interview' this chap. But you let me send out a general alarm, an all-out hunt . . ."

"Er—you wouldn't like to have a word with your friend Sir Henry Merrivale on the matter?"

"Sir, there's no call to trouble the old man about this!

16

Just give me the word to go ahead . . . thank you, sir . . . and wherever he is, so help me, we'll nobble that bounder inside a fortnight!"

Masters was wrong.

These events took place eleven years ago, with smoke and death and the wreckage of continents in between, but they did not catch Roger Bewlay. He had all the luck. His unshakable self-assurance did not desert him. They would never catch him now; he was safe.

2

One early September night, with the street-lamps shining again to mark the end of Hitler's war, Mr. Dennis Foster made his way down lower Charing Cross Road towards the Granada Theatre.

Lower Charing Cross Road is not a very inspiring street. The back of the National Gallery with its blind windows, the bricked-up statue of Henry Irving, the air-raid shelter not yet pulled down, were ever-present reminders.

Yet the dazzle of those tall street-lamps, still a miracle after several months, changed everything. They shone reflected in the road. They seemed unearthly, a carnival after black years. They touched the old city with magic. And young Mr. Dennis Foster—junior partner of the law firm of Mackintosh and Foster—walked with an even more buoyant step.

"I'm looking pleased," he said to himself. "And I mustn't look pleased. It's fatuous."

For he was going to the Granada Theatre.

Not to see the play, which he had seen several times during its two-year run. No; he was going there at the request of Miss Beryl West, the producer; he was going back-stage to see his friend, one of the leading junior actors of the English stage; and afterwards they were going on to the Ivy Restaurant.

"This," thought Dennis, "is seeing life!"

Dennis Foster was a sound Conservative, a member of the Reform Club, one of those people who View with Alarm. For his black Homburg hat to his brief-case and rolled umbrella, he was as correct as training could make him. To him the realm of the stage was a strange, dangerous jungle, filled with a romance and glamour of which he did not quite approve. If the truth must be told, Dennis was something of a stuffed shirt.

But this does not tell all the truth. Dennis Foster, recently demobbed from the Royal Navy after wounds gained from four years' service in three destroyers, might be a little too serious-minded. But he was so thoroughly honest, so much himself and without affectation, that everybody liked him and everybody trusted him.

In his heart, he admitted to himself, he was secretly pleased at this more-than-nodding acquaintance with the world of the theatre, just as he was pleased at being acquainted with a real-life Chief Inspector from Scotland Yard. But there were some puzzling things in it. For instance . . .

The Granada Theatre is just below the Garrick. Over the iron canopy of the doors to the foyer, staring white metal letters read BRUCE RANSOM in PRINCE OF DARKNESS. Across withering posters, in the same place for two years, had now been pasted diagonally a narrow strip of paper reading *Final Performance September 8th*. And at the foot of the poster, below all the other names, you could see "The play produced by Beryl West."

"Dennis! Hullo!" called a girl's voice.

And Beryl herself, looking a little anxious and

20

uneasy, was waiting for him at the entrance to the foyer.

Dennis had never quite got used to the idea of a woman producer. He had expected producers to be people who tear their hair and jump up and down in the aisles (which, God knows, they often do). But he had attended a rehearsal once, long ago, and marvelled at the deft, quiet way in which this comparatively young girl handled Bruce Ransom.

"I understand him, you see," she had explained. "He's a baby, really."

"Don't let Bruce hear you say that."

"No fear! I won't."

The clock of St. Martin's-in-the-Field now indicated a quarter to nine, that empty time just before the theatres are out. Under its high pale lights, Charing Cross Road was so quiet that Dennis could hear a radio talking in the amusement-arcade between the Garrick and the Granada. He hurried forward to greet Beryl.

Her face was partly in shadow, with the lights of the deserted marble-paved foyer behind her. Beryl had a light coat thrown across her shoulders, and a blue silk scarf bound peasant-fashion round her very thick, very black and glossy hair. In contrast the eyes were dark blue, set wide apart under thin brows, and a little prominent as in the case of very imaginative people. Her complexion was exquisite, set off by a soft mobile mouth which expressed many moods.

For Beryl was a person of impulses—all of them generous ones—moods, quick eagernesses, of a breathless and rather ethereal quality. She never seemed in repose. Her hands, her quick-moving eyes, every line of her slender body expressed it. Her face lighted up, her arms went out, when she caught sight of Dennis.

"Darling!" said Beryl, and put up her face sideways

21

to be kissed.

Dennis kissed her with reluctance, inclining his head slowly and stiffly like a man about to be beheaded. Beryl laughed delightedly as she drew back.

"You don't like it, Dennis: do you?"

"Like what?"

"This awful theatrical habit of people rushing up and kissing each other when they meet?"

"To be quite frank, I don't," retorted Dennis, with what he hoped was immense dignity. He had not intended to make the next remark; but it had been in his mind for so long that he blurted it out. "When I kiss a girl," he said, "I want it to mean something."

"Darling! Does that mean you might go berserk and sweep me all over the foyer?"

"I never meant anything of the kind!" Dennis said hotly—though perhaps, in his heart of hearts, he had.

Then Beryl's mood changed. She took his hands and drew him into the deserted foyer.

"Dennis, I'm most awfully sorry!" she told him, with a pouring contrition out of all proportion to the offence. It was as though, spiritually, she wanted to grovel on the floor. "You see, I asked you here because I need your advice. I do so want you to talk to Bruce. You seem to be one of the few people who have any influence over him."

Aha!

This was much better. Dennis Foster inclined his head gravely and pursed up his lips with a suitable portentousness.

"It *is* serious!" the girl assured him, with her great eyes searching his face.

"Well! We must see what we can do. What's the trouble?"

Beryl hesitated.

"I suppose you know," she nodded vaguely in the

22

direction of the posters outside, "the show's closing day after to-morrow?"

"Yes."

"And I can't even stay for the farewell party, I'm afraid. I'm off to the States to-morrow afternoon."

"To the States, by George! Are you!"

"It's to oversee the Broadway opening of the show: American cast, of course. I shall only be gone for three weeks. In the meantime," she hesitated, "Bruce is going down for a long holiday to some poky country place he selected out of Bradshaw. He's going under an assumed name (isn't that *like* Bruce?), to fish and play golf and vegetate."

"It'll do him good, Beryl."

"Yes! But that isn't the point!" She threw out her arms. "We've got to talk to him *now,* don't you see? Otherwise, by the time I get back, he'll be so set in his mind that nobody will be able to move him. It's about this play."

"Prince of Darkness?"

"No, no! The new play he means to do when he's had a long rest."

Beryl's teeth fastened into her smooth pink lower-lip. The colour that came and went under her too-fair skin, making her seem a decade younger than her thirty years, all the intense vitality which added to this youthfulness, became heightened by doubt and indecision.

"The curtain will be down in ten minutes," she added abruptly, and glanced at her wrist-watch. "Shall we have a look inside?"

They descended the curve of a long flight of padded steps between narrow walls in this old over-decorated theatre, a subterranean hush of dim-white and rose-pink, and emerged into the darkness at the back of the stalls.

A faint haze, as though from the dust of make-up, tingled in their nostrils. Dennis saw the stage as a bright enchanted blur, with bullet-heads and motionless back silhouetted against it. Hardly a cough or rustle struck against that hollowness. Miss Magda Verne, who played opposite Bruce, was mopping up the stage in one of her famous emotional scenes which intensely annoyed actors but enthralled out-of-town visitors. Bruce's own fine voice and personality—odd, off the stage, how stolid he often seemed!—flowed out over the footlights as a palpable force larger than life.

But Beryl West, after contemplating this for some time, wriggled and shifted from one foot to the other and drew a deep breath and finally made a gesture of utter hopelessness.

"Oh, dear!" she whispered.

"What's wrong?"

"Dennis, it's a good thing this show *is* closing. It's ghastly! They keep on drying . . . Bruce did it again just now . . ."

Dennis stared at her in the gloom.

"You mean they forget their lines after two years?"

"But that's just the trouble!"

"How so?"

"They know the words so well that it's become automatic. They play a scene and think about something else. In the middle of some tense situation Bruce will find himself thinking 'H'm, that's a nice-looking blonde sitting third from the aisle in the fourth row; wonder who she is?' Then all of a sudden he has to deliver a line, and he can't remember where he was before; so he dries."

"They must all be pretty well fed up, I imagine?"

"Terribly!" Beryl shook her head with some vehemence. "And they *will* insist on playing the part differently, anything for a novelty from the way I've

24

taught 'em, and upsetting everything. And they get fits of the giggles over nothing at all; they're just as apt to burst out laughing in each other's faces. Look at that dreadful exhibition there! Just look at it!"

To Dennis it seemed no different from the play as viewed on other occasions. But he had a disturbing glimpse into the essential humanity, the utter boredom and nerve-strain, behind this façade of make-believe. He glanced sideways at his companion.

"You were saying, Beryl?" he prompted. "About the new play Bruce plans to do?"

Beryl was silent for a moment, lifting her shoulders, while voices from the stage rang thinly.

"Heaven knows," she declared, "I don't object to Bruce's playing a murderer."

"A murderer?"

"Yes. For one thing, it'll be such a lovely change from all those plays where he's the urbane aristocrat in diguise, who penetrates into the bosom of a suburban family—God, darling, a play about family life *can't* fail in England!—and solves all the tangles, and in the third act discovers he's been in love all along with the girl he's been treating as a Good Friend."

Beryl laughed under her breath, with rather more thoroughness (it seemed to Dennis) than the subject called for.

"And," he suggested, "you don't like the idea of this new play?"

"On the contrary, Dennis! It's got a tre-mendous theme. That's why it mustn't be bungled. That's why . . ."

"*Sh-h-h!*"

A curving hiss, boiling up into several hisses like a snake-pit, echoed out of the gloom. Angry faces were craned round to protest at this mutter of voices from the back of the stalls.

"Come on," whispered Beryl, and plucked at his arm.

They crept round to the left, down the end aisle to the iron-door that led back-stage. Dennis, the back of his neck hot with embarrassment, felt that all eyes were following him. Only beyond, in a dust-breathing dimness shadowed by tall flats, where the voices of the actors had a disembodied quality which seemed to come from the air all about, did his ruffled feelings smooth down.

They found Bruce Ransom's dressing-room empty except for Toby, the dresser, who was on his way out to fetch Mr. Ransom's Guinness.

"Sit down," said Beryl, flinging her scarf and coat across a sofa. "I want you to be ready to tackle him."

The dressing-room was a spacious airless place, rather like a well-furnished hotel sitting-room except for the big mirror over the dressing-table, the wash-basin with hot and cold, and the built-in wardrobe covered by a flowered curtain. Its lights were yellow, subdued, and soothing. Noises penetrated here only with a muted and muffled quality, shut away from the world. Bruce Ransom's mascot for the run, a stuffed spotted dog, contemplated them with dispirited glass eyes from among cosmetics on the dressing-table.

Dennis, sinking back into a brown-upholstered easy chair with his hat, umbrella, and brief-case beside him, frowned across at Beryl.

"You said," he continued, "something about a murderer. What is the thing, anyway? A mystery play?"

"No, no, no! It's based on the real-life case of Roger Bewlay. Did you ever hear of Roger Bewlay?"

Dennis sat up as though he had been stung.

"You don't mean," he said incredulously, "Bruce is going to play the part of Roger Bewlay?"

"Yes. Though he's called by another name in the

26

play, of course. Why ever not?"

"No reason at all, except . . . it's an ugly business, Beryl. Bewlay's probably still alive, you know."

"And," smiled Beryl, "the police are still looking for him. They'll hang him if he's ever found. Somehow I don't think he'll sue for libel."

"No; but it wouldn't be pleasant for your leading lady to find him in her dressing-room one night. And how are you going to solve the mystery?"

"What mystery?"

Beryl shook back the glossy black hair which hung almost to her shoulders. She was sitting forward on the edge of the sofa, her hands clasped round one knee, and an eager rapt brooding look on her face. Now the dark-blue eyes woke up.

"My dear Beryl, listen! Roger Bewlay killed at least four women."

"Horrible!" said Beryl dreamily. "Audiences would eat it up." And she nodded very vigorously.

Dennis disregarded this.

"Bewlay," he pursued, "specialised in women without relatives. His first victim was a clergyman's daughter, his second a music-student, his third a palmist's assistant, and his fourth . . . well, they never could find out *who* she was, or anything about her."

"Dennis! How on earth do you know so much about this?"

"As it happens, one of my friends is the Scotland Yard man who handled the case."

"Oo-er!" breathed Beryl, with a quaintly childlike inflection and widening of the eyes. She sat up straight. She was really impressed.

"The point it, Beryl, that Bewlay killed these women. Then in some fashion that looked like black magic he disposed of the bodies. How did he do it?"

"Buried 'em, maybe," answered Beryl, with the

27

casualness of one who has never met such horrors in the flesh. "Burnt 'em perhaps. *Anything!*"

"I'm afraid that won't do."

"Darling, why not?"

(He wished she wouldn't call him "darling" in that casual fashion she applied to everybody.)

"Chief Inspector Masters," he went on, "quite properly won't tell you much about the final murder. That's reserve-evidence, a card up the sleeve, if they ever do catch Bewlay. All I can gather is that they have a witness who actually saw the fourth victim after she was dead.

"The point is, it's an impossibility! On the night of the murder, two policemen were watching the house front and back. They testified that not a soul, except Bewlay himself, left that house between the time the woman died and the time they broke in next morning. The victim was inside, and remained inside. Yet, by the time they broke in, Bewlay had disposed of the body."

"I . . . I didn't know that," said Beryl, a little troubled. She flung this away. "And, anyway, it doesn't matter."

"Doesn't matter?"

"Not for the purposes of the play."

Beryl got to her feet. She began to pace about the soft-carpeted room, her arms folded, with little short stiff-kneed steps. Again she was deep in a dream.

"If only," she cried, "if *only* Bruce will agree to alter that utterly impossible ending, I think I might do fine things with it." She broke off. "What does matter, Dennis, is the character of Bewlay. That's what I keep thinking about. It repels me and yet it fascinates me. What was the man like, really?"

Dennis grunted.

"He was abnormal. There can't be much doubt about that."

28

"No; but," she hesitated, "I mean, what was he like to live with? What did he think of any of these women? Did he ever have any pity? What did he think about, for instance, when he was lying beside her in the dark after they'd just . . . am I shocking you?"

"Damn it, woman, I'm not exactly a child in rompers."

"No, but you're a darling old sludgy slow-coach," said Beryl, suddenly rushing over to pat Dennis's cheek with exaggerated if genuine tenderness, and suddenly rushing away again. She resumed her pacing, with dignity. He could have laughed at her if she had not been so sincere.

"I won't touch it," she declared vehemently, "if Bruce keeps that awful ending. I won't! But I want to *see* Bewlay. I want to understand him. You see, Dennis,"—she swung round—"I said it didn't matter how he disposed of the bodies. And it doesn't. Because the theme of the play isn't, what happened to Bewlay while he was committing the murders? The theme is, what happened to him—afterwards?"

3

"Afterwards," Dennis repeated.

The curtain was down. They could tell this by the distant sound of applause, first a faint spatter, then deepening and shaking and running through the corridors of the old theatre like a noise of heavy rain. It rose, died, and rose again; by it you could mark the number of curtain-calls.

In this brown-upholstered room, with its drowsy yellow lights, that noise seemed to come from another world. Beryl West scarcely heard it.

"Afterwards!" Dennis said again.

"Take Bewlay," the girl pursued, "or Jack the Ripper, or any other mass-murderer who's never been caught."

"Well?"

"Well! The series of murders ends. Maybe his—his wish to kill is satisfied, or maybe he just gets scared because the police are so close. Anyway, it's finished. But he's still the same man. What happens to him then?"

"All right; what does happen to him then? And, by the way, who wrote the play?"

A shade of perplexity crossed Beryl's face, whose

expressive colour came and went with each new enthusiasm.

"It was written," she answered, "by somebody I never heard of. It came to Bruce out of the blue."

"How do you mean?"

"Well, hundreds of people keep sending manuscripts to Bruce. Mostly he hires a reader to deal with 'em. But occasionally, when he's got nothing better to do, he picks up one himself. That happened in this case. Then he rang me up at one o'clock in the morning and said it was the play for him."

"And it is a good play? Technically, that is?"

"Dreadful!" said Beryl instantly—as all producers do. "I mean, it's written by somebody with a sense of the stage, but with absolutely no experience. I shall have to rehash it. And the ending: dear heaven, the ending!"

"Then . . . ?"

"Bruce has written to the author; at least, I hope he has; he's terribly careless about things like that." Beryl brooded. "But in spite of everything it's got a terrific idea . . ."

"It's a dangerous idea, Beryl."

Beryl stopped pacing and looked at him.

Distantly, they could hear the theatre orchestra strike up The King. Its strains floated back, stately, against a shuffling hush; then the shuffle became a crescendo, rumbling inside this shell, as people pressed toward the exits. Little Beryl West looked as though all the troubles of the world, which she had done nothing to deserve, were now piled on her shoulders.

"Dangerous?" she cried.

"May I remind you again that Bewlay is still alive? And that it mightn't be pleasant to find him back-stage one night?"

"Sometimes, Dennis Foster, I think you have a

32

horrible mind."

"I'm sorry. There it is."

"You make the whole thing sound so *real!*"

"Why not? It is real."

"Somehow," muttered Beryl, "I don't think of it as that. At least, I don't want to." Again she folded her arms, the dark-blue eyes intent on problems of production.

"How to convey," she said, "that character across the footlights! How to get the smarmy charm that changes into something else! And the heroine, Dennis! How to convey the heroine's stupidity! For practically the whole play she never dreams, or at least refuses to believe, that this man . . ."

"Hel-lo, Dennis!" said a new voice. And Bruce Ransom stood in the open door of the dressing-room.

Off the stage, as Dennis had so often noticed, Bruce was tallish and wide-shouldered, unobtrusive and quiet-spoken. You saw a personality there, of course; but you only saw it after a second look. The dark hair cut close to the head; the broad face with its high cheek-bones under sleepy-looking eyes; the broad mouth accentuating the cheek-bones with its slow-curving smile: all these were unobtrusive. It was only on the stage that he blazed up into a kind of incandescence, an amiable *diablerie*.

And every quality was heightened by costume and make-up.

If you saw *Prince of Darkness* during its long run at the Granada, you may remember that in the third act Bruce wore evening-clothes, with a diamond cross under the white tie, and a great black cape lined with scarlet silk. These gaudy fripperies lighted the dressing-room now, like the colours of make-up. That orange-pink make-up, staring at close range, turned his face into a high-cheekboned mask: twinkling brown eyes outlined in black, and gleaming teeth, very different from the man in real life.

For it was not difficult to determine the reason for Bruce Ransom's immense personal popularity among his own people, among stage-folk. He may have possessed conceit. But he never showed it. Bruce knew his job. He really was a first-class actor, despite the hokum in which he so often played. And yet, though he could hardly be called a youngster (Bruce was forty-one), he was as serious-minded and unaffected as one just learning.

Dennis Foster had expected to find him dog-tired. But to an actor the end of each performance brings a buoyancy, a lift of relief, that the infernal thing is finished for one more night. Standing in the doorway in a ripple of scarlet silk, Bruce roared over his shoulder to Toby, his dresser, who was following him along the passage.

"Toby!"

"Sir?"

"Got the Guinness?"

"Coming, sir."

"I could eat a house," declared Ransom, rubbing his hands together. He shooed Toby ahead of him into the dressing-room, and then closed the door. "Somebody's remembered to book a table, I hope? Good, good, good! Won't keep you five minutes."

Putting down bottle and glass on the dressing-table, Toby deftly removed Ransom's scarlet-lined cape. The dress-coat and waistcoat followed, then tie and collar, then starched shirt. Ransom drew the trouser-braces back over his shoulders, put on the dressing-gown Toby held out for him and sat down with a thump at the dressing-table.

He poured out a glass of stout, slowly. He pushed the stuffed dog to one side, took a cigarette out of a brass

34

box, and lighted it. He took a slow, deep pull at the glass of stout, and a slow, deep drag at the cigarette; then he released his breath with an expiring sigh which seemed to leave him, momentarily, as limp as a straw doll.

"Aaah!" breathed Ransom with deep satisfaction.

And, dipping his hand into a jar of cold cream, he began to smear it on his face to remove the make-up.

"Bruce," Beryl West said softly.

All this time, Dennis noted, she had not spoken. In fact, she had been standing with her back turned to him, rather too casually.

Dennis could see Bruce Ransom's face reflected in the mirror over the dressing-table, the only bright surface in that dim brown room. It seemed to him that Bruce had given her a quick and somewhat guilty glance, like a large urchin, before applying himself with concentration to the cold cream.

"Well, poppet?" he said.

Beryl swung round.

"Do you know," she asked, "why I wanted Dennis to come here to-night?"

"Always glad to see you, old boy." Bruce's reflection beamed at him out of the mirror, the slow-curling smile. "Have I been getting into trouble about my income-tax again?"

"It isn't income-tax," Beryl said impatiently. "But somebody's got to persuade you, if I can't. Bruce, you *must* change the end of this new play!"

"Now listen—!" Bruce began with a sudden powerful roar, a note of intensity. Then, seeming to remember that he was always friendly with everybody, he checked himself and adopted an elaborately gentle air.

"Must we go into this, Beryl?"

"Yes, we must! It's a shame and a disgrace and you'll be laughed out of the theatre!"

35

"Pity," murmured Bruce.

"Bruce, it won't *do!* I appeal to Dennis!"

"Here! Oi! Wait a minute!" protested that gentleman. He felt flustered and uncomfortable. Yet in his heart he was deeply flattered at being appealed to, so he put his finger-tips together and prepared to be very judicial.

"You forget," Dennis added, "that I haven't even heard the story of the play."

"I'm going to tell you," said Beryl. "After Bewlay's committed his fourth murder . . ."

"Hold on." It was Bruce Ransom who intervened here. "Has Dennis heard anything about this fellow?"

"My dear Bruce, he knows *all* about it! He even knows the Chief Inspector who—"

Ransom did not appear to have heard.

"Bewlay was a fine one, he was," the actor observed, with his eyes fixed steadily on the mirror. "That little detail of the woman peeping through the window curtains, and seeing the victim rumpled-up and strangled on the couch, while Bewlay lights a cigarette under the lamp: there's your keynote on how to play the part."

"Go on, Beryl," prompted Dennis.

The girl hesitated slightly, as though first thinking of one thing and then changing her mind, before she resumed.

"Well! After Bewlay's committed his fourth murder, the inference is that he's frightened. He'll reform. He'll behave himself. So he goes to a sleepy village, and puts up at a country pub. And there he falls in love.

"I mean," explained Beryl, spreading out her hands, "he *really* falls in love, this time. With a fair-haired innocent, very sweet and healthy and country, whose parents are the local bigwigs. She'd have suited you exactly, Dennis.

36

"The whole thing begins like a romantic comedy in the usual style. Then slowly you begin to realize—a slip here, a slip there—that something's wrong. The story of the past crimes starts to splatter out, aided by a burbling character who's the village gossip. Gradually you realize that the engaging stranger is actually a murderer who can no more reform than a cat can keep off tormenting mice."

Beryl paused.

It was very still in the theatre, now that the end-of-performance clatter had died away in the passages back-stage.

With fingers and heel of hand, in hard opening-and-shutting dabs, Bruce Ransom continued to knead cold cream into his face. His eyes in the mirror were expressionless. His cigarette, balanced on the edge of the dressing-table, sent up motionless smoke in a close, airless room.

"The person who first tumbles to it," pursued Beryl, "is the girl's father. Grey-haired business man; you know the type; Edmund Jervice could play it. We see him begin to understand, and get closer and closer, though he can't prove anything and he's helpless. The girl, of course, refuses to believe anything, though there's one point where we can swear Bewlay loses his head and is going to kill her. The author . . . really, I'll admit it! . . . builds up the tension in such a way that if you played it properly you'd have the audience almost screaming.

"Third act: climax. Bewlay persuades the girl to run away with him. The father catches 'em. Big scene. Father goes berserk and tries to shoot Bewlay. And then—oh, dear!"

Dennis Foster jumped in his chair.

Beryl's voice rose to a wail. She spread out her arms as though appealing to the universe.

"It turns out," she explained piteously, "that the so-called murderer isn't Bewlay at all."

"Isn't Bewlay?"

"No! He's an eminent novelist in search of copy, pretending to be Bewlay so as to get people's reactions. Really, now! I ask you!"

Bruce Ransom finished applying cold cream. He pushed the jar to one side, picked up a cloth, and commenced swabbing at his face to remove the cold cream. In the mirror, one eye peered sideways at Beryl past the cloth.

"You've got to give 'em a happy ending," he declared.

"Oh, Bruce dear! No! No, no!"

"You've got to give 'em a happy ending," Bruce insisted stolidly. "Besides, what's wrong with it?"

"What's *wrong* with it?"

"I'm asking you."

"Listen," crooned Beryl.

She moved a little closer to him. With her flushed cheeks, the half-shut luminous eyes, the rise and fall of her breast under the grey frock, she might have been pleading for somebody's life. Also, when wound up she was so infernally attractive, an attractiveness flowing from her in a strong wave, that it made Dennis Foster half dizzy. Bruce Ransom was evidently conscious of this himself, for he turned his head away.

Beryl still spoke softly.

"It's anti-climax, Bruce. It's emotionally and artistically wrong. Don't you see that? Your whole play collapses with a ker-whoosh. . . ."

"I deny that."

"Listen to me, dear. Your whole play collapses with a ker-whoosh unless this man *is* Bewlay. I'll go further than that. As it is now, this play is just simply utterly impossible."

"Why so?"

"Well, what happens after 'Bewlay' is revealed as the eminent novelist in search of copy? What do you get?"

"A happy—"

"Please, Bruce! Whereupon, mark you, the girl rushes weeping into his arms. The father, practically with a tear in his own eye, shakes hands and say all is forgiven: blessings on you! The mother comes rushing in to do the same. Bruce, could that possibly happen in real life?"

"I don't see why not. What would have happened?"

"The old man," answered Beryl with conciseness, "jolly well *would* have shot him."

"There's no point in trying to be funny about this, Beryl."

"Darling, I'm not trying to be funny! I mean it! Don't you see the girl would never have spoken to him again? The family would have had him chased out of town. Could anybody forgive being made guinea-pigs in an experiment like that?"

"Yes, I think they would. If he really did happen to be a famous writer with a big reputation."

"Never, Bruce! Never in the world!"

"Look here, Beryl! Don't *you* see that—"

"And that," she swept aside his retort, "is the situation when you bring down your curtain. That's what you send 'em home with. After working for three acts to build it up, what have you got?"

"A happy ending."

"Oh, rats to your happy ending!"

Bruce flung down the cloth with which he had been cleansing his face, and got up from the dressing-table. But he did not lose his temper; he very seldom did. Swathed in the blue silk dressing-gown, his hands dug into his pockets, he began to turn to pace the room, while Toby the dresser waited patiently in the

39

background with his street-clothes.

When Bruce turned round again to face Beryl, it was with the smile which had melted the hearts of so many women on the other side of the footlights. His voice was soft and persuasive.

"Come on, now! Little girl mustn't lose her temper. The play has faults, I'll admit . . ."

"Yes. And evidently the author knows it."

His glance flashed across at her, suddenly vivid.

"Oh? What makes you think that?"

"Some pages are written on a different typewriter. A whole chunk of the last act is written on a different typewriter. I can show you exactly where he couldn't make up his mind, and—" Beryl stopped. "Where's the script, Bruce?"

"I sent it to Ethel Whitman's to have a dozen copies made. They'll take a devil of a long time over it, I'm afraid."

"Bruce. You *did* write to the author?"

"Yes, of course." His gesture dismissed this as being of no importance. "There's been no reply."

"Three weeks ago? And there's been no reply?"

"That's right."

"But, Bruce! You can't think of going into production without getting the author's consent and a contract made!"

Bruce threw back his head and laughed.

"My dear girl, who's talking about going into production yet? I'm fed up. I need a long rest. I'm going away for a holiday, and . . . Great Scott, what's the matter with you now?"

For Beryl, her mouth partly open and the dreaminess of a great inspiration in her eyes, had slowly pointed her finger at him like a prophetess.

"I've got it!" she cried.

"Got what?"

"I said the ending of that play was absolute bilge. And I'll prove it. I'll prove it, I'll prove it!"

"Prove it how?"

Beryl nodded to herself. She picked up the cigarette, still smouldering on the edge of the dressing-table, and drew at it twice before stubbing it out on the glass top of the dressing-table. Then she raised her head.

"Bruce," she said, "why don't you *be* Roger Bewlay?"

4

Long afterwards, when the horror had descended on them, Dennis Foster remembered that last pleasant evening before certain persons began to tamper with forces they did not understand.

Best of all he remembered Bruce Ransom in that position as though caught by a camera-shutter: hands thrust into the pockets of the dressing-gown, staring at Beryl in utter astonishment.

"I don't understand you," observed Bruce.

"On Saturday, when the show closes, you're going away for a holiday. To some poky little place on the east coast. Aren't you?"

"Yes!"

"And you've already booked hotel accommodation there—under an assumed name?"

"Yes. I . . ." Bruce took his hands out of his pockets. Quick alertness sprang into his eyes and remained there as a sort of glaze. His lips curled back from his teeth, emphasizing the high cheek-bones.

"God Almighty!" he said. "You mean—?"

Beryl nodded.

"I dare you," she said, "to do exactly what the man does in the play. He's supposed to be a well-known writer; you're a well-known actor; but the principle's just the same. You see?"

"Yes. I see."

"Go down to this place: what's its name?"

"Aldebridge, in Suffolk. Or near there, to be exact."

"Go down to this place," pursued Beryl, "and establish yourself at the pub. Then start making slips and dropping bricks; follow the line of the play. Gradually get the whole air of the village poisoned with the idea that you're the one and only original Roger Bewlay, on the prowl again.

"In the meantime, make passionate love to some local girl." Beryl turned her eyes away, casually. "That—that shouldn't be too difficult, should it? Preferably the daughter of someone who's important or at least well-known in the village. —Bruce! Are you listening to me?"

"Eh? Oh, yes."

Bruce opened and shut his hands. His thoughts were miles away.

"The girl," Beryl laughed, "probably won't have a father who'll want to shoot you. That only happens in plays and books. But she'll have *some* relative or boy-friend who'll take a pretty dim view of this Little Bird in the clutches of Roger Bewlay."

"Yes. I suppose so."

"Then, when you've got everybody really frantic . . . how long do you plan to stay in Aldebridge?"

"A month." Bruce spoke mechanically. "I've got a broadcasting date in October, but I can stay there the rest of the time."

To the disquiet of Dennis Foster, who had sat speechless throughout this, Bruce appeared to be taking the matter as already half an accomplished fact. Beryl gritted her teeth.

"All right! And I should be back from America in

just over three weeks. By that time, Bruce, you really ought to have raised the devil if you play your part properly. (Please be quiet, Dennis!) Then explode your third-act bombshell. Tell 'em you're not the sinister murderer, but dear old Bruce Ransom in search of copy; and just *see* what they say." Beryl's voice rose on such a note of breathlessness that she almost choked. "Will you do that? Go on! I dare you!"

There was a long silence, marred only by Beryl's cough to get her breath back.

"I never thought of that," Bruce muttered. "I never thought of it."

He contemplated the opposite wall with a strange, slow, hard-eyed look. He drove his clenched right fist into the palm of his left hand, and nodded. Then he moved slowly back across the room, with a soft and heavy tread like a tiger, to sit down again at the dressing-table.

"I wonder if I could get away with it!" he breathed.

"Of course you can get away with it! Why ever not?"

Bruce drummed with his fingers on the glass top of the dressing-table.

"Suppose somebody recognizes me?"

"That's not very likely, Bruce. You look different off the stage. *Much* different. And you loathe and despise film-work; you won't accept a film-offer as long as you have sixpence in the bank. It's only films that get people's faces known in a Suffolk village."

"Or,"—he grinned up at her, the twinkling eyes half shut up—"this may not work. There may not be any girl."

"There'll be a girl all right! Rest assured of that."

"Or," the honest voice continued, "she may not give me a tumble. Or she may make me fall for her, and then laugh ha-ha. I'd deserve it, God knows."

"That," interposed Dennis Foster firmly, "is the first

45

sane and sensible remark that's been made." Though he saw the exasperation in Beryl's face, he rose to his feet and continued in the same firm if concilatory tone.

"Look here, you people!" pleaded Dennis. "I don't want to seem a death's head at the feast every time I meet you. And I admit it's an intriguing idea. But you don't seriously mean to go through with it?"

"Why ever not?" cried Beryl.

"For one thing, doesn't it strike you as being a little cold-blooded?"

"Well . . ." said Bruce. He frowned at his clenched fist on the dressing-table, and then opened and shut the fingers. But Beryl would have none of this objection.

"You mean about the girl?" she cried.

"Yes," said Dennis.

"No, I can't say it does," declared Beryl in a cool and poised voice. "After all, you know, it's being done in the name of . . . well! Of art."

"Pardon me," returned Dennis, with a smile that made her lower her eyes. "You know perfectly damned well it's not being done for any reason of the kind."

"Oh, Dennis, don't be so stuffy!"

"The idea," he pursued remorselessly, "sweeps you both off your feet as being a new and exciting game. You're like children preparing a butter-slide for the schoolmaster." He extended his hands. "But you can't play with people's lives and people's emotions like that. It's dangerous. It gets out of hand. This isn't the stage. It's real life."

"But that," Beryl cried, "is exactly what I've been trying to tell Bruce! If he'll only change the frightful ending of that play . . ."

"I will *not* change the ending of the play," said Bruce Ransom.

"Darling, it's BILGE!"

"I say it's not bilge," announced Bruce, with his eye on the mirror. "And I'll prove it in a way that may surprise you. Furthermore . . ."

He broke off; and, deeply engrossed though they were, both he and Beryl twisted round to stare. For Dennis Foster was laughing.

Sinking back again in the easy chair, Dennis fished after his cigarette-case, took out a cigarette, and lighted it. He laughed so much that he choked over the smoke. For, in that last outburst between these two, it suddenly seemed to him that values altered and shrank. It seemed to him that he had perhaps been making too much of his protest.

After all, it was unlikely that Bruce would come to any real harm. It was all make-believe, like the rest of their lives. You do not suffer hurt in a house of make-believe, or meet real spectres aboard the Ghost-Train.

He, Dennis, had made his protest. He had done his duty. If Bruce chose to go ahead now, he could only sit back and watch. Dennis was consumed by a reprehensible curiosity to know just what the devil *would* happen. And, come to think of it, he could always arrange matters so that Bruce kept out of the only sort of trouble he was likely to encounter.

So Dennis sat and laughed, spluttering amid smoke, while the other two regarded him with a sort of offended consternation: as though, during a performance, some austere dramatic-critic had suddenly risen in the stalls and given them a loud raspberry.

"What's so funny, old boy?" demanded Bruce.

"I don't like it," said Beryl, opening her large eyes wide. "I think it sounds sinister. —Bruce!"

"Well?"

"I told you a while ago, though I don't think you took it in, that Dennis knows Chief Inspector Masters.

47

The man who handled the Bewlay case! You don't think Dennis is going to queer our pitch?"

"Chief Inspector Masters," said Bruce. He turned back to the mirror. He picked up the small stuffed dog which was his mascot, and put it down again. "Isn't that the fellow who goes about with Sir Henry Merrivale?"

Dennis nodded.

"Yes," agreed Dennis, not without satisfaction, "I believe Masters is a friend of Sir Henry Merrivale. And I am proud to record the fact."

"Why so, old boy?"

"Sir Henry Merrivale," Dennis answered, "is greatly interested in crime. It's sufficient apology for my own interest in crime when I'm accused of having—er—low tastes. I've never met Sir Henry, but he has been described to me as being the perfect pattern of the English gentleman."

"Yes," said Bruce, "there's undoubtedly—" Then Bruce stopped dead. Slowly he craned his neck round. "Sir Henry Merrivale," he added, "has been described to you as *what?*"

"As the perfect pattern of the English gentleman." Dennis was himself again: sedate, briskly nodding. "I don't care what you say, Bruce: it's a relief to know there's someone of the old school, someone of dignity and good manners, left in England to-day."

"Yes," said the polite Bruce. "Yes, old boy. No doubt." His expression changed. "But Beryl was asking you . . . !"

"Dennis dear," cried Beryl, "you won't interfere, will you?"

"In this hare-brained scheme of Bruce's?"

"Yes! Please!"

"No," replied Dennis, contemplating them indulgently, "I won't interfere. On the contrary. If Bruce insists on going through with it, I may be able to help him."

"Help him? How?"

"Never mind that, for the moment. We can discuss it presently. In the meantime, it's getting late. Hadn't we better go along to the Ivy while there's still some food left?"

This was the point at which they heard a discreet tap at the dressing-room door. Toby, the dresser, still waiting patiently in the background with a martyred expression, and with Bruce's street-clothes over his arm, hurried to answer it. After a muttered confabulation outside, Toby returned with a sealed envelope bearing Bruce's name in small, neatly inked capitals.

Puzzled, Bruce got up from the dressing-table.

"For me?" he inquired somewhat superfluously.

"Yes, sir."

While Beryl went to collect her coat and scarf from the sofa, and Dennis stubbed out his cigarette before gathering up his own possessions beside the chair, Bruce tore open the envelope. It contained a folded sheet of notepaper with a dozen lines of writing. Bruce read it through once. He read it through again. He folded up the sheet, replaced it in the envelope, and thrust the envelope into the pocket of his dressing-gown.

Then Bruce cleared his throat. And the whole atmosphere changed as palpably as though the temperature had altered.

"Er—Beryl," he said. "You and Dennis go along to the Ivy. I'm afraid I won't be able to join you for a little while."

"Bruce!"

"Ask Mariot," continued Bruce, in his most winning

voice, "if he'll save me some cold ham and salad, anything at all, in case I'm very late. You don't mind, do you?"

"I see," Beryl murmured without expression. "No, of course I don't mind."

Before Dennis or Bruce could move to help her, she swung the light coat loosely over her shoulders. Drawing the silk scarf over her head, she fastened it under her chin with a little gold pin: all this with very deliberate movements, and her eye on the door.

"I'm off to America to-morrow, Bruce."

"I'm sorry," said Bruce, answering her meaning rather than her words, "but there it is! It can't be helped. I've got to see someone about—anyway, it's very important. And it's not as though . . ."

Beryl whirled round.

"Oh, go down to Aldebridge and *make* love to your beastly wench!" she burst out.

And with the tears starting to her eyes she ran out of the room, banging the door in a hollow slam which echoed through the theatre.

The last remark was so unexpected, and so contrary to everything she had just been urging, that it took Dennis Foster off balance. He blinked at the still-quivering door.

"What in blazes," he demanded, "is the matter with her?"

Dennis said this although, being no fool, he guessed very well what was wrong with her. For some time the theatrical world had speculated as to whether there was anything between Bruce Ransom and Beryl West. And, even in a profession where everybody knows everybody else's affairs to an almost gruesome extent, no certainty existed. Dennis, who liked both Beryl and Bruce, had long hoped they would make a match of it. He was still hoping.

"What in blazes is the matter with *her?*"

"Well! You know what women are," said Bruce, in the conspiratorial tone men employ to discuss these matters. Then a great kindliness shone from him. "Dennis!"

"Eh?"

"Run after her, will you? Take her out through the front of the house. Don't let her go out by the stage-door."

"But it's much shorter to . . . Oh! I see."

"You don't see," Bruce assured him. "Tell her it's not what she's thinking! Tell her . . . For God's sake rally round, can't you?"

"Right," said Dennis. "You may rely on me."

And he hurried out after Beryl.

For some time afterwards Bruce Ransom stood motionless, his arms folded, staring at the door. Then Bruce smiled.

It was a curious smile, which Toby the dresser did not understand. A sleepy smile, an ineffable smile, a Puck-like smile. It narrowed the eyes to amiably gleaming slits. It barely showed the strong teeth, so tightly did it compress his lips as it travelled wider and wider, up and up. Thus Bruce smiled in the dim light; you would have said he was thinking himself into a part.

Once more he sat down in front of the dressing-table. He looked into the mirror, unseeingly, and seemed to be meditating. From his pocket he took out the envelope containing the note; he smoothed it out in front of him. As though idly he picked up a soft black eyebrow pencil, to make a brief notation in figures on the envelope.

The black pencil traced out 7, 4, 28-36. And again, as though to remind himself or in a certain quirk of triumph, 7, 4, 28-36. Bruce Ransom put down the pencil softly, and returned the envelope to his pocket. His expression smoothed itself out, became easy and unobtrusive, as he caught his dresser's eye in the mirror.

"Toby!"

"Yes, sir?"

"Ask the lady to come in."

5

It was only a few minutes later that Dennis Foster met Sir Henry Merrivale, under circumstances of a somewhat regrettable kind.

Dennis, as he hurried out after Beryl, found there was no need to steer her away from the stage-door. Instead Beryl deliberately marched out through the front of the house, stumbling in the dark. He overtook her in the foyer, amid a mud-tide of discarded ticket-stubs and cigarette-ends.

"Dennis. What did you mean when you said you could help Bruce?"

It was as though that little outburst in the dressing-room had never occurred. Beryl's upturned face was composed, ethereal again. The very tone of her voice implied that it hadn't happened; that she would not refer to it; and he was tactful enough not to refer to it either.

"Well," he smiled, as he pushed down the iron rod of one of the creaking glass doors into the street, "there are one or two little things that don't seem to have occurred to either of you."

"Such as?"

"Suppose Bruce plays his part too well and really

53

gets the police after him?"

Beryl halted in the doorway.

"But he won't be doing anything against the law! Or will he? You're a lawyer. You ought to know."

"No, he won't be doing anything against the law unless some question of fraud arises: which of course it won't."

"All right, then! And if they do get tiresome, Bruce can always explain who he really is and what he's doing."

"True, Beryl. But the police can make themselves infernally unpleasant if they choose. There are all sorts of pretexts on which Bruce could be 'detained',"—he saw the alarm in her face—"and questioned, and chivvied all over the place, without actually being arrested. Unless . . ."

"But we don't want Bruce in *prison!*" She stopped short. "Unless?"

"Unless the police know all about it to begin with."

"How do you mean?"

"Beryl," he continued, as they emerged into Charing Cross Road, "I want your permission to go to Scotland Yard and tell this whole story to Chief Inspector Masters."

"But . . . will he like it?"

"You bet he won't like it. He'll probably threaten reprisals of no uncertain kind. But I think, if I argue it all out, I may persuade him to keep quiet. Then (don't you see?) he can pass the word to the Aldebridge police. 'If you hear Roger Bewlay is on the prowl, don't pay any attention to it; it's only Bruce Ransom acting the fool.' Then Bruce can do exactly as he likes without anyone to interfere."

"Dennis!" exclaimed Beryl, and walked faster beside him and raised a radiant face. "Would you really do that?"

54

"Of course. I'll go to-morrow, if you like. I can . . . Good Lord!"

Dennis broke off, and stared.

Next door to the Granada, as he had already noted, there was an amusement arcade. In the past few years these noisy halls have sprung up all over what might be called the east side of the West End. This one, described as PLAYLAND in red letters over the broad open front, looked much the same as any other.

Inside a dingy low-ceilinged cavern stretching well back, there were lines of pin-ball machines against each wall. You put a penny in the slot to have five tries at a high score amid ringing bells and flashing vari-coloured lights. Down the middle of the cavern, dividing the pin-ball machines into two aisles, were glass cases from which you attempted to wrest prizes with the aid of shaky metal arms and paralytic toy derricks. Another machine told your fortune; you could throw darts or look at peep-shows; and there was a small shooting-gallery at the rear.

In this arcade, halfway down the left-hand aisle, stood Chief Inspector Humphrey Masters himself.

Masters, urbane and burly in his blue serge and bowler hat, was bending with mild interest over a pin-ball machine. They watched his boiled blue eye follow the run of the ball, and the dancing lights of the indicator.

"I don't know what Masters is doing here," Dennis muttered, when he had explained to Beryl. "But it's just possible he's here on business. This may not be the time to intrude."

"Oh, couldn't we see him? Couldn't we see him now?"

"You—er—don't object to going into a place like this?"

"I'd love to," Beryl answered simply. "Only nobody

has ever invited me to, and I haven't had the nerve to go alone."

"There's nothing for you to be afraid of. These arcades are the quietest places in London. Only . . ."

"Please!" urged Beryl.

Playland, at this hour, was only sparsely filled with loungers and troops. Its atmosphere, a damp musty smell, blew out at them as they advanced.

There was a *ding-ding* as another pin-ball machine sprang into chuckling metallic life. They heard a heavy jingle of coins as the manager, a large white bag of coppers clung over his shoulder, moved about to make change. From the rear a .22 target-rifle spat, and spat again. Over everything, in the somnolence of the cavern, radio dance-music flowed from a loud-speaker.

Chief Inspector Masters did not turn his head or seem to notice the newcomers. But a ventriloquial voice faintly reached Dennis.

"Don't speak to me, sir," growled Masters. "And better get the young lady out of here. There may be trouble."

Ding-ding went a bell across the room.

Dennis took a quick glance round. He could not see the opposite side of the arcade, which was hidden behind garish glass cases illuminated by tiny electric lights, nor could he see much of the back. There appeared to be nothing very ominous here, under the blare of dance-music. But Dennis nodded.

"Right," he agreed in the same ventriolquial voice. "We only wanted to tell you something about Roger Bewlay."

And he took Beryl's arm to turn away.

"Hurrum! Stop a bit!"

Perhaps no other words Dennis could have chosen would have swerved Masters from the hair-line of duty. But this was different. For eleven years, as his

56

colleagues could have testified, that name of Bewlay had on Masters the same effect which is produced by feeding tobacco to an elephant.

So Dennis turned back again, to find Masters glowering at him with a doubtful and angry eye, torn between emotions.

"Hurrum!" said Masters. "The chap I'm expecting"— he darted a quick glance towards the door—"can't possibly be here for another ten minutes. So, if you've got anything to tell me? *Or* the young lady? Eh?"

And his eyebrows went up in a powerfully suggestive way as he looked at Beryl.

"I beg your pardon!" said Dennis. "May I present: Miss Beryl West, Chief . . ."

"Don't mention my name," groaned Masters under his breath. "The chap I'm looking for may have pals in this place. Now, then!"

"Sorry. This is Miss Beryl West, who has produced Bruce Ransom in most of his successful plays . . ."

"Bruce Ransom?" Masters moved his neck, indicating. "Show next door?"

"That's right."

"Oh, ah. And did *you* ever meet Roger Bewlay, miss?"

"I? Good heavens, no!"

"Oh," grunted Masters.

His momentary hope had been dashed. He rattled the handle of the pin-ball machine. Finding it empty, he dropped in another penny, jabbed at the handle, and brought the metal balls back to position with a clattering rattle and roll. The indicator above the board, depicting a gaudy motor-car race, flashed into light.

"Then what do you know about Bewlay, miss?"

"Nothing, I'm afraid. Except what's in the play, and what Bruce and Dennis have told me. And, of course, the accounts of him in Conant's *Remarkable Criminals* and the Detection Club's *The Anatomy of Murder*. Bruce asked me to read those, because of the play."

"Play, miss? What play?"

"Someone," explained Dennis, "has written a play based on the career of Bewlay. Mr. Ransom's going to play the part."

Masters frowned.

"But what I'm trying to get at," he persisted with a sort of heavy patience, "is what you've got to tell me about the fellow? What new information, like?"

"Well!" said Dennis. "The fact is, to be strictly accurate, we haven't got any new information. But . . ."

"Is that so, now?" mused Masters, and again jabbed at the handle so as to bring a ball up on the runway. "You haven't actually got any new information!"

Dennis exchanged a glance with Beryl, and their hearts sank.

Beryl was very nervous. She kept glancing over her shoulder towards the door, obviously wondering whether a row might not start at any moment. But she was so absorbed in studying a real-life detective-officer, in noting each gesture and inflection for professional use afterwards, that she almost forgot this. Beryl didn't want the interview to end.

"No, we haven't any information," she confessed. "But I do hope you catch him, Mr. Masters. I do so hope you catch him!"

"Thank you, miss. In the meantime, I must just ask you both to . . ."

"It must have been a pretty awful business," insisted Beryl. "Especially, as Bruce says, that little detail of the woman looking through the window-curtains and seeing the victim lying strangled on a couch. And (what was it?) Bewlay lighting a cigarette under the lamp."

58

The effect of this remark was extraordinary.

Masters, who had drawn back the handle to its full extent, released it so suddenly that the metal ball shot up the runway. The whole pin-table whirred and clicked. White, green, and then red lights danced to a maniacal dinging of bells; phantom motor-cars flickered wildly across the screen as it rang up score after score. It might have expressed Masters's state of mind.

"Well, well!" said Masters, in a soft and agreeable voice. "So that's what our witness saw, is it?"

"Is—is anything wrong?"

"She saw a strangled victim lying on a couch, eh? And Bewlay lighting a cigarette?"

"Yes!—Didn't she?"

"She did, miss," agreed Masters, nodding almost affably. "But how do you happen to know that?"

Long pause.

"You see, miss, we gave a lot of publicity to the first three crimes. We had to. There was a hunt on, and the public might have helped. But the evidence in the fourth murder, the evidence that can hang Mister Bewlay, we kept to ourselves."

Here Masters looked very hard at Beryl.

"Barring the fact we *did* have a witness," he said, "no one single detail was ever released to the Press or as much as breathed outside the police-force. Oh, ah! Then how do you come to know all about it, miss?"

Dance-music still jingled in that reverberating cavern; the target-rifle cracked again.

"But,"—Beryl raised guileless eyes, after hesitating again,—"it's in the play!"

"You mean this play Mr. Ransom's going to do?"

"Yes, of course!"

"And who wrote the play, miss?"

Once more Dennis Foster saw on Beryl's face a

59

strange expression she had not worn at some point earlier in the evening, though he could not place just when.

"We don't know the author personally," she replied. "It's some man whose name I can't remember. He submitted it to Bruce."

"But you've got this man's name and address?"

"Yes! Or at least Bruce has."

"Where's the play now, miss?"

"You mean the script? It's—being copied. I daresay Bruce could get you the original."

Masters nodded.

It was remarkable how his manner had changed in the last few moments. Masters was animated now by a sort of catlike benevolence, confidential and bland.

"Now, now, miss!" he urged, in his blandest and most soothing way. "No call to go and get alarmed. I'm sorry I spoke a bit sharp to you a minute ago; and to you too, Mr. Foster. But I wonder," he lowered his voice confidentially, "whether you'd mind telling what you've just told me to Sir Henry Merrivale."

"Sir Henry Merrivale?" repeated Dennis, and peered round. "Is he here?"

"Oh, ah! Very much so. You see, miss," Masters continued to Beryl, "it'd come better from you than from me. The Bewlay case is the one case I daren't mention to the old ba—the old gentleman, even after eleven years."

"Why ever not?"

"Well, miss, he got mad."

"How do you mean?"

"I didn't consult him," Masters confided. "I thought I didn't need him. So he just looks at the ceiling every time I try to say a ruddy word about the case. And nowadays, when he's taken up golf again for the first time since the war, he's not what you might call sweet-tempered. No," ruminated Masters, shaking his head, "he's not what you might call sweet-tempered."

"But where is he now?" demanded Dennis.

"The last time I saw him," returned Masters, peering round rather suspiciously, "he was looking at the peepshow where you put in a penny to see the strip-tease."

Dennis Foster was conscious of a slight sense of shock. There could not, he thought, be two Sir Henry Merrivales?

"I let him come along to-night," said Masters, "and bring that Scotch professional golf-teacher he's always got in tow nowadays, provided he promised on his Bible oath to behave himself."

"Behave himself? Why shouldn't he?"

"Come with me, please," requested Masters.

He turned round, not without a quick uneasy glance towards the front door, and led the way towards the back. In the light of later events, it may be considered just as well that Masters was on hand.

At the back of the arcade, beyond a largish open space, a slightly drunk Australian corporal was leaning against the counter of the little shooting-range, endeavouring to focus what seemed to him a steady rifle on an unsteady target. The arcade manager stood by, jingling coins in the white sack.

At the line of peep-show machines, a French sailor was earnestly peering into an exhibit labelled *Nuit de Paris*. Two American G.I.'s, and a lanky Royal Navy sub-lieutenant who was smoking a cigar, listened with keen interest to a violent argument now going on between two gentlemen in civilian clothes.

They stood beside another of the amusement-devices. This consisted of a heavy wooden frame, supporting a heavy wooden canopy from which hung a punching-bag. You dropped a penny into the slot, and an indicator-dial on the frame showed the power of

61

your blow.

Of the two who argued, one was a gnarled, stern-looking little man in tweeds, Mr. Donald Fergus MacFergus of the Killiecrankie Golf Club.

The other was a large, stout, barrel-shaped gentleman in a black alpaca suit. Shell-rimmed spectacles were pulled down on his broad nose, and he peered over them with an expression of terrifying malignancy. Even his corporation, ornamented by a large gold watch-chain, seemed to bristle. His fists were on his hips, one hand clutching the rim of a bowler hat, and his large bald head gleamed under the ceiling lights.

Then Sir Henry Merrivale spoke.

"Looky here, son," said the perfect pattern of the English gentleman. "Are you tryin' to tell me you can hit this goddam punching-bag harder than I can?"

"Aye," said Mr. MacFergus.

The two American G.I.'s, and the Navy sub-lieutenant with the cigar, continued to listen with fascinated interest.

"Look!" said H. M., slowly flexing the biceps of his right arm, and pointing impressively to it like Sandow the Strong Man. "Oi! Look! Feel that?"

"Under Mr. MacFergus's patient voice could be heard the beginnings of a slight hysteria, as one who has dwelt many weeks in the company of Sir Henry Merrivale.

"I keep telling ye," he said, "it's no' a question o' muscle!"

"No, son?"

"No! It's a question o' muscular co-orrdination, as I keep telling ye whiles I try tae teach ye golf."

"What's the matter with my golf?" demanded H. M., suddenly lowering his arms. "I'm the most promisin' natural golfer," he explained to the listening G.I.'s, who nodded approvingly, "I'm the most promisin' natural golfer that ever teed up a ball."

"Aye," said Mr. MacFergus sternly. "And ye concede yersel' a twal'-foot putt, ma mannie, when ye think I'm no' luking. But we werena speaking o' golf. We were speaking,"—he extended his finger—"o' yon poonching-bag."

"And you think *you* can paste it harder'n *I* can?"

"Aye."

"You want to bet?"

Mr. MacFergus considered this.

"Saxpence?" he suggested.

"I said bet," repeated H. M., with his countenance turning slightly purple. "Lord love a duck, your recklessness is goin' to land the whole Clan MacFergus in the poor-house." Then inspiration seized him. "Oi! Wait a minute! I got it! What about a forfeit-bet?"

"Forfeit-bet?"

"Sure. Whoever loses has got to go and kick a policeman in the pants. Or stand outside a big cinema with a roll of toilet-paper, and hand a piece to everybody who goes in."

In the background, Chief Inspector Masters uttered a strangled cry. Beryl West and Dennis Foster stood rooted to the spot. But the two American G.I.'s were now listening in a kind of stunned admiration. It went to their hearts as being the most sporting proposition they had heard in England.

"Boy," crowed the first G.I., and suddenly slapped his thigh, "has this old guy got what it takes? Go on, pop! Soak the hell out of it. My money's on you."

The Navy sub-lieutenant took the cigar out of his mouth.

"Hoots!" said the sub-lieutenant richly. With his cigar he pointed towards Mr. MacFergus. "Yon mannie'll hi' it twice as hard as any Sassenach, bein' Sco'ish. Wud ye care tae mak' a wee bet yersel'?"

"Will I *bet?*" said the first G.I., staring back at him. "Boy, oh, boy, will I *bet?*"

Feverishly he dived into his pockets, and produced a crumpled roll of notes.

"Five pounds," he declared, "five pounds says the old guy's got what it takes. Five pounds says he knocks the living be-Jesus out of it."

"Thank'ee, son," said H. M. with a modest cough.

Deliberately the Navy sub-lieutenant took out a note-case. He extracted five pound-notes. With a gloomy and sepulchral air, rather like Marley's ghost rebuking Scrooge, he held up the money under his companion's nose.

"I'll tak' ye," he said.

It cannot now be stated whether Mr. MacFergus acted out of horror at his countryman's insanity, or out of obscure pride. But it is certain that he lost his head and dropped a penny in the slot. It is certain that the spirit of Bannockburn inspired him and blazed out of his pale eyes.

"Stand ye back!" said Mr. MacFergus sternly. "Sco'land for ever!"

And well and truly he smote the bag.

It was a noble effort, in truth a lusty swipe. The leather bag crashed and flapped and rebounded in a flickering blur. Its indicator-needle swept round the dial and jumped quivering within a quarter-inch of the top.

There was a startled silence under the blare of the dance-band.

"Can ye beat *that?*" inquired Mr. MacFergus.

"Jeez, Tom," the second G.I. muttered apprehensively, "this don't look so good. The little guy packs a wallop. I think there goes our dough."

"Have no fear, son," said H. M., raising his hand majestically with palm outwards. "I'm the old man."

And he tapped himself on the chest.

Whereupon H. M. handed his hat to the second G.I. He dropped a penny into the slot. He hitched up his trousers. Slowly lifting his right hand in the air, he brought it down so as to moisten the thumb with his tongue in passing. Then, squaring off with a glare of indescribable malignancy, he lunged at that punching-bag as Samson lunged at the gates of Gath.

As to what happened next . . .

H. M. has since argued, with some show of reason, that it was not his fault. And this, up to a point, is true. Admittedly he could not have foreseen that the cord supporting the punching-bag, weakened by long use, would snap as a rotten thread snaps.

But that, unfortunately, was what happened.

The heavy pear-shaped bag whizzed across the room like a projectile from a rocket-firing Typhoon. The manager of the arcade got it squarely in the face, making him spin round like a teetotum so that they saw his glazed eyes on the second whirl, before it glanced off full and true into the neck of the slightly drunk Australian just as the latter was raising his rifle.

"So-and-so!" said the Australian corporal.

Seizing the bag as it fell, he put down the rifle. He turned round from the counter. Holding the bag like a football, he released it in a low, vicious drop-kick which sent the heavy projectile whizzing back across the room straight into the stomach of Sir Henry Merrivale.

"Long live Austrylia!" he shouted.

Then things began to happen all at once.

6

Dimly, above the inferno of noise in what he had described as the quietest place in London, Dennis Foster heard the bellow of Chief Inspector Masters's voice.

"Don't do anything, sir!" Masters was yelling to H. M. "Stay where you are! Put the thing down! Put it . . ."

This good advice went unheeded.

H. M., now so infuriated that he was completely cross-eyed, did not even wait to get his breath.

As one who had played rugger for Cambridge in '91, he instantly kicked in reply. But his wrath-blurred eye, or perhaps the impressive size of his corporation, sent the missile wide. The improvised football curved past the Australian, curved past a startled French sailor, and crashed through a glass case containing a toy crane with which you fished for prizes.

There are times when a corporate madness enters into the minds of men. This is especially so in post-war London, where browned-off troops and equally browned-off civilians find their nerves scratched by so many small annoyances that at times life becomes unendurable. Then a spark sets them off. And they do things, and know not why.

Hardly had the bursting jangle of glass died away when the first G.I. was racing after that improvised football. He snatched it up, and, with a sheer elemental howl to express his feelings, he deliberately flung it through another glass case.

Mr. Donald MacFergus thereupon seized H. M.'s hat from the second G.I., dropped H. M.'s hat on the floor, and jumped on it with both feet. The second G.I., after staring at him for a second, laid hold of Mr. MacFergus and threw him six feet into a fortune-telling machine, which collapsed in a deafening din of wheels and weights. The lanky sub-lieutenant then dropped his cigar, thrust money back into his pocket, courteously tapped the G.I. on the shoulder, and, when the latter swung round, waded in with both fists.

Meantime, the French sailor had not been idle. Crying out, "Zut, alors!"—presumably at the tameness of the peep-show—he laid frantic hands on that apparatus and yanked it to the floor. The Australian corporal, himself inspired, had raised his rifle and was now employed in shooting out the ceiling-lights.

"M.P.'s!" the cry went up out of the gathering darkness. *"Watch it! M.P.'s!"*

How Masters managed what he did, Dennis Foster could never afterwards quite remember. Masters was a whole rescue-squad in himself.

Holding Beryl's arm with one hand and Dennis's arm with the other, he swept them towards the back of the arcade. Using them as a kind of scoop, he gathered up a gesticulating H. M. and a dizzy Mr. Mac-Fergus on his way.

"There's a back door here somewhere," snarled Masters. "Open it!"

"But looky here, Masters!" rose H. M.'s protesting bellow. "I . . ."

"Open it, sir!" hissed the Chief Inspector.

The arcade was now an eerie gloom starred with coloured lights where an overturned pin-ball machine rang like a demented cash-register. The radio sang, *Smoke Gets in Your Eyes,* to crashings as the military and civil police arrived.

"I've got it!" said Dennis groping for the door. "Are you all right, Beryl?"

"I feel g-ghastly," quavered the girl's voice. "In a few minutes I'm going to start laughing. But not yet."

Masters swept this aside. "Is there a key in the door, Mr. Foster?"

"Yes!"

"Through you go, now!" said Masters, impelling them into cool intense darkness. "Lock the door on the outside; then shove the key through under the sill. If they find the door locked and the key lying inside, they may not twig it."

"Right!"

"Me, a police-officer," Masters gritted out of the darkness, "helping disturbers of the peace to get away instead of running 'em in! Lummy!"

"What do you mean, disturbers of the peace?" howled the mortally injured voice of Sir Henry Merrivale. "Burn me, Masters, what did *I* do? I didn't do a single . . ."

"No, sir?"

"I say, Masters." There was a faintly apologetic note in H. M.'s voice. "We're not far from the back door of a pub I know. The proprietor's an old pal of mine."

"As it happens," said Masters grimly, " I was aware of that. I'm counting on it. Straight ahead, now!"

In the confusion Dennis had lost all sense of direction. He only knew that they were in a narrow paved way with high brick walls on either side, the stars brilliant in a black sky and a cool wind blowing. They

69

blundered forward for about twenty steps, H. M. in the lead.

It was H. M. who opened the door into the tiny rear passage of a very vile and sweating public-house. From ahead of them, beyond an arch covered by a bead curtain, a din of voices in a smoke-mist blattered above the thump of beer-pump handles. The bead curtain was instantly drawn aside by a stocky man with a battered face, in his shirt-sleeves, who peered in suspicion.

"'Lo, Alf," said H. M.

The change was instantaneous.

"Wot-cher, Sir 'Enry!" cried the proprietor. His countenance opened and smiled like a distorted gold-toothed flower. But this again changed to anxiety as he hurried towards them. "Ayn't in trouble again, areyer?"

"It's nothin' much, Alf. Spot of bother with the cops, that's all."

"Your friend there's a copper, ayn't 'e?"

"Sure, Alf. But he's not on duty. Is the back room empty?"

Alf shut one eye in a significant leer.

"In yer go," he said briskly. "Lock the door and don't open it 'less you 'ear three taps; that'll be me. You leave it ter me, cock. I'll see yer don't get lagged."

That was how they found themselves in a small room, so full of stale tobacco-smoke that it blurred the feeble lights. The windows were sealed up with blackout frames of wood and heavy cardboard, although there was now no necessity for blackout. There had recently been a party here: wet rings from glasses spotted a big round table, and chairs were pushed wide. Over the mantelpiece and rusty grate hung a steel engraving of a Highland stag.

Yet, even in this sanctuary, thunder stirred.

With an ominous air Masters locked the door. He

70

went over to Sir Henry Merrivale, who had sat down beside the table, and stood in front of H. M. with his fists on his hips.

"Well?" said Masters.

"Well, what?" asked H. M. querulously.

"Aren't you ashamed of yourself?"

An expression of patient martyrdom overspread H. M.'s face.

"Masters," he said, "will you just tell me why these things have got to happen to *me?* I go through life as good as gold, comportin' myself like Lord Chesterfield on his best behaviour,"—H. M. quite seriously believed this—"and yet I'm always the victim of a goddam conspiracy. Will you just tell me why?"

"Certainly I'll tell you why," returned Masters without hesitation.

"Oh?"

"It's because you lay yourself open to it, that's why. If you'd been sitting quietly at your club, or at home with a good book, or doing anything a man of your age ought to do, you wouldn't *get* into these messes."

Then Masters's colour came up.

"Wrecking amusement arcades!" he said. "Handing out toilet-paper in front of a cinema. God's truth!"

"I didn't hand out toilet-paper in front of a cinema, burn it! I only said . . ."

"And you, Mr. MacFergus!"

Mr. MacFergus, turned away from them with his elbows on the mantelpiece, was sunk in an abyss of Caledonian remorse.

"The de'il was in me," he said in a hollow voice. "I canna blame the whusky this time. The de'il was in me."

"As for you, Sir Henry, it'll serve you right to find one of our blokes on your doorstep to-morrow morning. I tell you straight: it'll serve you right if you get six weeks without the option."

"I don't see how they can ketch me, Masters."

"You don't, eh?" inquired the Chief Inspector. "Where's your hat?"

H. M.'s hands went to his big bald head.

"You left it behind, didn't you? And it's got your name in it."

"I jumpit on it," groaned Mr. MacFergus. "The de'il was in me, and I jumpit on it."

"That," Masters was remorseless, "is the first point. The second point is that I let you come along to-night to see me nab Joe the Mole, *if* Joe showed up at Playland when he was supposed to. But would Joe be likely to show up, eh? With you smashing the whole place to blazes? Not bl—" Masters checked himself, glanced at Beryl, and swallowed hard. "Not very likely, is it? The fact is, sir, you've got me into plenty of trouble as well."

Despite his brave words, H. M. was in fact peering up at Masters with somewhat the air of a chastened Donald Duck.

"Now I don't say," pursued Masters, pointing his finger in H. M.'s face, "I don't say, mind you, but what I might be able to square this. I say I *might* be able to square it. But that's on one condition."

"Condition?"

"That you come off your ruddy high horse," said Masters, whacking his hand down on the table, "and give me a bit of advice about the Bewlay case."

There was a long silence in the smoke-fogged room with the sweating walls, while Mr. MacFergus half wept under the engraving of the Highland stag.

"Blackmail, hey?" demanded H. M.

"No, sir, it is *not* blackmail."

"It sounds awful like it to me, son."

"If we had no new evidence," Masters said doggedly, "oh, ah! Well! I might not have brought it up for the umpty-umph time. But it looks as though we've got some new evidence."

"So? What evidence?"

"This," Masters thrust Beryl forward, "is Miss West, the theatrical producer, who's done so many of Mr. Bruce Ransom's shows. This gentleman is Mr. Dennis Foster, who is . . . hurrum! . . ."

"Mr. Ransom's solicitor," supplied Dennis.

Masters could have made no happier introduction than the first. Anything to do with the stage instantly rivets the attention of Sir Henry Merrivale, whose own leanings in that direction have sometimes led to regrettable results. H. M., who had taken a cigar-case out of his pocket, regarded Beryl with ghoulish interest.

(Beryl, Dennis noticed with a stab of uneasiness, was as white as a ghost.)

"Now, sir!" Masters continued. "When I sent you that big file on Roger Bewlay, did you read it?"

"No," said H. M. mulishly.

"Come on, now! Fair's fair! Did you read it?"

"Well . . . now," growled H. M. He glowered at the black cigar he was turning over in his fingers. "I might just have peeped into it, yes. I might just have *glanced* at it, maybe, to see what you people were kickin' up such a fuss about."

"Do you remember about our witness at Torquay?"

H. M. grunted.

"Red-haired gal named Mildred Lyons," he replied. "Typist who got flummoxed with a bad ten-bob note. She looked through a window, and saw—a lot of things."

"So you do remember!"

"Maybe," H. M. said very thoughtfully, "I got a reason for remembering. But looky here, son! What's all this got to do with a noble profession like play-

73

acting? Ma'am," he added to Beryl, partly getting up to make as stately and ponderous a bow as his corporation would permit, "ma'am, I'm your very obedient servant."

"Th-thank you, Sir Henry," smiled Beryl. But the smile did not extend to her eyes.

Masters swept aside the amenities.

"Some unknown author," he explained, "wrote a play about Bewlay and sent it to Mr. Ransom. And this author knows too much. He knows the witness was a woman; where she looked and what she saw; every smacking thing that's been supposed to be known only by the police, by you, and by the Lyons girl herself."

Again there was silence. But this time it had a different quality.

Sir Henry Merrivale, who had bit off the end of the cigar and put it into his mouth, was just snapping the wheel of a pocket-lighter. As Masters said those words H. M. stopped suddenly, motionless, with the flame of the lighter two inches from the end of his cigar. Over his face, blurred in smoke-mist, flashed an expression very difficult to read.

But Dennis Foster became aware of a different aspect to this indecorous figure who kicked punching-bags through glass cases. For this was the Old Maestro.

H. M.'s face smoothed itself out. He blew out the flame of the lighter, and put both cigar and lighter down on the table.

"That's very interestin'," he observed in a mild voice. Then he blinked at Beryl. "Has Bruce Ransom accepted this play?"

Beryl lifted her shoulders.

"Yes, I suppose you could call it that."

"So of course he's met the author?"

"As I keep telling everybody: no! Bruce wrote to the author, yes. But we haven't had any answer."

"So? How long ago did he write to the author?"

"Three weeks."

"But that's rather rummy, ain't it?"

"How so?"

H. M.'s little eyes behind the big spectacles were fixed on her, with a disturbing and almost creepy quality Dennis had not seen there before.

"In my experience, d'ye see, when an unknown writer bungs in a play and has it accepted, the first thing he does is shoot back a letter by return of post. Then, as a rule, he goes and camps on the management's doorstep until they have screamin' hysterics."

"I'm afraid I haven't thought very much about it." Beryl drew a deep breath and turned out her wrist. "All sorts of things can happen, you know."

"They can, my wench. They do. All the same, Ransom is definitely goin' to use this play?"

"He's going to do more than that," interposed Dennis Foster. "He's going down to a place called Aldebridge, in Suffolk, and pretend to be Roger Bewlay so that he can see whether the end of the play is justified."

"What's that?" shouted Chief Inspector Masters.

And Dennis told him.

While the silence lengthened, and Beryl coughed, and even Mr. MacFergus forgot the enormities burdening his soul, Dennis explained the theme of the play. He outlined the plan for Bruce's masquerade. He told them in short, everything he could remember of the conversation in the dressing-room. And Masters's expression changed; but not H. M.'s.

"So he's going to Aldebridge, hey?" mused H. M. "Does this feller Ransom know anything about Aldebridge? Has he ever been there before?"

"Never!" It was Beryl who answered. "Bruce simply picked out the place at random."

"Then he's goin' to get something of a shock," said H. M. "Because I know a gal there who exactly fulfills the specifications for the heroine of the play. Her name's Daphne Herbert. Her father is—"

H. M. paused.

"I say, Masters," he added, and twiddled his thumbs over his stomach. "It'd be very curious, wouldn't it, if this play started actin' itself out line for line in real life?"

Masters threw back his head and snorted like a bull.

"Oh, ah!" he agreed darkly. "It might be what you call curious, sir. It might be. *If* I allowed it to happen?"

"You're not going to allow it to happen?"

"Sir, do you think I'm off my chump? Stand by in a tom-fool trick like this and maybe interfere with our chances of catching the real Bewlay?"

Dennis Foster glanced quickly at Beryl, and back again.

In the excitement of the moment a while ago, in the lightness and rashness with which we make promises, it had seemed to him that persuading Masters would not be too difficult. A little tact; a little amused comment; the thing would be done. But he had not reckoned with Masters's obsession on the subject of Roger Bewlay.

"May I point out, Chief Inspector," Dennis said sharply, "that Bruce won't be doing anything against the law?"

"I didn't say he would be, sir."

"Well, then?"

"But if Mr. Ransom thinks he can get away with this," Masters's colour came up again, "then he'll have another think coming. You leave it to me, sir. *I'll* spike the gentleman's guns good and proper."

"Oh, no, you won't," said H. M. calmly. "If you want any help from me."

Masters stared at him.

"You'll let the feller strictly alone," amplified H. M.

76

"What's more, you'll instruct the Aldebridge police to let him strictly alone. I'm tellin' you."

"Sir, are *you* crazy?"

"No."

"But why should you ask me to do that? Yes, I know!" Masters interrupted himself in haste, as H. M. started to make a powerfully impressive gesture. "You're the old man! I know all that! But just give me a reason!"

For a time H. M. did not reply. He seemed to be trying, with a hideous scowl, to place some elusive memory.

"Roger Bewlay," he muttered, "Roger Bewlay."

The top of the big round table was wet with spilled beer and the marks of glasses. Dipping his forefinger into the beer, Sir Henry Merrivale traced out on the table the letters *R. B.* He traced them out again, and craned his neck to study them sideways.

"I say, Masters," he went on. "Has it ever struck you how funny things look when they're written backwards? Remember the scene in *David Copperfield—*"

Masters said things about *David Copperfield* which would have been considered harsh even by the late William Makepeace Thackeray.

"Shut up," said H. M. austerely. "The scene (I was sayin') where the boy sees the mysterious words, 'Moor Eeffoc' on the back of the glass window, when it really reads 'Coffee Room'? And there was a chap who wrote a book about boozin' under the pen-name of Rab Noolas, which is rather a noble conception."

Then H. M. woke up out of his musing, vaguely.

"By the way, Masters. Were you askin' me something?"

Masters pressed his hands firmly to his bowler hat.

"As it happens," he roared, "I was asking you something. I want to know . . ."

77

"Oh, yes," said H. M., sweeping aside as unimportant what Masters wanted to know. "That reminds me I got a question for *you*. Looky here, son. You think this play about Bewlay is real red-hot new evidence?"

"I think it may lead us to new evidence, yes! Don't you? With somebody knowing too much?"

"Well . . . now. We got to make sure it hasn't an innocent explanation."

"Such as?"

"Lord love a duck, Masters, you talk as though it was impossible for somebody to blab. This gal Mildred Lyons, for instance. Suppose she told her terrible adventure to somebody, and it got to the ears of an aspiring writer? Can you, as a married man yourself, think of any way to prevent a woman from talkin'?"

"Oh, ah! I certainly can! If her life depends on it."

Masters tapped the table with his forefinger.

"Bewlay's a killer, sir," he went on. "If he ever learned the name of the witness who can hang him, the girl's life wouldn't be worth *that*." He snapped his fingers. "We told her so."

"Uh-huh," agreed H. M., although he gave Masters a very curious look.

"What's more, Mildred Lyons was so scared of Bewlay that she had a nervous breakdown afterwards. No, sir. That woman's never opened her mouth since, or I'm a Dutchman. I admit eleven years is a long time. I admit it'd be a good story to tell round the fire. But—!"

H. M. continued to survey Masters with that same odd expression.

"I was only," he grunted, "pointin' out one possible explanation. The other explanation (and oh, burn me, I prefer it!) is that . . ." Here H. M. looked at Beryl. "Anything wrong, my wench?"

Beryl had backed slowly away from them.

"No, of course not! What on earth could be wrong?"

"Sure, my wench?"

"It's this poisonous atmosphere." Beryl blinked smarting eyes and moved her hand in the air, trying to dispel smoke. Eagerly she elaborated this explanation. "Did you ever see such an awful fug in all your life? It's making me lightheaded. I can't breathe."

"Well, miss, that's easily remedied," said Masters. He coughed in his turn. "Come to think of it, it is a bit on the thick side."

Masters strode over to the nearer of the two windows.

"But the main point is," he persisted, laying hold of the wooden blackout-frame, and addressing H. M. over his shoulder, "the main point is: what do you THINK of this whole business?"

"The Bewlay business in general?"

"Yes! Here's a man who murders women, and then makes their bodies vanish as though they'd been hit by an atom bomb. How does he do it?"

"I'd appreciate it a lot, Masters, if you'd send me that file again to-morrow morning. Also any information you've been able to dig up about our friend's early life, before he became the smilin' murderer. In the meantime,"—vaguely troubled, H. M. ruffled his hands across his big bald head—"in the meantime, I think I can tell you the source of all your trouble."

"Well, sir?"

"You don't know what your problem is."

"What's that?"

"You don't know what your problem is," repeated H. M.

"Our problem," said Masters, "is what in lum's name happened to Roger Bewlay and how he disposed of four bodies. Isn't it?"

"Not exactly," said H. M.

79

Masters, as though not for the moment deigning to reply, pulled down the blackout-frame from a grimy window. The maddened Chief Inspector propped this frame under the window; and he was raising his head again when he stopped, as though paralysed, staring out the window. Five seconds crawled by before Masters spoke.

"Put out the light, somebody," he said.

"Eh, son?"

"Put out that light!"

The urgency in Masters's voice jabbed at the nerves and set them quivering. Dennis Foster hurried over and pressed the switch beside the door.

Darkness, an extinguisher-cap, added to the oppressiveness in throat and nostrils. But faint light showed outside the window, against which they could see Masters's silhouette as he stood with his fists on the sill. With one impulse Dennis Foster and Beryl West ran to his side.

And at last Dennis found his sense of direction. This pub, of course, must face St. Martin's Lane, and they were in a room on the south side. They had doubled back on their tracks. They were now looking out, straight across a paved alley hardly fifteen feet wide, at the stage-door of the Granada Theatre.

(A conductor had lifted his baton, a wheel had begun to spin, for a movement of quick and evil events which should not now ease in their rapidity until the last strangling.)

"Look!" said Masters. "Know who that is?"

A lamp burned above the stage-door, showing the dull and blistered green paint of the door as it was pushed open. In the aperture stood a hatless woman in a grey mackintosh, on her way out of the theatre.

This woman had a furtiveness of movement, yet a quick-breathing excitement. She glanced first left and then right, as though uncertain of the way out into Charing Cross Road. The light shone down on her pale red hair. She was not pretty; far from it, to judge by what could be seen amid shadows. Yet you noticed her. Her pale-blue eyes glittered with some emotion between fear and triumph.

Then Masters spoke again.

"That's Mildred Lyons," he said. "Excuse me."

And he turned and ran for the door. They could hear him blundering in the dark, fumbling for door and key.

Also in the dark Beryl groped for Dennis's hand, and gripped it hard. The red-haired woman, after a quick glance behind her, closed the stage-door. Through the grimy window-pane they saw her hurry away, her head down, in the direction of Charing Cross Road.

A cat squalled at a rubbish-bin, whose iron lid rattled. Sir Henry Merrivale was swearing. But Beryl (which was all an emotionally upset Dennis could take in) now pressed against his side as though for protection. When he put his arm reassuringly across her shoulders, Dennis felt her whole body tremble. A warm, breathing bundle of nerves, she emanated emotion before she had spoken a word.

"I started this," she whispered. "It's all my fault. But now I'm afraid." Her voice rose. "I'm afraid. I'm afraid. I'm afraid!"

7

The telegram read:

ARRIVED BACK FROM AMERICA YESTERDAY TRIED
TO PHONE YOU AT OFFICE BUT YOU WERE OUT CAN
YOU GO WITH ME TO ALDEBRIDGE TOMORROW
FRIDAY ONE OCLOCK TRAIN LIVERPOOL STREET
SOMETHING DREADFUL HAPPENING LOVE BERYL.

Dennis Foster found it in the letter-box at his flat
when he returned there, lonely, on the night of
Thursday the fourth of October.

Nearly a month had gone by since that night in the
pub. Its blankness, its apparent dearth of news despite
one ugly incident, filled him with even more disquiet.
He tried to brush this away by concentrating on his
work, of which there had been more than enough. Mr.
Mackintosh, senior partner of the old and crusted firm
of Mackintosh & Foster (it dated from 1741) was
getting on in years.

For a moment, when he read Beryl's telegram,
Dennis thought he couldn't possibly make it.

Friday, his diary told him, was a heavy day. His head
buzzed with things to be done. But a tempter whispered

that he had two capable juniors. If he could apportion out all the work by the end of Friday morning, he might catch that one o'clock train.

Dennis very nearly missed the train, in spite of miraculously getting a taxi. He charged through the barrier at Liverpool Street Station, clutching an overnight-bag, just as the train began to glide out.

"Something dreadful happening."

Dennis ran like hell.

Then he saw Beryl in the corridor of a first-class carriage, leaning out of the open window, and waving frantically. With a burst of speed he made it, slamming the door behind him. Breathing hard, he stood in the corridor and looked at Beryl, while they rattled out through the gloom of an overcast day. This train, he saw with surprise, was almost empty.

"Hello, Beryl," he said.

"Hello, darling."

"You're looking very fit, Beryl. Did you have a pleasant trip?"

"I'm all right, thanks. I—I had a lot of good food. But there was too much of it, really; it digusted me. And I bought a lot of lovely new clothes."

"The Broadway opening was a success, I hope?"

"I'm afraid not, darling. They gave it an awful raspberry. But I always said they would, and it doesn't matter anyway."

To tell the strict truth, Beryl was not looking very fit. The exceptional smartness of her clothes, something in green with gold costume-jewellery, showed in contrast to a white, apologetic, smiling face. Her soft sleek hair trembled against her cheeks to the jerking, swaying motion of the train. Beryl stared out of the corridor windows.

"Dennis dear," she burst out, "what's been *happening* while I was away?"

"But I don't know! I thought you did!"

"Have you seen Bruce?"

"No."

"Why on earth not?"

"Well . . . I didn't want to seem inquisitive. It's not quite the thing."

"Oh, Dennis!" She surveyed him in helpless reproachfulness. "Bruce is your friend. It surely wouldn't have seemed inquisitive to—anyway! Have you seen Mr. Masters?"

"I talked to him once on the telephone."

"Yes, Dennis?"

"It seems that Sir . . . oh, let's call him H. M.; everybody else does! . . . it seems H. M. gave Masters strict instructions to keep away from Bruce. That nearly sent Masters through the roof. But he soon got an excuse to call on Bruce just before Bruce left town, though Masters still didn't let on the police knew anything. Do you remember that last night at the amusement arcade and the pub?"

"Do I remember it! With Bruce completely disappearing, and not even showing up at the Ivy for dinner? I—I didn't even see him to say good-bye."

It had been a lugubrious meal, Dennis conceded. But he swept this aside.

"On that same night," he went on, "there was a burglary at the office of Ethel Whitman & Co., the typewriting place in Bedford Street. Somebody stole the script of the Bewlay play, the only script there was."

"Oh?" said Beryl in a very curious voice.

"By H. M.'s order it's been kept a dead secret; nothing in the papers, and everyone concerned, including Bruce, sworn to secrecy."

"What did Bruce have to say when he heard about it?"

"Apparently he just laughed like a fiend and said it

didn't matter. But, look here! What have you got to tell me? Your telegram . . ."

The train-whistle screamed. Beryl opened a gleaming new handbag, took out a crumpled note, and handed it to him. Its printed letter-head read, *The Leather Boot Hotel, Seacrest, near Aldebridge,* and in Bruce's quick sprawling handwriting it was dated September 27th.

ANGEL-FACE:

Your cable says you'll be back by the Queen Elizabeth about the fourth or fifth. If you love me come down here as soon as you can. Can't explain now, but I'm in trouble. I need you.

Yours in haste,

BRUCE.

P.S. Hope you had a good time in the States. Sorry to have been so remiss about writing.

"It's the only line he's written since I've been away," said Beryl, taking back the note. "Sam Andrews, that's our stage-director, says he won't even answer business letters. But the point is, darling: he isn't one to get the wind up about nothing."

"No. He certainly isn't. What do you think's happened?"

Beryl, shutting up her handbag with an angry click, was about to reply when the sound of a new voice struck her dumb.

They were standing in the corridor between two compartments, all the compartment doors being closed. But the door of the one just beyond Beryl had its glass panel pushed a little way down. A girl's voice— very clear, with the soft ringing quality of youth—rose up with a kind of shivering stubbornness.

"I'm sorry, Dad. I can't help what you say, or

86

Mother says, or anybody in Aldebridge says. I think I'm in love with him."

"Daphne, listen! With a man who may be . . . well!"

"Please go on! Why do you always stop there, and not want to face it? Who may be what?"

"Very well, my dear; let's face it. Who may be a murderer."

Beryl and Dennis exchanged a slow, startled glance. While you might have counted ten, they stood motionless.

Then Beryl moved backwards for a quick look into the compartment. She was instantly hauled back by Dennis, who made a fierce pantomime of one who is about to wallop her; but not before Dennis himself, insistently impelled, had caught a brief glimpse of three persons inside.

In the far corner seat facing the engine sat a fashionably dressed woman, ageing but still pretty, who could only be the mother. In the place beside her, swung round so that his back was towards the watchers in the corridor, sat a grey-haired man with a harassed voice.

The girl stood up, facing them, her back to the outer door. Despite the dim gritty light outside, Dennis and Beryl in the corridor had a clear glimpse of her.

Ordinarily, he guessed, this girl would be inarticulate. She had been too obedient, too restrained, too well-brought-up. Even now, in fighting back, she kept her eyes lowered and a flush of sheer embarrassment stained her cheeks. It was only strong emotion that brought the words tumbling out. And emotion was strung to a dangerous pitch in that compartment.

Dennis could not see them now. But he could hear the voices.

"Daphne, listen!" urged the voice of the grey-haired man.

"Yes, Daddy? I'm listening."

("Daphne Herbert!" whispered Beryl, with her lips against Dennis's ear. "I knew I'd heard that name before. Daphne Herbert!")

"Your mother and I decided long ago, Daphne, that when the time came for you to think of . . . well! of getting married, or anything like that, we wouldn't stand in the way of your choice. Didn't we decide that, Clara?"

The other woman's voice spoke in a pleasant but not very intelligent-sounding tone.

"Of course, Jonathan. But it's so silly for our Daphne to talk about being in love!"

"Why is it silly?" cried the girl.

"Don't ask foolish questions, my dear."

"But *why* is it silly? Didn't you fall in love with Daddy?"

(Now when an English family gets to talking as frankly as this, you may bet that they have forgotten themselves in the presence of something serious.)

"Yes. I—I suppose I did."

"And didn't it turn out happily?"

There was a slight pause. Mrs. Herbert's voice softened.

"Terribly happily!" she said. It was a cry from the heart, which you could not hear unmoved. "But that's a very different thing, Daphne."

"Why is it different?"

"I was of mature years and—and everything. Oh, do stop it! I wasn't a silly little schoolgirl."

"Clara my dear," Mr. Jonathan Herbert observed mildly, "we might at least have the decency and justice to treat Daphne as being grown-up. Which, after all, she is."

"Thanks, Daddy! Thanks terribly!"

"But the point I'm trying to make," persisted Mr.

Herbert, "is not Daphne's age. After all, she's twenty-four. What I'm talking about is the *man* in question. Provided the man's all right, I've got no objection whatever her choice is. I don't care whether she marries a duke or a dustman, or a—or a confounded artist or actor! But this fellow What's-his-name: do you realize he may well be a murdering lunatic the police have been after for years?"

Daphne's voice sounded stifled.

"So you've been listening to the poisonous gossip too."

"Haven't you, my dear?"

"What I can't understand," said Daphne, "is how all this horrible talk got *started.*"

"Come now, my dear! Be fair and reasonable!"

"I am being fair and reasonable!"

Trailing another scream from its whistle, the train plunged into one of those many tunnels which shut away the railway-line from the suburbs.

Darkness descended, smothering even the noise of the whistle. Then, a second later, four bright little lights flashed on in each compartment. The watchers had no longer any need to look in. On the black corridor-windows, backed by ghostly white steam billowing past, these lights threw a reflected image of Mr. Herbert, of Mrs. Herbert, and of Daphne. Every colour, every line, was reflected with spectral vividness in the glass.

If Daphne Herbert had possessed more animation, less shyness, she would have been genuinely beautiful. Even as it was, the sedate Dennis Foster felt his heart contract with an emotion he had seldom known.

The broad low forehead, the short nose, the arched eyebrows, were framed in brown-golden hair which gleamed under the lights. Her figure had that virginal yet mature air which was only emphasized by a white frock of a pattern rather too young for her. Despite Daphne's fiery embarrassment, hard-breathing, she could no longer keep her eyes lowered. The eyes were of a light grey, black-fringed, puzzled and appealing.

("Beryl!" Dennis whispered. He was so bowled over that he had to say something. "What's the matter with you?")

("Those people!")

("Well?")

("They're exactly like the long descriptions of the characters in the play. It might have been written for 'em!")

("Sh-h!")

Mr. Jonathan Herbert had to raise his voice above the hollow tumult of the train roaring through the tunnel.

"Listen, Daphne! On the very first day your paragon arrives at the Leather Boot, he absentmindedly starts to write the wrong name in the hotel register. He writes: 'Roger Be—' and then hastily scratches it out."

"You haven't any proof of that!"

"Commander Renwick saw it, my dear. Renwick's the proprietor of the hotel; he ought to know."

"But . . . !"

"And I was there myself, and so was Chittering, in the smoking-room of the Leather Boot, when your Mongolian-faced gentleman gave that little lecture on how easy is it to strangle people. My word, it made our hair stand on end. There's been nothing like it since I saw Richard Mansfield in *Jekyll and Hyde*."

("Good lord," whispered Dennis, "Bruce is overplaying his part like . . . like . . .")

("Sh-h!" hissed Beryl.)

"What put the tin-hat on it, Daphne, was when Chittering got him to talking about famous criminal cases. Chittering led him on to the subject of Bewlay.

When this fine fellow of yours spoke about Bewlay's second victim, that music-student Elizabeth What's-her-name—"

"Please, Daddy!"

"—he gave some details that Chittering swears, and the vicar agrees with him, have never been published in any book or article."

Daphne's spectral image in the glass was contorted by more than the vibration of the train.

"I c-can't stand this," she said. "It's all so utterly fantastic!"

"Granted, my dear. But it happens to be true."

Daphne's eyes brimmed over.

"And if you think he's—what he oughtn't to be, which he *isn't*, I tell you, he *isn't*, because he's a darling and I'm in love with him—if you think that, Daddy, why don't you try to be fair to him instead of just muttering in corners? Why don't you go to him and ask him?"

"That, my dear, is exactly what I propose to do."

"Jonathan," cried Mrs. Herbert, "for heaven's sake don't let's have a scene! Wouldn't it—wouldn't it be simpler to go to the police?"

"To be perfectly frank, Clara, I've already been to the police."

"You've . . ." Daphne's grey eyes, with their tear-damped black lashes, opened wide. For a moment she hardly seemed to breathe. "You've *been* to the police?"

"Yes. Three days ago."

"And what did they say?"

"They laughed at me."

Mr. Herbert lifted his fist. The train emerged from its tunnel in a white whirl of steam, destroying mirrored images, but almost immediately plunged into another.

"I went to the police-station," said Mr. Herbert, unclenching his fist bewilderedly. "Inspector Parks is

91

an old friend of mine. I . . ."

"Please go on, Daddy!"

"Confound it, how *is* one to approach a subject like that? I hemm'd and haw'd; and finally I asked Parks straight out if he'd heard any rumours about Bewlay being in Aldebridge."

"Yes?"

"Parks just smiled in a confoundedly peculiar way and said: 'Don't you worry about that, sir; we're not worrying.' Then he ushered me out. That was when they all started to laugh."

"Laugh? Who laughed?"

"First the inspector, then the sergeant, and then the constable." Mr. Herbert's voice went up. "The windows of the police-station were wide open, and I could hear them distinctly. They stood there and laughed like maniacs while I went down the path."

Daphne's face was radiant. A healthy, triumphant girl seemed to emerge from nightmare.

"But, Daddy! Why couldn't you have told me this before? Don't you see it changes everything?"

"How does it change everything?"

"Because it puts an end to this filthy gossip! The police would know, wouldn't they?"

The badgered Mr. Herbert hesitated and wavered.

"Yes. I dare say they *ought* to know. That was what shook me up. All the same—"

"I'm sorry, Daddy; but I'm afraid I'm in love with him."

"Look here, my dear. I don't want to do the fellow an injustice. All your mother and I want is for you to be happy. But I think he's a wrong 'un; and somehow or other I'll prove it."

Again Daphne's voice had a stifled sound.

"If you're not careful," she said, "I'll run away with him to-morrow. Yes, I will! He's asked me to."

Mr. Herbert sprang to his feet.

"This fellow's asked you to run away and marry him?"

"Yes!"

Out in the corridor, Dennis Foster and Beryl West exchanged glances.

("Let's get away from here," Beryl muttered, with her face turned away. "Hurry! Quick! Please!")

Dennis agreed with her. The clackety-roar in their ears, the lights jolting on dingy woodwork and grey upholstery, the claustrophobia induced by the tunnel, had begun to press in on them like the unpleasant possibilities that were gathering.

Breathing cinder-dust, they walked back along the corridor. Beryl dragged open the door of another compartment, and she had taken a step inside before they realized it was not empty.

A stoutish comfortable-looking man, bald except for a few strands of brown hair brushed across his skull, was sitting in the outside corner seat, idly turning over the pages of a well-thumbed book. A little inquisitive eye was turned towards them as Beryl dragged open the door, and the man smiled.

"I beg your pardon!" shouted Beryl, who wanted a place where they could talk and talk and talk. "Wrong compartment!"

"Not at all," the other said politely.

He smiled again, directed another sidelong glance, and settled down to his book as comfortably as a cat by the fire. Dennis, with an irrational sense of shock, had noticed the title of that book as the stranger momentarily closed it. You could not miss the title; it ran in staring black letters across dust-grey cloth, as clear as the train-whistle in the tunnel.

Its title was: *The Art of Writing Plays.*

8

It was only when they were alone together in a different compartment, with the train emerging from the last of its tunnels, that a pent-up torrent of words burst out.

"Beryl," said Dennis, in a voice he very seldom used, "has Bruce gone clean out of his mind?"

Beryl gave a quick glance, and then wouldn't look at him. Beryl sank down, as though furtively, in a seat with her back to the engine.

"Why do you say that, Dennis?"

"Because this 'experiment' is beginning to scare me." Then his voice poured with bitterness; he discovered, in some surprise, that his arms and shoulders were trembling.

"I mean," he went on, "when Bruce takes up some casual love-affair to prove an academic theory, is it customary for him to ask the girl whether she'll elope and marry him? Is that your God-damned theatrical habit?"

Beryl, looking rather shocked, was now regarding him with wide-eyed astonishment.

"Dennis!" she exclaimed.

"Never mind my language. *Is it?*"

Beryl transferred her attention, with the utmost absorption, to a metal ashtray fixed underneath the window. Outside, the last white shreds of steam-cloud eddied past against an overcast day.

"When a man gets excited over a love-affair," she answered, "he's apt to say anything. You ought to know that, Dennis, even if you won't admit it. But . . ."

"But what?"

"I've never known *Bruce* to talk like that. His—his attitude is: 'I like you, and you like me, so let's enjoy ourselves and not get serious and make a Thing of it'."

"Indeed. That must be very satisfactory."

"It's not satisfactory," said Beryl, concentrating fiercely on the ashtray. "It never works. Because, when you try that, one party or the other always does get serious. Then it's: 'Why did you lead me on, in that case?' And the most awful scenes. And . . . oh, what does it matter? All I can tell you is that it's not Bruce's technique."

Dennis drew the back of his hand across his forehead.

"Then the only explanation," he said, "is that Bruce really has fallen with a bang for—for Miss Herbert. Lord knows, I couldn't blame him if he has."

"Yes. It struck me you were rather smitten."

"I am not 'rather smitten'," retorted Dennis, in a voice that sounded very loud in the compartment. "May I point out that I have never exchanged a word with the young lady, or seen her for more than ten minutes? In any case," he added bitterly, "what chance would I stand against Bruce Ransom?"

Beryl, huddled up in the corner with her arms folded, did not reply.

"The point is," Dennis insisted, "that we've got to stop this nonsense at once!"

96

"What nonsense?"

"Bruce's masquerade! The old man down there,"—his gesture indicated the direction of Mr. Jonathan Herbert—"is nearly out of his mind. There's going to be trouble. Bruce has got to stop boasting of Bewlay's crimes on the strength of information he got out of somebody's play."

"He didn't get the information of that play," said Beryl very quietly. "It's not in the play."

There was a long pause.

"What's that?" demanded Dennis.

There had been something in the very quietness of Beryl's tone which swept the protest out of his mind, and momentarily swept away even the image of Daphne Herbert's face. While he stared at Beryl, she sat up straight. He could not read her expression.

"Dennis, do you remember that last night in the dressing-room? And Bruce said something like: 'That little detail of the woman peeping through the window curtains, and seeing the victim rumpled-up and strangled on the couch, while Bewlay lights a cigarette under the lamp: there's your keynote on how to play the part.' Do you remember, Dennis?"

"Of course I remember. What about it?"

Beryl moistened her lips.

"I thought it was funny at the time, if you noticed. But I didn't say anything." She nodded like a somnambulist, "I—I only started to get the wind up when those same words gave Mr. Masters such a shock in the amusement arcade. So I said it was in the play. But it wasn't in the play."

Suddenly a premonition of horror began to crawl through Dennis Foster.

He started to get up, but at Beryl's gesture he sat down again.

"It wasn't written in the play, you see," she continued

97

in the same hypnotized voice. "It's supposed to be known only to the witness and to the police. *But Bruce knows it.*"

Beryl paused.

"Bruce," she said, "is forty-one years old. That would make the dates about right. And why does Bruce loathe film-work so much? He *says* it's because film-work ruins your acting for the stage. He says that in front of a camera you can't even raise an eyebrow to express surprise without its making your whole face go lopsided like this." Here Beryl made a hideously distorted face. "Is it really because he can't be recognized on the stage, whereas he might very well be recognized in a film close-up?

"Dennis, please wait before you say anything!" Her voice rose. "Where I got the wind up worst that last night, and I'm afraid I showed it, was at the pub when Sir Henry Merrivale started talking. The old devil (remember?) said it was awfully funny how things look when they're read backwards. He even drew some initials on the table to illustrate. Don't you see, Dennis, don't you see that the initials of 'Bruce Ransom' are just 'Roger Bewlay' read backwards?"

Softly the train-wheels clicked, softly the carriage swayed, while you might have counted twenty.

Then Dennis's voice sounded strange and wild and hoarse in his own ears.

"What in God's name are you trying to tell me? That . . ."

"Sh-h! Please!"

"That Bruce *is* Roger Bewlay?"

"I want you to tell me I'm the world's ghastliest idiot," said Beryl, swallowing hard and then appealing to him with all the strength of her nature. "I want to be comforted. I want you to prove I'm c-crazy. But I've been thinking about it, over and over, day and night, no rest or peace, until I had to tell somebody or die."

"But it's preposterous!"

"I know, dear. Utterly fantastic!"

"Impossible!"

"Yes! Out of the question! I couldn't agree more. Only," added Beryl, slowly reaching for her handbag on the seat beside her, "there is that little matter of Mildred Lyons."

"Mildred Lyons? What about her?"

"Don't you see, Dennis? It was Mildred Lyons who called on Bruce at the theatre that night! The mysterious person who sent in the note, and Bruce threw us out of his dressing-room as soon as he read it? It—it didn't occur to me at the time, of course. I was simply blind-jealous. I suppose you guessed that?"

Dennis looked very hard at the floor.

"Yes, Beryl. I guessed it."

Fumblingly, trying to keep her head lowered, Beryl opened the handbag and sought after a compact. Her fine green suit was rumpled, like the new nylon stockings.

"Bruce," she said, "can no more stay away from women than—than he can keep from over-acting, unless you hold him down. I thought it was a new affair. But it wasn't. It was Mildred Lyons."

"Wait a minute, now! Why should Mildred Lyons be calling on Bruce?"

"Oh, Dennis! Have you forgotten? The Lyons girl was an expert typist, with an office of her own in Torquay."

"Well?"

"Well! What's more likely, with the war and all, than that her office folded up? And she went in with a bigger firm like Ethel Whitman? Then along comes this play, which Bruce sends to be copied . . ."

"And Mildred Lyons reads it? Is that what you're

trying to say?"

"Yes! The play is a perfectly harmless piece of imagination. But it would naturally rouse Mildred Lyons's curiosity. The woman, in all innocence, goes along to Bruce to see whether he knows anything about the author. And in Bruce's dressing-room she comes face to face with . . . with a murderer. With Bewlay himself. With the man she can hang. Do you remember her face, when she slipped out of the theatre that night?"

Dennis remembered it.

In imagination he saw again the red-haired woman furtively hurrying out by the stage-door. He saw the hollows under her eyes. He saw the shift and gleam of those eyes, right and left, glittering with some emotion between fear and triumph. He heard the squall of a cat, the rattle of a dustbin-lid.

Masters hadn't caught up with Miss Lyons, that night. She vanished in the crowds of Charing Cross Road, vanished heaven knew where. It suddenly occurred to Dennis that if Mildred Lyons were to be found dead . . .

"They'll hang him," said Beryl. "Don't you see the police suspect? That's why H. M.'s giving him all this liberty, so he'll put the rope round his own neck. They'll hang him."

"Stop it, Beryl!"

"They'll hang him," said Beryl, in a frenzy. "Please, for God's sake, don't let them hang him!"

And, uncontrollably, she began to sob.

Dennis's wits were whirling. He got up from his seat, and took Beryl by the shoulders. He shook her with violence, in a frenzy of his own, until the sobs partly subsided; but her shoulders felt soft and limp under his fingers, and her neck as limp as though it had been broken.

"Beryl! Listen to me!"

"Y-yes?"

"I want you to look me in the eyes. Go on: do it! I want you to look me in the eyes, and tell me you don't believe one word of this rubbish."

"But I don't believe it, Dennis! Not really and truly."

"Then why the devil are you carrying on like this?"

"Because it *might* be, Dennis. And if it is . . ."

Now in his imagination, very clearly, he saw Bruce Ransom. He saw the high cheek-bones, the slow-curving smile, the powerful hands. He saw Bruce stepping softly across the dressing-room, and remembered certain enigmatic looks out of a mirror. A chill of horror had got into Dennis's bones. But Bruce was his friend; he couldn't entertain even a suspicion of this.

So Dennis fought his way through the fog.

"Does it strike you as likely, Beryl, that if Bruce were really this fellow . . . well! that he'd want to, or even dare, play his own part on the stage?"

"Yes, it does. Out of conceit."

"Conceit?"

"The sheer vanity, the awful urge to show off, that no murderer like that can help."

"But Bruce isn't conceited!"

"You mean he doesn't show it. And, if you remember, the play ends by proving that the central figure isn't Bewlay at all. So he'd think it was safe."

"If you go on like this, Beryl, you'll have *me* uneasy. I tell you it's fantastic! Putting the theatre to one side, would the real Bewlay go and play his own part in a Suffolk village? Stirring up everybody and probably getting the police on his track?"

"N-no. There is that. Unless . . ."

"You've got too much imagination, Beryl. It poisons your life. It won't let you stop worrying. But you've got to get this nonsense out of your mind! The real Bewlay

101

may be dead, for all we know. In any case he's hundreds of miles from Aldebridge. The real Bewlay—"

A new voice said:

"I beg your pardon." And Dennis, as though he had got a blow under the heart, released Beryl's shoulders and jumped back. Embarrassing scenes, he thought, were becoming the order of the day.

Neither of them had heard the door to the corridor roll back. In the aperture, steadying himself against the motion of the train, stood a tall lean man who was regarding them with a polite smile.

Everything about this newcomer breathed of the retired naval-officer. He seemed to be wearing a uniform, brushed and straight-backed, even though he wore country tweeds and a soft hat. Twinkling eyes that radiated wrinkles contemplated them above a straight nose and thick, close-cropped beard and moustache of gleaming dark-brown.

The newcomer had lost an arm, presumably the reason for his discharge from the service. His empty left sleeve was tucked into the jacket-pocket, and he carried one shoulder higher than the other. In his right hand he held a small suitcase, with cardboard label attached— and Dennis Foster's overnight bag.

The bearded man cleared his throat.

"Er—forgive me for intruding," he continued in his pleasant, heavy voice. "But may I inquire, madam," he held up the two valises, "whether these belong to you? I found them both in the corridor."

Beryl had instantly recovered her composure. She had taken her compact out of her handbag, and was opening it with every evidence of coolness.

"The larger one is mine," she answered. "Thanks awfully!"

"And the smaller one is mine," said Dennis. "I left it

102

in the corridor, and I'm afraid I forgot it. Hope you didn't trip over 'em?"

"Not at all," smiled the stranger. He put one bag on the seat beside Dennis, and the other on the seat beside Beryl. On the crumpled cardboard label attached to the suitcase Dennis could see the red letters: "Cunard White-Star Line," with Beryl's name, ship, and cabin-number printed below in ink.

"May I also ask," pursued the newcomer, after a slight hesitation, "whether you are the Miss West who wired for two rooms at the Leather Boot Hotel?"

Beryl looked up quickly from the compact.

"Yes!" she said. "But . . ."

"My name is Renwick," explained the stranger, with faint apology. "I'm the proprietor of the hotel."

"Commander Renwick!" said Beryl. "I knew I'd heard somebody use that name! Commander Renwick!"

"Not 'commander,' if you please." Wrinkles of amusement deepened round the eyes in Renwick's long, weatherbeaten face. Teeth gleamed white against the beard when he smiled. "I'm a publican now, Miss West. All I can hope is that I'm a good one."

"I'm sure you are," said Beryl. "Up in town for the day?"

"Yes." Commander Renwick's tone was whimsical. "Quite a number of local people seem to have made the same decision. Mr. and Mrs. Herbert and their daughter, and Mr. Chittering too. But what I wanted to tell you, Miss West—"

"Forgive me," interposed Beryl. "Is Mr. Chittering a stoutish rather ugly-looking man with an inquisitive face? Reading a book on how to write plays?"

"Well!" said Commander Renwick. "As to his personal appearance . . ."

"I knew it!" said Beryl. "The village gossip!"

Commander Renwick, obviously, was very pukka. Very much the sort of person who, despite his affability in the bar, does not let you forget that he has been an officer and a gentleman. He stood there stiffly and a little awkwardly with his empty left sleeve, eyebrows raised and a thread of silver glinting in his beard when he turned his head.

"I—I beg your pardon?"

"It's in the play," Beryl said rather wildly. "All the characters are coming to life. If the old man does lose his head and try to shoot . . ." Catching Dennis's warning glance, she stopped dead.

For a moment there was no sound except the rattle of the train. Commander Renwick opened his mouth to say something, but thought better of it. It was Renwick, however, who broke the silence.

"Chittering—er—certainly does like to talk. His best friends couldn't deny that." The smile returned, engagingly, amid wrinkles. "Nevertheless! What I wanted to tell you, Miss West, is that I'm afraid we can't put anybody up at the Leather Boot."

Beryl sprang to her feet.

"You see," Renwick hastened on, "we've had the military in our district for years. There was a battle-school, and it's been a prohibited area."

"But—!"

"The golf links are in good condition, because the colonel's staff used it; and they've taken the mines and barbed wire off the beach. But I've been trying to get the poor old hotel repaired, and it's been a bit of a job. Next spring, of course, I should be delighted to . . ."

"But you've already got—" Again Beryl checked herself.

"Yes," said Renwick. "I've already got one guest. A Mr. Bruce Egerton from London. I let him have a bedroom and a sitting-room. And, quite frankly, I wish

I hadn't."

Dennis's throat felt dry. "Oh? Why do you wish that?"

"Because," replied Commander Renwick. "I shouldn't like to see him lynched."

"Lynched?" cried Beryl.

(We are being drawn into a situation, thought Dennis, which grows worse and worse with every click of the train-wheels.)

"Yesterday," said Commander Renwick, "somebody threw a stone at him from behind a hedge. It hit him in the temple and almost knocked him out. You—er—wouldn't find the atmosphere soothing. Now I must really apologize again for intruding on you."

And with another courtly smile, raising his hat so as to show a glint of silver in the thick dark-brown hair, he turned round and moved rather awkwardly towards the door.

"Commander Renwick!" said Beryl.

The other halted and looked back.

"I don't," Beryl spoke very clearly, "I don't expect you to understand or sympathize . . ."

"My dear lady!"

"But please believe me when I say that it's terribly, vitally important for us to be at that hotel. For a reason I can't explain now, I think it's the most important thing in my life. Can't you *please* possibly give us a shakedown of some kind, even if it's only for one night?"

Renwick hesitated. He looked at the floor. He studied Beryl through somewhat pouchy eyelids. The fingers of his right hand, long and sinewy, twisted a leather-covered button on his coat. Then he cleared his throat.

"You wouldn't object to roughing it?" he asked.

"Does anybody object to roughing it nowadays?"

"Well. I'll see what I can do."

"Thank you, Commander Renwick!"

"Not at all. This gentleman is . . . ?"

"Mr. Foster. He's—my solicitor." .

Renwick inclined his head gravely. "You know your stop, of course?"

"Know our stop?"

"You don't go on into Aldebridge," the other explained. "Your stop is Seacrest Halt, about a mile this side of town. I can't go with you, I'm afraid; I've left my car in Aldebridge and I must go on to get it. But if you get out at Seacrest and cut straight across the golf links, you can't miss the hotel on the edge of the beach. Only: please take care."

"What do you mean by that?"

"Just what I say, Miss West. Take care."

With a final smile, ineffably sympathetic, he went out into the corridor and dragged shut the door. The whistle screamed again as he wandered off in the direction of the compartment occupied by Mr. Chittering.

Beryl stood motionless, the open compact still in one hand and her handbag in the other. She threw out her arms, spilling powder from the compact. When she spoke, in a husky frightened voice, she did not explain the meaning of what welled up from her heart; but Dennis thought he understood.

"My God!" said Beryl. "My God! My God!"

And, after that, she shivered.

9

From where they stood, on the high ground beside the railway-line at Seacrest Halt, they had a clear view eastwards.

It was a quarter-past four in the afternoon, drawing towards twilight. A wind from the North Sea, sullenest of waters, stirred across that expanse and crept into their nostrils with what at first was grateful coolness.

A salt wind, carrying a faint wash of the incoming tide. It blew across a shingle beach, up past a rambling weather-boarded structure, once painted white with green shutters, which could only be the Leather Boot Hotel. It touched the low, rolling hills of the golf links, with bunkers like prehistoric graves and sand-traps glimmering white, with greens still vivid under their red flags but fairways already dulled by autumn. It fluttered the leaves of tall trees along the edges of the rough, yet it seemed to make no sound there because the leaves were yellowing and damp.

"Ugh!" said Beryl.

Nobody except Beryl and Dennis got out at Seacrest Halt. Or, to be more exact, they saw nobody. The rumble of the train died away towards Aldebridge, leaving an immensity of silence.

"Beryl," Dennis began abruptly, "what are you going to say to Bruce?"

"I don't know," she answered just as abruptly.

"You're not going to tell him this nonsensical idea that he's Bewlay?"

For a time she did not reply. They descended a long flight of wooden steps, carrying them down from the high ground so that they no longer had a view of the sea. Nothing can be lonelier than a wayside station. No dog barked; not even a signal-arm stirred. They crossed a road, beyond which lay open ground then a fence with a stile, then, longways as they faced it, a brambly stretch of "rough" on the edge of the links. Through the stems of tall trees along this edge, they could again see the melancholy links beyond.

It was perhaps this loneliness, this sense of intimacy, which wrung the words from Dennis Foster.

"Beryl," he said, "you're very much in love with Bruce. Aren't you?"

"Yes. I'm afraid so."

"Would you still be in love with him even if he *is* . . . you know?"

Beryl turned a white face.

"If he's Bewlay," she said, "I'm going to kill him myself."

"Beryl! Easy!"

"I mean it, Dennis. I don't know if I have the nerve, but I'll try. When you think of all those women, buried and rotting in the dark . . . !"

"But we don't know how the fellow disposed of those bodies! That's what's driving everybody mad. You don't think Bruce, Bruce of all people, could devise a way to make them disintegrate?"

"Is my idea so nonsensical, Dennis? Is it?"

"Yes!"

"Then if it is, Dennis, just tell me why Sir Henry

108

Merrivale talked like that? Just tell me why he set this careful trap for Bruce?"

"Trap, my foot!" protested Dennis. "It was only H. M.'s way of talking. He didn't mean anything by it. He's probably forgotten the whole business by this time."

"Has he?" inquired Beryl, and nodded ahead.

For the first person they saw at Seacrest was Sir Henry Merrivale.

The great man, at first, did not see them. He was standing deep in the rough, under the branches of a chestnut-tree, facing out towards the links. The great man wore a suit of plus-fours, immensely broad in the beam, together with a bowler hat: constituting a sight so aesthetically horrible that the stoutest might have recoiled. From one hand trailed a heavy golf-bag containing a dozen clubs. But what struck Dennis was the great man's curious behaviour.

H. M.'s attention appeared to be fixed, with casual unconcern, on something in the branches of the tree. He looked up, steadily, looked up innocently. At the same time his right foot, as though disassociated with his body, moved out. It moved still farther. It touched something on the ground. A golf-ball, hitherto hidden deep in a rut, popped out of that rut and trickled from the rough to the edge of the fairway.

"Ahem!" said Sir Henry Merrivale very briskly.

A man reborn, a man virtuous and of inflexible purpose, H. M. was just seizing a mid-iron from the golf-bag when a new noise made him give a convulsive start.

"I'm watchin' ye," said a terrible voice.

And Mr. Donald Fergus MacFergus, like the Spirit of Conscience, stepped out from behind a nearby tree.

Now it has been observed that H. M. in any large deceit, any vast and thundering piece of misdirection, can keep a face as expressionless as a wooden Indian. But a small deceit, a slight fall from grace, is different. His look of awful and outraged majesty, with the spectacles pulled down on his nose, would not have deceived a baby.

"I dunno what you're talkin' about," he bellowed.

"Ye ken fine what I'm talkin' aboot," said Mr. MacFergus implacably. "Mon," said Mr. MacFergus in a voice of awe, "I wudna hae what's on your conscience for all the meelions o' Rockefeller!" The voice rose to a plaintive yelp. "Are ye no' a releegious mon at all?"

"Sure I'm a religious man! I'm as religious as hell. I . . ."

"Not content," said Mr. MacFergus, "not content wi' conceding yersel' any putt that isna actually off the green; not content wi' claiming a sax on the eighth hole forbye it's twal' or thirteen; not content wi' losing yer fiend's temper and jumpin' in the water-hazard when ye cudna drive across it . . ."

"Looky here, son. Are you accusin' me of hokey-pokey in this game?"

"Aye."

H. M. flung down the golf-bag among the brambles. Still gripping the mid-iron, he lumbered over to where the ball lay on the edge of the rough. With a glare of malevolence beyond description, and his face a rich purple colour under the bowler hat, he pointed his club at the ball.

"Look at it," yelled H. M.

"I'm luking at it."

"It's alive," said H. M. "It leers. It's got a soul. Son, there's more concentrated meanness packed into one golf-ball than in a whole Congress of the Gestapo after singin' the Horst Wessel and eatin' hashish."

Here H. M.'s corporation began to shiver.

"I come out in the morning," he said, "and tee up for my first drive. Me bein' as good a golfer as I am, I ought to wallop him two hundred yards straight down the fairway. And what happens? The little swine curves off in a slice like a homin' boomerang. Why?"

Mr. MacFergus clutched at his iron-grey hair.

"I keep telling ye . . . !" he began.

"No," screamed H. M.

"I dinna follow ye."

"If I hear one more word about keeping my eye on the ball and not moving my head," said H. M., pointing at him malevolently with the mid-iron, "I'm goin' to cut your heart out. That's got nothin' to do with it, and I'll prove what I say.

"It slices, d'ye see? And sort of a red mist swims in front of my eyes. And I think to myself: 'You want to slice, hey? All right, you bounder; I'll fix you!' So I stand sideways on the tee . . ."

Mr. MacFergus uttered a moan.

"I stand sideways on the tee," persisted H. M., "and drive like blazes at right angles to the hole. By any sane computation, that ought to carry the perisher round and land him slap on the green after all. Only this time, instead of slicin' a hundred yards to the right, the little swine hooks two hundred yards to the left and busts the club-house window.

"I'm only human, son. I can't stand it. The only way to treat that blighter is to pick him up and chuck him where he ought to go. Even then, y'know, I wouldn't be surprised if he jumps up out of the cup and squirts water at me in revenge."

"Sir Henry," Beryl called softly.

Dennis, who had been on the point of exploding with laughter in the great man's face and perhaps giving H. M. an apoplectic stroke, glanced at Beryl and checked himself.

111

For this wasn't funny. It wasn't funny at all.

All the rage faded out of H. M.'s expression. He looked deflated and a little embarrassed. He lumbered back up into the rough, twiddling the mid-iron.

Beryl climbed over the stile. In that twilight hollow of silence, you could hear her footsteps swish among weeds and brambles as she walked up to H. M.

"How long have you been here?" she asked.

"Me?" said H. M. "Oh, about a fortnight. —I been playin' golf," he added, by way of explanation.

"Is that all you've been doing?"

"I dunno what you mean, my wench."

Beryl suddenly pointed across the links. "You haven't been staying at . . . ?"

"At the Leather Boot? Well," growled H. M., turning the club over in his hands and scowling at it, "well, no. Y'see, I've met your friend Bruce Ransom once or twice in the past."

"Yes." Beryl nodded. "From something Bruce said in the dressing-room, I rather guessed you had."

"So, naturally, I didn't want to queer the feller's pitch by interfering with him. I'm on a holiday, my wench. That's all there is to it."

Along the white road they had just crossed, the road that presumably led to Aldebridge, clanked the motor of an ancient station-taxi. Dennis, shifting uneasily with Beryl's suitcase in one hand and his own bag in the other, paid no attention to the taxi until, at a sudden word of command, it ground to a stop. Leaning out of the back seat, adding a touch of the sinister, was Chief Inspector Masters.

"Ah, sir!" Masters called grimly.

He got out and paid off the cab, slamming the door with even more grimness.

"So we all meet again," observed Masters. "Well, well, well! Nobody told me Aldebridge was one stop

112

beyond where I wanted to go. Otherwise—"

"Were you on that train too?" demanded Dennis.

"Ah," assented Masters, with something that might have been a smile. "But coppers' expense-sheets don't run to first-class tickets, Mr. Foster. Now, Sir Henry!"

He climbed the stile, with Dennis following him. H. M. stood motionless.

"Masters, you crawlin' snake," said H. M. in a faraway voice. "Lord love a duck, I never did expect to see *you* here!"

The Chief Inspector stopped short and stared at him.

"You didn't expect me? Then what in thunderation *did* you expect, when you write to me and say Roger Bewlay really is here after all?"

Dead silence.

Dennis, who had dropped the bags, gripped Beryl's arm in a warning pressure; it stopped the beginnings of a stifled shriek. But Masters did not seem to notice. He was concentrating on other matters.

"After all I've been through from that gentleman's doings, did you think I'd just say: 'Oh, ah? and forget it? You can be smacking well certain I'm here! Why shouldn't I be?"

"Because you're wastin' your time. Unless, burn me, I can get an awful inspiration!"

"This chap *is* Bewlay?"

"Oh, yes."

"You can prove it?"

"I think so."

"Then what are we waiting for?"

"Masters," said H. M., scratching the side of his jaw in a ruminating way, "there's a few things you ought to be told here and now." Then he looked steadily at Beryl and Dennis. "And it's only fair, you young 'uns, that you should hear 'em too. I say, Masters. Would you like me to give you some very broad pointers on what

113

we'll call The Problem of Disposing of the Body?"

"Would I!" breathed Masters. "Lummy!"

All about them was the scent of autumn, of melancholy and decay. The leaves of the chestnut-tree, tattered and yellowing, moved uneasily as another breeze crept across the darkening links.

H. M. sat down comfortably on the stump of a felled tree. He removed his objectionable hat, and dropped it among weeds. He also dropped the mid-iron, which fell across the golf-bag at his feet. He sat there for a time glaring at his shoes, as though to marshal cogent thoughts, and then he sniffed and peered up at Masters over the spectacles.

"First," he said, "let's consider the tactics of the average murderer who kills his victim (this victim generally bein' a woman) and then hides the body and tries to pretend no murder's been committed. You follow me, son?"

"Naturally!"

"Well!" said H. M. "This murderer, usually, is a very dull dog. In nine cases out of ten he makes exactly the same mistake. Instead of buryin' the body miles away from where he lives, which would make him reasonably safe . . . after all, Masters, you coppers can't dig up every square foot of ground in a country . . . instead of doin' that, I repeat, the silly dummy goes and buries it in his own house or his own garden.

"Dougal did that. Crippen did it. Norman Thorne did it. For some mysterious reason, d'ye see, the feller seems to feel safer if he's got the body near him. And you coppers know that, Masters; you come to expect it. Now don't you?"

Masters was studying him in a puzzled way.

"Oh, ah. It's true. That's what hangs 'em."

H. M. pointed his finger.

"But occasionally, son, along comes a murderer

114

who's not a dull dog by any manner of means. Take Bewlay, for instance. I was very much interested in that information you dug up about his past life, before he took to killin' women as a profession."

Beryl shivered. H. M. was now looking at her very steadily and disconcertingly.

"Bewlay, my wench, comes of a very good family."

"Why tell *me* this?"

"Ain't you interested?"

"Yes, of course! But . . ."

"Bewlay," continued H. M., "comes of a very good family: all dead now. He was born in Jamaica. His old man was governor of the island, what they call captain-general, for years and years. As a lad he studied law, and he was whackingly clever at it. He was also a first-class amateur actor; but the point is that he studied law.

"He was supposed to be a dazzler, in classroom theory anyway, at constructin' ingenious tricks to upset the law. A kink, d'ye see. Like his other kink. Because he seems to have suffered, as a lad, from an awful inferiority complex with regard to women."

"Inferiority complex?" exclaimed Beryl. "With regard to women?"

"Uh-huh. Thought they wouldn't look at him. My eye, how we change! But he did get into some kind of trouble with a woman, a Negro woman it was. There was a scandal that had to be hushed up. He hared off for England in the middle nineteen-twenties; and disappeared. I say, Masters: don't you find all this very fetchin' and interesting?"

Masters, exasperated and bewildered, had taken out a notebook. Now he thrust the notebook back into his pocket as not being needed.

"'Interesting'," he snapped. "Oh, ah! Maybe! But it doesn't tell us how our man disposed of the bodies, does it?"

"So? You don't think it helps?"

"No, sir, I don't!"

H. M. waved his hand.

"In that case, son, let's go on to my second point. Let's forget the first three murders, Angela Phipps and Elizabeth Mosnar and Andrée Cooper. Let's concentrate on that nasty business in Torquay eleven years ago.

"Bewlay, alias R. Benedict, rents a furnished bungalow and arrives there with a brand-new wife. The local police-inspector gets a wee bit suspicious and puts a night-watch, front and back, on the bungalow. On the night of July 6th our fetchin' Bluebeard strangles the umpteenth Mrs. B., and walks away next day. Correct?"

"Yes!"

"Now, Masters,"—H. M. bent forward as far as his corporation would permit, with a hideous earnestness— "I defy you to read that evidence and not realize one thing. Bewlay knew he was being watched."

The Chief Inspector blinked.

"But I've never denied he knew it!" Masters said. "After all, sir, he walked straight up to a constable who was hiding, and wished the constable good morning. Both Harris and Peterson told me they were sure he'd twigged it several days before that."

"That takes the cokernut," said H. M., after a slight pause. "That takes the cokernut and wraps it up in nice pink tape. Bewlay knows he's bein' watched. Yet he goes blithely ahead with the murder, and doesn't even draw the window-curtains properly. Oh, my son! Does *that* strike you as significant?"

Masters drew his sleeve across his forehead.

"All you're telling me," he roared, "is that Mr. Bloody Bewlay has got a fool-proof way of disposing of the bodies. And odd as it may sound, sir, I KNEW

116

THAT ALREADY."

"Now, now, Masters! Keep your shirt on!"

"But—"

"Mustn't lose your temper, Masters. Be like Me."

(In the background, Mr. MacFergus uttered a stifled groan.)

"My next point," continued H. M., very seriously and sincerely, "concerns the wife that was polished off. Who was she, Masters? What was her name? Where were they married? What bank did she keep her money in, if any? I've grubbed through every record you sent; and burn me if I can find anything more than a great big X."

"He wasn't after her money! He was after her jewellery! And, if he married her under still another name . . ."

"Uh-huh. But you still don't see the point. Maybe I can make it clearer in another way."

H. M. was silent for a moment, ruffling his hands across his big bald head.

"Masters," he went on, and when he raised his head again Dennis saw that H. M.'s face was white in the gathering twilight, "these mass-murderers who prey on women are all alike. Remember Landru? And Pranzini? And Smith who drowned 'em in tin baths?"

"Well?"

"They're as stingy as a French peasant. They're sexually cold in spite of all their rompin'. They've all got a twisted poetical streak that runs to flowers and verses. And (this is the point I want to make) there's always one woman they *don't* kill."

It seemed to Dennis that H. M.'s eyes flickered, very briefly, towards Beryl. But there was a yellow sky, an evening sky, behind the high line of the railway-embankment at their backs; it threw changing lights under the damp shadows of the chestnut-trees; and

Dennis could not be sure.

"I mean, son, there's always a woman they go back to. A woman they live with, between murders, as cosy as Darby and Joan. A woman (oh, my eye!) who forgives 'em even when they stand in the dock. I just want you to remember that Smith had his Edith Pegler. Landru had his Fernande Segret. And Roger Bewlay . . ."

The silence stretched out interminably. H. M. reached down beside the tree-stump and fished up a short length of dead branch, weighing it in his hand like a golf-club.

Chief Inspector Masters was impressed, though for the life of him he could not have said why he was impressed. He hesitated, a picture of indecision, and then cleared his throat.

"Hurrum!" he said. "And have you any other points," he added sarcastically, "to tell us how the bodies were disposed of?"

"Uh-huh. A fifth and final one. I sort of hate to tell you, Masters, because it's goin' to be a bit of a shock. But here you are, straight in the face. If you nabbed Roger Bewlay at this minute, are you sure you could convict him?"

"What's that?"

"Easy now!" H. M. urged sharply, as Masters lifted both fists. "Are you sure, son?"

Masters got his breath.

"Even," said the Chief Inspector, "with Mildred Lyons giving testimony in the witness-box?"

"Even," H. M. agreed sombrely, "with Mildred Lyons givin' testimony in the witness-box. Remember your Assistant Commissioner?"

They could now hear Masters breathing, noisily and thickly.

"Old Sir Philip? What about him? He died a year ago."

"Sure. But when you first phoned through to him and said you'd got a witness, *he* wasn't sure: now as he? Phil Pembrook was a lawyer. Have you gone into this business with the D.P.P.?"*

"No! It's not necessary, until we nab Bewlay!"

H. M. sniffed.

"They might risk a prosecution, son. It's possible. But, if they did, let the old man tell you exactly what would happen."

"Well?"

"'Now, Miss Lyons,' says counsel for the defence, 'you tell us you saw a dead body?' 'Yes!' 'Please tell the jury, Miss Lyons, how you knew it was a dead body. Did you feel for the pulse? Test the heart-beat? Hold a mirror up to the mouth? Come, come: you only *saw* it'?"

Masters stared back at him, motionless, while H. M. continued the mimicry of a court-room.

"'Members of the jury,' says counsel for the defence, 'you have heard the prisoner testify that his wife, in good health left the bungalow that afternoon when it was not watched by the police. Yet this witness, Miss Lyons, dares speak of a *dead* body in spite of the fact that the police have found no trace of it.

"'Miss Lyons admits that the light was very dim. Can she, in fact, take her oath that what she saw was not a shadow, an arrangement of sofa-cushions, or the effect of her own overheated imagination? For until we have proof of *(a)* a woman's body and *(b)* a dead body, I submit that you dare not pronounce this man guilty'."

H. M. paused.

He somewhat marred the effect of this stately

* Department of Public Prosecutions.

119

peroration by adding: "Phooey!" and whacking at the brambles with the dead branch in his hand. But Masters understood.

"And that," Masters asked huskily, "that'd work?"

"Sure it'd work, son."

"But—"

"Judge and jury and everybody else would realize the defence was eyewash. But even if they lost their heads and said: 'Burn it, we know he's guilty; hang the blighter!' . . . well, Masters, the sentence would be quashed as dead as Moses by the Court of Criminal Appeal."

Chief Inspector Masters turned away. He stood motionless, and they could not see his face. When he spoke again, it was not loudly.

"I see, sir. So Bewlay has all the luck again, as usual?"

"I'm sorry, Masters. There it is."

Masters swung round. "Sir, is he *always* going to get away with it?"

"Not necessarily," said H. M. It was in a tone that made his listeners jump.

"Masters," he resumed, "from the first I had a sort of vision of this case. Your biographical stuff confirmed it, I saw that boy growin' up in a sub-tropical climate, with a native nurse and native companions he could belt about as he liked: learnin' not only the law, mind you, but all hocus-pocus from the craft of fightin' with a knife to the art of performing Voodoo rites . . ."

"Curse it all, you're not trying to say he makes women vanish with a magical spell?"

"Easy now! Lemme finish. Masters, the first time Bewlay realized the police were after him was when he'd killed that girl Andrée Cooper. Her boy-friend went to the police. That was when you started tearing houses to pieces. And I saw, with a shivery kind of

120

clearness, just what Bewlay *would* do." H. M.'s voice rose in a groan. "If I could only think of one more thing, Masters! Oh, burn me, just one more thing!"

"But if you can't think of it, sir, how does it help us?"

"Because he's walked straight into our hands, son. His vanity's got him over that play. That's why I set my little trap. He may, I only say he may, make a mistake. But if he does . . ."

H. M. took the length of dead branch in his hands, and broke it in two. It cracked with a sharp cleanness grisly to hear, like the cracking of a neck.

"Beryl!" cried Dennis.

He could restrain Beryl no longer. She tore loose from his grip on her arm. Stumbling in the crackly undergrowth, out across the fairway, swerving at a bunker, but always in the direction of the white weatherboarded hotel glimmering in the distance, Beryl ran from that place in blind terror.

And Dennis ran after her.

10

It was almost dark.

The muddy yellow sky had faded. Eastwards, the sea lay black and whispering. The Leather Boot Hotel, its front door facing the golf links and its back to a little promontory over the beach, was just beyond a motor-road that curved along the far edge of the links. Long and low, chipped and dingy, it showed no lights except a dim one shining out through the open front doors.

Beryl, her green suit whipped by the sea-wind, stood motionless in front of those doors when Dennis caught up with her. A chill of dew was in his nostrils, perhaps a chill of death.

"If this were the play," Beryl said unexpectedly, "I could tell you exactly what we're going to see inside."

"You mean one of the scenes of the play is laid in—?"

"Yes! In a country hotel. If this were the play, I could describe every detail to you. And there would be a fat waiter with sandy hair."

"Listen, Beryl: you've got to pull yourself together! You're not going in there and make a scene; understand? Just . . ."

But she had already gone into the hotel.

Inside, under the dim light of a few electric wall-candles, they found themselves in a large low-ceilinged lounge with decrepit wicker chairs. The glass windows of the bar-hatch were firmly closed. On the left an open door led into a darkened smoking-room; at the back, beyond an alcove, were fresh-painted doors bearing the words: "dining-room"; and there was a reception-desk on the right. The whole place had that mildewy air of being knocked about by the military, just as one of the wall-candles was a little off-blanace.

In one of the wicker chairs sat Miss Daphne Herbert. And in the middle of the lounge, looking at them, stood a fat waiter with sandy hair.

There is somewhere a very fine ghost story which describes the mounting terror of a man who dreams, year after year, the same nightmare, and then finds it taking form in real life. It sings to the evil refrain of: *"Jack will show you to your room; I have given you the room in the tower."* A very similar emotion shook the heart of Dennis Foster as he dropped their two valises on the floor.

Commander Renwick, clearly, had not yet returned from Aldebridge. The waiter, who was expecting nobody, looked at them inquiringly.

"Yes, miss? Yes, sir?"

"We should like to see Mr. Ra—Mr. Egerton," said Beryl, correcting herself hastily with the assumed name Bruce was using. Her voice rose clearly in the melancholy lounge. "We're friends of his from London."

"Mr. Egerton's not in, miss." The waiter's face hardened. "This young lady's waiting for 'im too."

And he nodded towards Daphne Herbert.

Daphne, who now wore a fleecy tan-coloured coat turned up at the neck, was sitting by the empty fireplace near the smoking-room door. Dennis, watching her out of the corner of his eye, saw her give a little start as Beryl spoke.

124

Daphne turned that stolidly pretty face, those grey dark-fringed eyes which could have so demoralizing an effect. She hesitated, and looked away. Then, almost against her will, she got up and walked over towards them.

"I do beg your pardon," Daphne said, with an uncertain glance between Beryl and Dennis. "But—you say you're friends of Mr. Egerton?"

"That's right, dear," Beryl answered mechanically. Beryl gave her a quick look, and then looked elsewhere. The emotional temperature of the lounge shot up several degrees.

But Daphne faltered.

"Oh. Yes. I see," she murmured.

Dennis knew what was the matter. The girl was too shy, too desperately well-mannered, to say: 'Who is Mr. Egerton?' She could not even think how to approach the subject, though it shone in her eyes and coloured her face and breathed on her lips; it shook her whole placid soul.

And she turned away.

"Where," Beryl asked the waiter, "is Mr. Egerton's room?"

"Mr. Egerton's rooms," the waiter corrected her, "are up in the north wing down at the end. But 'e's not in."

"We'll go up and wait for him there," said Beryl. "We're *very* old friends."

She smiled at Daphne. Daphne, in the act of turning away, stopped dead and looked back. And, just before Beryl hurried towards the little staircase, something flicked between those two girls like an electric spark; not emotion of any kind, merely understanding. It was a deep instinct; both of them knew.

For a second Dennis thought that Daphne was going to follow them up. But the notion plainly struck her as so unconventional, so open to what people might say, that Daphne hesitated in agony. She followed them only with her eyes. It was the last thing Dennis saw— Daphne, with the glow of one or two battered wall-lamps touching her brown-golden hair, the soft line of her chin and neck, the half-jealous wonder in her eyes—as they went up the stairs into the stuffy, sour-smelling atmosphere of the upper hall.

"It's Angela Phipps all over again," muttered Beryl. "The clergyman's daughter! It always is! Don't you see?"

"Easy, now!"

"Was it true what H. M. said, Dennis? That they can't possibly convict Bruce if—if he murdered that woman at Torquay?"

"Oh, yes. Now the Old Maestro points it out (and I can understand why they call him that), it's as plain as print you'd get an acquittal. I simply didn't think of it, that's all. If," he added hastily, "Bruce really is . . ."

"They think so, don't they?"

Doors stood open on dismantled bedrooms, a gutted shell. Groping in the gloom of the north wing, Beryl halted doubtfully at the second door from the end of the passage, facing front, and rapped on it.

There was no reply. Beryl opened the door on a dusky, silent room with two glimmering windows facing the links. Faint traces of the yellow sky gleamed outside. Feeling on the left of the door, Beryl found a light switch and pressed it.

It was Bruce's sitting-room, coloured grey and blue from carpet to curtains and walls. A bag of golf-clubs stood in one corner. On the writing-table lay a huge drift of opened letters: all unanswered, for a portable typewriter, covered and dusty with name-tag attached, was beside them. The *Radio Times,* the *New Yorker,* and a thick book called *Genius and the Criminal,* were

126

strewn on grey-and-blue easy chairs and settee as though someone had restlessly occupied each in turn. The whole room shone bleakly, like the little telephone-table by the mantelpiece.

"Bruce!" cried Beryl. Dennis jumped in spite of himself.

"What's the good of shouting like that? Didn't you hear the waiter say he's out?"

"He's here," said Beryl. "I *know* he's here. Bruce!"

And, furtively, they heard the creak of a footfall on a shaky floor.

It came from behind a closed door towards the right, a door which presumably led to Bruce's bedroom at the end of the wing. After five seconds the knob turned. Bruce Ransom, wearing the same silk dressing-gown in which they had last seen him, came into the sitting-room and closed the door behind him.

Nobody spoke.

On Bruce's face was printed a fixed, agreeable expression. What was it Mr. Herbert had called him? Mongolian! That was it. And there was in fact a very slight suggestion of the Tartar about those high cheek-bones and narrow eyes, in contrast to the hearty English mouth and jaw. But this was not what they noticed now. On Bruce's left temple was a purplish, swollen bruise, a devil's brush against amiability.

Bruce walked over to the little blue-marble mantel-piece into which was set an electric heater. He took a cigarette from a packet on the mantelpiece, and a match from its box. He lighted the cigarette with a steady hand, and dropped the match on the hearth.

"Hello, you two," he said.

Still Beryl did not speak. Dennis Foster, for no reason he could determine, felt his nerves jerking like a hooked fish. Beryl was looking very steadily at the bruise on Bruce's temple, and Bruce was compelled to

127

notice it.

"This?" he said, touching it. His laughter rang in the bleak room. "I always was a clumsy ox, Beryl. I must have had one or two in the bar downstairs, because I walked straight into the edge of that bedroom door there . . ."

"Bruce," said the girl, "why do you keep on lying to me?"

Long pause.

"Lying to you, angel-face?"

"You got that bruise because somebody threw a stone at you. Why lie about it?"

"Oh," murmured Bruce, as though he had expected something else. He kept on smiling, though his eyes looked strained. "I've been overplaying my part as usual, angel-face. That's because you weren't here to direct me."

"Yes," agreed Beryl. "You've been overplaying your part."

(For God's sake *say* something! If the girl's going to explode, let her explode. But not this!)

Beryl opened her handbag, and slowly unfolded the sheet of notepaper.

"'Come down here as soon as you can'," she read aloud from Bruce's letter. "'Can't explain now, but I'm in trouble. I need you'."

"Pay no attention to that," said Bruce impatiently. He took a quick draw at the cigarette. "I wrote it one night when I was depressed." Then he burst out: "This damned 'experiment' . . . !"

"Yes," said Beryl, "the experiment. If you've really asked the girl to run away and marry you, don't you think that's going a bit too far?"

Bruce looked at her.

He did not stop to ask how she knew; he accepted the information as understood, and answered in the manner of honesty he always used.

128

"I'm in love with her," returned Bruce, with a forthrightness and sincerity it was impossible to doubt. "I've genuinely and sincerely fallen this time. I feel like a callow kid of eighteen. She's the sweetest . . ."

Taking a deep draw at the cigarette, with a breath that quivered deep in his chest, Bruce wandered over to the settee. His eye caught the title *Genius and the Criminal,* and he sent the book spinning across the room. He sat down, elbows on knees and head in hands.

"Beryl," he went on, with what sounded like a real warmth of affection as he looked up again, "I'm a hound, you know. I ought to have written to you. Daphne even pinched her old man's typewriter so I could answer my letters (that's how sweet she is). But you know what I am."

"Yes," said Beryl. "I'm beginning to know."

"And you, Dennis! You were right too!"

Dennis's throat felt still more dry. This unnatural calmness of Beryl's couldn't go on much longer.

"I was right, Bruce? How?"

"'You can't play with people's lives and people's emotions like that.' Remember? That was what you told me in the dressing-room. And, by God, you can't!" Bruce whacked his fist down on his knee. "I've now got everybody hereabouts, including the father and mother of the girl I'm in love with, believing I *am* Roger Bewlay . . ."

"Well!" said Beryl. "Why don't you tell them you're not?"

Bruce studied his clenched fist.

"Because I can't."

"Why not?"

"I can't, I tell you! Not just yet. If I'm to bring down the curtain in the only proper way, and justify myself and—" His left hand, holding the cigarette, hovered in the air. He took another fierce inhalation of smoke, which must have made his head swim. "You don't understand," he added plaintively.

"No, Bruce?"

"The old man hates me. Damn him!" said Bruce. "What right has he got to dictate to Daphne? He's only a footling J.P. and would-be country squire; it's Daphne's mother who's got all the money.

"But I like to have things pleasant about me. I don't want to have to tell my prospective in-laws I've been playing a joke on 'em: unless of course I can end the play in a proper way, and then they'll all forgive me.

"Beryl, Daphne is scared out of her wits. She says she found the old man cleaning a revolver, just as though this were a bad melodrama. If he tries any funny games with me I'll land him one that'll put him to sleep for an hour; but it's not *pleasant*. Commander Renwick's ordered me to get out of the hotel by Monday. Even that ass Chittering . . ."

"Then why don't you tell them, Bruce. *Why don't you tell them?*"

"Angel-face, how many times must I repeat it? I can't! Maybe, this morning, I could have. I tell you straight, I was just about to call the whole thing off. But not now."

"Why not now?"

Then occurred something that froze Dennis Foster's blood.

Bruce got to his feet. He stretched out his hand towards Bruce. Over his face, as though it were moulding itself there like moving wax, crept a smile. It was a smile of contrition, a smile of repentance, a smile that begged you to take no offence; and yet, at the same time, the smile of one who is deeply misunderstood.

"Well, you see," said Bruce, "there's a dead woman in my bedroom."

11

"She's—er—dead," Bruce repeated. "I'm afraid she's
been smothered or strangled."

For a moment Dennis could not have moved to save
his own life. Then Beryl cried out with one of those
inspired guesses which can come to women where
someone they love is concerned.

"It's Mildred Lyons, isn't it?" Beryl said. "It's
Mildred Lyons!"

"Yes," said Bruce. "She . . ." A terrifying change
came over his face. His eyes widened. The lips curled
back, showing the teeth. With a broad thumb he
crushed out the cigarette in an ashtray on the writing-
table.

"What do you know about Mildred Lyons?" he
demanded.

Beryl flew at the door of the bedroom.

"Don't go in there!" said Bruce, with his face
whitening. "She's . . ."

Beryl threw open the door. The bedroom with its
four windows, two facing north and two facing west,
held just enough light to show faintly the outline of
something sitting lolled in an easy chair near the bed.

And Beryl did not go into the room. Faintly they

heard the humming of a motor-car, approaching along the road outside the hotel. A reflection of its white headlamps, at that very bad moment, brushed briefly through the bedroom; it showed the face and the disarranged red hair of the thing that sat in the chair, and Beryl retreated. Dennis thought she was going to be sick.

"Bruce, you *fool*," she screamed.

"I know I'm a fool! All right! But . . ."

"That woman couldn't have convicted you," said Beryl, fighting for breath. "Her testimony didn't amount to a row of beans. We heard H. M. say so. But now you've gone and killed her, and they'll hang you for certain!"

Bruce put up a hand to shade his eyes, as though it were a gesture to ward off a blow.

"What in hell's name are you talking about?" he asked hoarsely.

"They're on to you, Bruce! They've set a trap for you, they hoped you'd make a mistake, and now you have! They'll hang you!"

Bruce stared at her.

"Listen, Beryl," he said in a dazed voice, not loudly. "Are you scatty?"

"Yes! Yes! Yes!"

"I'm Bruce Ransom: remember me? We planned this whole thing together: remember? It was your idea: remember that?"

"You're Bruce Ransom now," she flung the words at him, "but who were you before then? I first met you when you came up from the Bristol Rep in '35: who were you before then? Have you ever been in Jamaica?"

Bruce made a fighting gesture.

"Long Island, you mean? I stayed with some people there when I was doing *Captain Cutthroat* in New York . . ."

"I mean the island of Jamaica. Where Roger Bewlay came from!"

"My God, Beryl," faltered Bruce, "you don't mean you really think I *am?*"

This man, thought Dennis Foster, *is telling the truth.*

It came to him with a rush and shock, a dizziness of relief. For some time he had been trying to balance his judgment in scale-pans that would not remain still. They would dip first in one direction, then in the other. And now, Dennis thought, he knew.

Bruce's sick pallor now matched Beryl's own. The utter sincerity with which he stumbled out in those words? "You don't mean you really think I *am,*" the incredulous horror as though the idea had only just occurred to him, carried conviction. It seemed to Dennis that no actor, living or dead, could have managed it. A shadow of wonder, of hysterical doubt, troubled Beryl's features as she stared back at him.

"Your initials!" Beryl swallowed hard. "R. B. backwards! The things you knew that weren't in the play! The . . ."

"Backwards," said Bruce. And he began to laugh.

It was laughter that seemed to hurt him deep inside: devilish, frantic laughter, ringing and roaring in that bleak room. It brought the tears to his eyes, made the veins swell out at his temples, pulled his mouth square like a greek mask. Beryl regarded him in terror.

"Bruce! Stop it! What's the matter?"

Half doubled up, stamping on the floor, laughing now in a way that was near a sob, Bruce groped for the drawer of the writing-table and yanked it partly open. There seemed to be nothing inside, Dennis noted from a distance, except some typewritten sheets whose topmost one bore the figure 7 in its upper right-hand corner, and a piece of thin crumpled wrapping-paper across which ran the pale green lettering: "Ye Olde Tea

133

Shoppe, Aldebridge."

"You thought," yelled Bruce, "that *I* . . . ?"

"The Lyons woman is dead, isn't she?"

"Yes! But I didn't kill her!"

"Easy!" Dennis interposed. His cool voice struck across the room, sobering the other two. "Listen, Bruce. Did Mildred Lyons come to see you at the Granada that last night we were all together?"

"Yes!"

"Well?"

Bruce wiped his eyes. He was shivering now. He plucked at the collar of his sports-shirt under the dressing-gown, though the collar was already open.

"Miss Lyons," he continued, "was supposed to come down here this afternoon. I've got her letter here somewhere." He made a vague gesture which swept papers off the littered writing-table. "She wrote to me she'd take the train that'd get her to Seacrest Halt at a quarter-past four, and said she'd walk across the links."

"But we were on that train!"

"Did you see her?"

"No."

"Anyway, she didn't turn up. I waited until a quarter to five. Then I phoned downstairs that I was going out for a swim, and said if anybody called to tell 'em to wait."

"You went for a swim?" cried Beryl. "In this weather?"

"Why not? It's not cold. Good for you!" Bruce swallowed. "There's an outside staircase in my bedroom; the military had it built so that they could get up and down in a hurry. I went by way of that, and swam until it started to get really dark. Then I came back by way of the outside staircase, and changed my clothes in there. I opened the wardrobe to get this," he touched his dressing-gown, "and the blasted woman's

134

body fell out."

"Fell out of the wardrobe?"

"Yes."

Again Bruce plucked at his collar. The purplish bruise showed livid against his pallor. He seemed to be suffering from a kind of delayed shock.

"God!" said Bruce, and pressed sinewy hands over his eyes. "*She* must have been down on the beach too."

"Why?"

"There was sand all over her face. Sand! Somebody'd grabbed her and choked her and then pressed her face into the sand until she smothered. There was sand in her teeth and nose and eyes. That's what I couldn't stand: sand on wide-open eyeballs that didn't blink. I wiped it off her face, but the eyes are still . . ."

He paused, letting the ugly picture sink in.

"Sand on wide-open eyeballs that didn't blink." Another motor-car hummed along the road outside, loud in loneliness; it seemed to shake the very hotel, and Dennis fancied that Mildred Lyons's body, lolling there in the dark, vibrated to it.

"She must have fought like the devil," said Bruce. "She was still warm, too. I . . ." Bruce took a handkerchief out of his dressing-gown pocket, showing the fine white grains of sand adhering to it, and hastily stuffed it back into his pocket as he saw Beryl's face.

"Then," he added, "you arrived. What delayed *you?*"

"We stopped for a long time to talk to Sir Henry Merrivale and Chief Inspector Masters. Bruce, they believe you're Roger Bewlay!"

"That's a lie," said Bruce, his muddy pallor increasing. "That's a lie."

"It's not a lie! H. M. . . ."

"I know H. M.'s here! I've talked to him!"

"You've—?"

"Yes! And he doesn't believe anything of the kind.

135

But if you, my friends, think . . . This isn't like a murder on the stage," Bruce said piteously. "It isn't like a murder on the stage at all! I'm just beginning to realize. There are people hereabouts who'd like to see me strung up to the nearest lamp-post. If I'm found here with a dead body, a murdered woman's body, by someone who doesn't happen to like me . . ."

There was a soft tap at the door to the corridor.

Almost immediately the door was opened by Daphne Herbert. Behind her, his hands in his pockets, stood Mr. Jonathan Herbert.

The door to the bedroom still stood wide open. Beryl instinctively made a gesture to close it; but, as though this would be too obvious, she dropped her hand again. True, the bedroom was so dark that you could no longer even see the outlines of the thing in the chair. But it loomed too close; their minds were poisoned by its presence. It was as though the dead woman, blind and dumb with the sand in her eyes and mouth, nevertheless cried out.

Dennis Foster's heart seemed to skip a beat, and then pounded with enormous rhythm in his ears.

"Mind if I come in, Egerton?" said Mr. Herbert.

"Daddy!" cried the girl. "You promised . . . !"

"It's all right," said Mr. Herbert, and gave her a smile.

It was the first time Dennis had seen Mr. Herbert face to face. Aboard the train, he had been sitting with his back to the corridor.

He was a middle-sized hardy man, with a young-looking face despite his grey hair. He had a manner that inspired confidence and respect. From under dark heavily-marked eyebrows, grey eyes of a quality like Daphne's looked out of a wind-roughened face with a cleft chin. He wore grey tweeds and a soft hat, removing the hat as he entered.

136

Bruce took a step forward. Bruce's voice went up.

"If you want a showdown, sir," he said, "you're ruddy well going to get one here and now."

"I should prefer," said Mr. Herbert, "not to call it show-down. You see . . ."

Daphne walked over to Bruce's side, and took his arm. A shadow of despair crossed Mr. Herbert's face, but he made no comment.

"Yesterday," he went on, "her mother and I took Daphne to London. We hoped it would . . . well! distract her mind. Instead she insisted on returning to-day. In fact, no sooner did we get to Aldebridge than she jumped out of the train and raced away. It was very plain where she had gone. I followed in her car; I thought perhaps . . ."

He paused, his face pinching up.

"Er—this lady and gentleman?" he added.

"May I present Miss West and Mr. Foster?" Bruce said very loudly. "Mr. Foster is my solicitor. Dennis, tell Mr. Herbert who I really am."

"Well . . ."

"Go on!" Bruce insisted fiercely. "Tell him!"

Dennis found his voice.

"The fact is, Mr. Herbert," he moistened his lips, "this man you know as Bruce Egerton is really Bruce Ransom. The actor."

There was a pause.

"If you haven't seen him on the stage," continued Dennis, his own voice becoming very loud and his face hot, "you've undoubtedly heard of him. About a month ago, a—a dispute arose as to how—how people would feel if somebody pretended to be a notorious murderer and then revealed that he wasn't."

In three sentences Dennis outlined the situation. A curious heaviness seemed to have got into everybody's limbs. Time passed slowly, too, very slowly; Dennis

137

could hear somebody's watch ticking.

"I see," observed Mr. Herbert in a level voice. But his nostrils were distended.

"It's been very unfortunate," shouted Dennis, "and— and perhaps not in the best of taste." He stole a glance at Daphne, who had backed away. "But I think you'll agree that no actual harm has been done."

"I see." Mr. Herbert spoke in the same level voice. "Then the whole thing, including the comedy of making love to Daphne, was a prearranged scheme?"

"I had another reason," gritted Bruce, "that even Beryl and Dennis don't know about! When you hear what it is, sir, I think both you and Daphne will forgive me. It's a matter I haven't discu . . ."

Mr. Herbert walked slowly forward. With no warning, without any change of expression, he let go a vicious right-hander at Bruce's face.

Bruce, off guard and thinking of other matters, only partly parried with his left. Mr. Herbert's hard knuckles grazed the cheek-bone, drawing a red swathe and two bright beads of blood against a face that was paler yet.

"I don't want to hurt you," Bruce said in a shaky voice, "so don't try that again. Though I suppose I deserve it."

"You deserve worse," said Mr. Herbert. Yet somehow, in his tone, there was relief. "It's very unfortunate I'm not young enough to give you worse. Come along, Daphne."

"Daphne!" cried Bruce.

The girl had backed away still farther, until an easy chair stopped her. Her lips were open; her eyes looked sick and hurt against a flush of heightened emotion. When Bruce cried out to her, his words sounded almost grotesque: like an eighteen-year-old protesting at the wicked world.

"Daphne! Don't you love me?"

"I don't know," whispered Daphne. "I—I want to think about it."

And then:

"I wish you had been a murderer," she said. "I almost wish you *had* been a murderer!"

Outside, where bright star-points were showing in a blue-black sky, the rumble of a very heavy lorry or military van rose along the road. It grew to a shattering din, making the window-frames rattle. As it swept past the hotel, its vibrations had their effect: the body in the dark bedroom rolled out of the chair and fell with a heavy thump on the floor.

Yet not a soul in that sitting-room noticed it.

"I worshipped you," said Daphne. "I—I always thought there was something of the stage about you. But I didn't care who you were or what you were. Until this happened."

"It's not a game, Daphne." Bruce took a step towards her; but, seeing her expression, he stopped. "It *started* as a game, yes! But it turned into something else. I meant every single word I said to you."

For a moment the girl wavered. There had been so much utter sincerity in Bruce's tone, the compelling force of his personality, that it flowed out and engulfed her. But she looked at Mr. Herbert.

"Please," Daphne said, "can we go home now?"

Mr. Herbert, his head down, was staring at the writing-table in so abstracted a way that Daphne had to repeat the question. Then he woke up. He took two steps towards the door before turning round, his hat half raised.

"Mr.—Mr. Ransom." He spoke formally, though his eyes looked congested. "I believe Commander Renwick has given you notice to leave this hotel by Monday. That will be just as well."

139

"Daphne!" said Bruce.

Mr. Herbert drew the back of his hand across his forehead.

"I propose, Mr. Ransom, to say nothing to anyone about who you really are, beyond assuring my friends you're not the murderer and that,"—he hesitated—"they can stop looking for Bewlay in this district. I won't say anything beyond that. I can't. You have shamed us enough already."

He hesitated again, and looked at Dennis.

"Thank you, Mr. Foster, for telling me what you have. You seem to be the only person concerned in this affair with any decent instincts."

"It isn't that!" Dennis protested. "On my word of honour, I can assure you Bruce really means . . ."

Bruce Ransom had not heard one word of all this.

"Daphne, I can't go with you now. There's a reason," Bruce's eyes flickered briefly towards the dark bedroom, "why I can't go with you and why I'm not exactly myself. But I'll ring you to-morrow morning, and I'll prove you've been doing me an injustice. It's only . . ."

"If you try to see my daughter again," said Mr. Herbert, "I'll kill you. I happen to mean that. Good-night."

"Daphne!"

And Bruce took a step forward.

Daphne's hands moved up to the collar of her fleecy tan coat. Her lips trembled and there was a glaze of approaching tears in her eyes. Repulsion, hurt pride, struggled with the hypnotic fascination Bruce exercised over her. Deliberately she avoided Bruce's glance.

"Yes, Mr. Foster. Thank you." Her eyes met Dennis's with an expression of friendliness, even of kinship, which exalted him even while it made him feel himself the villain of the piece. "I can't help thinking there were some things you omitted or slurred over.

140

That's what *I* thank you for. Good night."

She nodded to Beryl, gave Dennis a blurred kind of smile as though assuring him it didn't matter, and went quickly out of the room into the corridor. Mr. Herbert, following her, shut the door with great care. They saw his furrowed forehead and distended nostrils for a moment before the door closed.

In the long pause that followed, Dennis could again hear a watch ticking. Bruce stared at the closed door. Slowly his hand travelled up and touched the blood-mark on his cheek.

"Well?" inquired Beryl without looking at him. "Are you satisfied now how they'd take it?"

"I'll prove it!" said Bruce. "I'll prove it to both of them!—Beryl!"

"Yes?"

"Look here, angel-face. You don't honestly believe all that tommy-rot you were talking a while ago? About suspecting *me* of being—you know?"

"Oh, Bruce, I don't know what I think!" Beryl answered helplessly. "I'm like the clergyman's daughter."

"The what?"

"Never mind. It's just that when I'm away from you I get all sorts of funny ideas; and it's horrible. But, when I hear you burbling again, I can't see you as anybody but poor old foolish Bruce Ransom."

"Then will you do something for me?"

Beryl stared at him.

"Really, Bruce! You can choose the most outrageous times to—to—!"

"This is important," said Bruce. His eyes were rolling and glittering with that half-maniacal light which was to be seen sometimes on the stage.

"Daphne and her old man," he added, "mustn't leave this hotel for the next half-hour. I want you to go downstairs after them, Beryl. I want you to spin 'em a

141

yarn; tell 'em anything you like; only detain 'em here for the next thirty minutes. Will you do that? And hurry?"

"Why should I do that?"

"Because I want to borrow Daphne's car, and get far away from here before they know I'm gone."

"Borrow it to do . . . what's that?"

"Listen, Beryl. If I have anything like luck, in a few hours I'll demonstrate something that'll make Daphne fall on my neck and her old man shake hands instead of wanting to take a wallop at me. The Good Lord," Bruce addressed the ceiling with sincere trustfulness and appeal, "couldn't desert me after playing a filthy trick like landing me with that body. Will you do what I ask?"

"No."

"Beryl!"

"Can't . . . Dennis do it? If it has to be done?"

"Why Dennis?"

"After all," said Beryl, "he seems to have made something of a hit with the family. And he's fallen head over heels for Daphne Herbert."

"Has he, by George?" muttered Bruce. Bruce directed a quick, speculative look at Dennis, who was now so tongue-tied that the protest choked in his throat. "I suppose I ought to say, may the best man win. And I do say it."

"Look here—!"

"But the important thing now," Bruce swept out his hand, "is that I can't spare Dennis now. I've got to ask for his help in another matter."

"Hold on," said Dennis. "What other matter?"

"You and I, old man," Bruce announced, "are going to dispose of the body. I have a foolproof way of disposing of it."

12

And Bruce smiled again.

He smiled, soothingly, even though the breath whistled through his nostrils and they could see his chest heaving. Thrusting out his left arm, Bruce glanced at a wrist-watch; he nodded, as though at some inner secret. And the scale-pans of judgment wouldn't stay still.

"Disposing of the body?" echoed Beryl. She came up to the table and put her hands on it.

"Yes."

"In the same way that Roger Bewlay disposed of it?"

"No, of course not! Don't be an ass! I was just thinking of the battle-school, and . . ."

"Bewlay," said Beryl, "*is* in Aldebridge. That's definite. H. M. said so."

"My dearest poppet," retorted Bruce in a strained voice, "of course Bewlay's in Aldebridge. I've known it all along. That's why I'm here now. Don't you understand? *Bewlay wrote the play.*"

"You mean the play that . . . ?"

"The play that gives him away and betrays two or three secrets. Yes!"

"But that's just the trouble, Bruce! The play doesn't

143

give away any secrets!"

Bruce gave a sort of triumphant mirth.

"It doesn't *now*," he said. "Because I re-wrote some of it before I let anybody read the script. Look here!"

He yanked wide open the writing-table drawer he had opened a while before. Fully exposed lay the little pile of typewritten sheets, on top of a piece of crumpled wrapping-paper.

"These," Bruce tapped the sheets, "are from the original manuscript. I've had 'em witnessed and attested by a Commissioner for Oaths." He picked up the top sheet. "Act One, page 7!" He picked up the second sheet. "Act Two, page 4!" He picked up the rest of the batch. "Act Three, pages 28 to 36!

"Here's retrospect-mention of Bewlay's second murder, which was what made me sure the author was Bewlay. Here's an account of Andrée Cooper. Here's a lot of stuff about the last murder, references to the red-haired girl who gets a bad banknote and goes out on a bicycle and sees the blighter at work through the window. Glance at 'em!"

Beryl did so, and could not repress a cry.

"After all," snapped Bruce, "you needn't look so flabbergasted You noticed it!"

"I noticed it?"

"Yes! That last night in my dressing-room. You pointed out that parts of the script you read had been written on a different typewriter: a page here and there, and a whole chunk of the last act. Didn't you?"

Beryl's finger-tips, with their pink varnished nails, flew to her mouth. Bruce took the sheets from her and threw them back into the drawer.

"You thought," Bruce hammered at her, "it was because the author had changed his mind. It wasn't. It was because I changed the pages, and wrote in a lot of other stuff so that nobody who read the play would guess what I guessed."

"Meaning?"

"That Bewlay wrote the play. And I'm out to catch him."

Here Bruce's voice grew almost hysterical.

"Beryl, I've got to borrow somebody's car. Daphne and her father will be away from this hotel in two minutes unless you hurry down there now; and then we're all dished. Won't you please rally round and give me some help?"

"Bruce, I'm awfully sorry! I'm a nasty-minded little so-and-so! I never dreamed—!"

Conviction of Bruce's innocence, utter and complete, had come to Beryl at last. This was no half-hearted wish to be convinced. It really was conviction; and consternation, and abysmal loathing of herself. Still with her finger-tips pressed against her lips, she stood blinking at him while her eyes grew bright in a kind of radiant humility. Afterwards she nodded quickly, as she would have nodded if he had told her to jump from a high window.

"I'll detain them, Bruce," she promised. "I can't think how; but I'll do it."

"For half an hour, mind!"

"For half an hour," said Beryl. And she ran out of the room on her errand.

"That's better," said Bruce. "That's better!" He seemed a little shaken, as though he had played a difficult scene, when he turned back to Dennis. "You understand the situation, old man?"

"Yes. I think I'm beginning to."

"Ah!"

"But how did you learn the real Bewlay was here in Aldebridge?" demanded Dennis. "And why should he send you a play, apparently with a fake name and address? And why are you so violently interested in

145

nabbing him? And who is the real Bewlay?"

"That's just the trouble," snarled Bruce. "I don't know *who* the blighter is! As for your other questions . . ."

"Well?"

"They've got to wait!" Again Bruce consulted his wrist-watch; again his eyes grew feverish. "Do you know what time it is? It's getting on towards six o'clock! And we've got to get that body away from here, we've *got* to, before six o'clock!"

"Wait a minute, now! You're not going through with this crazy idea of disposing of the body?"

"Oh, yes, I am," said Bruce. "And you're going to help me. Look here!"

Dennis's uneasiness, at whatever mood Bruce might be in, was fast becoming panic. Bruce strode across to the dark bedroom. Motioning Dennis to precede him, he snapped on a wall-switch just inside the door.

Raw electric light from a couple of wall-candles frostily illuminated the disarranged room, with its two windows facing west and two windows facing north. Between the latter two windows, at the end of the wing, was another door: presumably leading to the outside staircase. But neither Dennis nor Bruce looked at anything except what remained of Mildred Lyons.

She had not been very pretty even in life. Now she seemed almost obscene. She lay on her back, in a cheap utility coat spotted with damp sand, beside the fat easy chair. Her face, clean-wiped, showed in contrast to the sand-streaks across the eyeballs and the sandy crust of her lips. From the mass of disarranged hair a few pale red strands straggled across her forehead. Beyond her the open door of the wardrobe, with its mirror, creaked a little as a draught stirred through the open windows.

The evil brutality of the murderer was a living force in this room. Dennis saw a few hairpins on the carpet.

He couldn't stand it.

"Put out that light!" he said.

"What's she doing on the floor there?" Bruce asked hoarsely. "*I* put her in the chair. Has somebody been in here?"

"Probably she rolled off. Put out that light!"

Darkness descended.

It wasn't a merciful darkness; you were too conscious of what lay on the floor, as though it might reach out and catch at your ankle. Bruce groped across the bedroom. A knob turned, a latch clicked. Another oblong of space, with a deeper gush of breeze, appeared against starlight as Bruce opened the outer door.

"Come here!" whispered Bruce.

Dennis joined him on a little wooden platform, with a handrail, from which a rather rickety flight of wooden stairs led down against the outside wall of the hotel. And Bruce pointed.

A yellow moon was rising, the hunter's moon. It unveiled the black sea, stretching away towards their right, in little slow ripples that glinted before they moved in to splash whisperingly on the shingle. White wreaths of mist drifted above it, never still. Far ahead of them, to the left of a white-edged coastline, twinkled the lights of Aldebridge. Just below, the wooden staircase led down into a gravelled yard—evidently used as a parking-place—whose outlines could dimly be discerned.

A solitary two-seater car, its parking-lights on, stood in the yard. Bruce's voice came soft and exultant out of the gloom.

"She's done it!" he gloated. "Beryl's kept 'em inside like the Ancient Mariner. Look there! That's Daphne's car."

Then Bruce's fingers fastened on Dennis's arm.

"Now listen! What I want you to do is this. Nip down

147

there as quietly as you can; turn out the lights; and back that car up against the foot of the stairway here. Then—"

"Wait a minute, Bruce. I won't do it."

The sea-wind blew very cold. Ghostly surf whitened under a yellow moon. It was as though he had struck Bruce in the face.

"You won't do it?"

"No."

"Dennis, old man!" Bruce's voice poured with reproachfulness. "You wouldn't help a pal in trouble?"

"Now look here, Bruce. It's no good trying your charm-act on me. Just give me one good reason *why* you want to do a hare-brained thing like this!"

"For one thing," cried Bruce, and shook the railing round the platform as though he wanted to shake it loose, "do you think I want the police to find that woman in my bedroom and maybe suspect me of murder?"

"If you're not Roger Bewlay, what difference does that make?"

And now Dennis could see the shift and gleam of Bruce's eyes. It was as though Bruce was seeking, questing, rapidly considering courses and then discarding them, while his physical presence seemed to tower in an effort at hypnosis.

"So you definitely refuse to help me?"

"Yes!"

"I see," said Bruce. "Then Beryl was right after all."

"How do you mean, Beryl was right?"

"You've fallen for Daphne Herbert. You'd *like* to see me get into a mess, you'd like to have Daphne and her family hate me, so you could have a go at her yourself."

Pause, while the surf whispered.

"That's a damn lie!"

"Sorry, old man; but I'm afraid it's true."

148

"You don't seriously think . . . ?"

"I'd handle the whole business myself," Bruce flung aside his protest. "Only, do you see, I can't drive a car. It sounds foolish; but there it is. I never learned; hadn't the patience. So I'm left stuck here with a dead woman, and prevented from catching the real murderer, because a friend of mine falls for my girl and tries to play me a dirty trick.

"Not that I blame you, mind!" Bruce interrupted himself, raising a hand. "All's fair in love and what's-its-name; and maybe I'd do the same thing myself. Only—it seems a bit thick. By George, hold on!" In a blaze of inspiration, Bruce snapped his fingers. "I've got it! I know what I'll do!"

"Easy, now!"

"I can't drive a car, Dennis. But I can have a ruddy good shot at trying to drive it."

"Don't be a . . . !"

"After all, I know the motions. I'm going to cram that woman's body into the back seat, and drive to the devil and gone. I mean it, Dennis! Even if I do wreck the car because you won't help me, and maybe involve Daphne herself, I'm going to . . . Excuse me."

And he started down the stairs.

"Bruce! Wait!"

Bruce stopped, without turning round.

Dennis Foster felt that his collar had begun to strangle him.

"May I point out for the last time," he said desperately, "that this isn't a stage-play? It's ugly, dangerous work. It means a prison-sentence for both of us if we get caught."

"It isn't dangerous,"—Bruce instantly swung round—"if you'll only hurry!" Bruce peered at the luminous figures on his watch. "A quarter to six!" he groaned. "A quarter to six already!"

149

"What's all this about six o'clock?"

"Sh-h! Keep your voice down! Did you notice Commander Renwick's bar and smoking-room downstairs?"

"I saw it, yes!"

"Renwick," gabbled Bruce, "can't do much for hotel-guests. But his drinks are in super-abundance. It's Black Market; bound to be; but you can get as many double Scotches as you want at four bob a go. Everybody in Aldebridge who's got any money comes out here in the evening."

"Well?"

"Well! The bar opens at six. From then on, or even before, cars will be pouring into this parking-space and we won't stand the ghost of a chance!"

Dennis tried to conquer a shaky throat.

"Bruce, what are you going to *do* with the body?"

"I'm going to hide it." The blur of a face looking up at him from the stairs, looking up under the yellow moon, seemed distended as though Bruce's mouth were wider than usual. "I'm going to hide it in a place where you can't see it even if you happen to be looking at it.— Will you help me, old son?"

And Dennis went down the steps.

"Good lad!" whispered Bruce. "I'll get ready and carry her down. We can be away from here in two shakes. Look sharp, now!"

I'm going to hide it in a place where you can't see it even if you happen to be looking at it.

But what Dennis saw most clearly in his mind's eye, as he descended the stairs, was the face of Mr. James Mackintosh, senior partner of the law firm of Mackintosh & Foster. He saw his own office, his flat, his whole daily round, as though through the wrong end of a telescope: infinitely remote, eerily lighted against blackness and sea-wash. He was doing an absolutely mad thing, and knew it. If it hadn't been for

150

that remark about Daphne Herbert . . .

Even now he clutched at an uneasy hope. It was ten to one that the ignition-key had been removed from the car. In that case, he would have a legitimate excuse for backing out.

The gravelled yard, with dingy whitewashed out-buildings, swam in half-light. In the middle stood a post which had once supported an arc-lamp. Beyond it was the car, a Ford V.8 in whose big dickey, or rumble-seat, you could easily hide a body. It seemed a long way across the yard, a very long way, while he heard his own footsteps crunch on gravel. He stopped by the car, and looked inside at the dashboard.

The key was there. He was committed now.

Gritting his teeth, Dennis felt the sea-wind blowing even more chill. He climbed into the car and, after a blank pause for resolution, he switched on. Then he trod on the starter.

The resultant throb, though it was not loud, affected his nerves as being loud beyond endurance. He revved the motor softly while it warmed up. When he engaged reverse gear, a pulse in the calf of his leg was shaking so badly that he stalled the engine, and had to begin again.

Steady! This wouldn't do!

The car shot backwards, spurting gravel under its wheels. And, at the same moment, a light behind him flashed on.

Dennis knew a second's blind panic before he identified the source of it. It came from the two north windows of the smoking-room, which, as he now remembered, was on the ground-floor directly under Bruce's suite. They were lighting up the smoking-room preparatory to receiving guests.

With his neck craned round, Dennis could see into a part of the smoking-room. He could see some chairs, and the edge of a Russian-billiard table. Most distinctly he could see a brown-faced clock, with gold numerals, on the west wall. The clock, fast as pub-clocks always are, said ten minutes to six.

Hurry! Hurry! *Hurry!*

The car shot backwards with such violence that it nearly crashed into the little outside staircase; Dennis saved it in time, and felt the sweat start out on his body. Then the car stood in shadow, softly throbbing.

If Bruce would hurry, now, and carry down what had to be carried down, they could be away in two minutes. Dennis got out of the car, and stared upwards.

"All right, old boy!" a voice whispered reassuringly.

The white wall of the hotel was colourless in shadow, with Bruce a dim blur against it. He heard Bruce's footsteps shuffle, creak, and steady themselves on the stairs. Down Bruce came, carrying something in his arms; the woman's hair streaming loose.

"Open the back, damn it!" Bruce whispered hoarsely. "I've got my hands full."

Dennis twisted the handle of the dickey and flung it open. His eyes kept straying to that brown-faced clock in the smoking-room. At any moment, now . . .

With a powerful heave, an exhalation of breath, Bruce dropped Mildred Lyons's body inside: doubled sideways, with her cheek against the red-leather cushion of the seat. The lights behind them seemed an accusing glare; the clock ticked on.

"Close it," whispered Dennis, "and let's get out of here!—What's the matter with you?"

Bruce, one foot on the metal step by which you reached the dickey, supporting himself with both hands on the edge of the seat and panting heavily, seemed racked by some puzzling point that just eluded him. He stared. He bit at his upper-lip. Then he jumped down with a soft thud on the gravel.

"Her handbag!" he said. "I've forgotten her hand-bag!"

"But we can't . . . !"

152

"Just a minute," urged Bruce.

And he was off again up the stairs.

(Eight minutes to six.)

Across the light from the smoking-room windows passed the figure of the stout sandy-haired waiter, who flicked with a cloth at one table and passed incuriously. Relentless was the clock, squeezing agony out of every second. The lid of the dickey gaped wide, as though it proclaimed what lay inside.

(Seven minutes to six.)

"Bruce!" He daren't call louder.

After what seemed an interminable time he heard Bruce's footsteps quickly racing down the steps. Dressing-gown flying, Bruce appeared out of the gloom brandishing a brown-leather handbag with a pair of gloves fastened to a strap across it.

"Got it!" he breathed, and flung the handbag into the back seat. "It was jammed down inside the wardrobe, where some swine put it. It took me a little time to . . ."

"Never mind that! Get into the car!"

"I just want to assure you, old boy, that I've got the best of reasons for what I'm doing. Where we're going isn't far from here, but I warn you we may be away for a very long time. We must wait until . . ."

Again Dennis saw Bruce stop, reflecting. Bruce's hands went to the lapels of his dressing-gown. Dennis's voice was not loud, but it was charged with repressed violence.

"In Christ's name, Bruce, what's wrong *now?*"

"This dressing-gown, old boy. I can't go rushing about the country dressed like this. It'd look funny if somebody stopped us. Just one minute more while I put on some clothes."

And he was gone again.

We have all, in the normal course of catching a train or going to the theatre, seen this sort of thing happen. We wait at the door, hat in hand, while someone goes back once, and yet again and again, before the process of departure can be complete. In normal life it is maddening enough. But, if you are pitched without warning into a situation with a prison sentence at the end of it, where your whole fate may depend on a few seconds' time, it reaches a point of something like hysterical laughter.

(Three minutes to six.)

Dennis paced up and down beside the car.

Assuming Bruce to be innocent, what was he up to? Those words "if somebody stopped us" rang ominously in Dennis's mind. They added to the dangers that fanged every step of the way. There was no reason to suppose a policeman might stop the car, or look in the back seat if he did. All the same . . .

A rug, a tarpaulin, anything to cover that body!

The lid still yawned open. Dennis jumped up on the metal step and peered down into darkness. The moon threw little illumination here. He took out a pocket-lighter, snapped on its flame, and held it down into the rear seat.

There was a carriage-rug, thrown down carelessly on the floor among one or two tools. He hated touching that body, the texture of its coat, even when he tried to drape the rug clumsily over her.

Mildred Lyons's mouth had fallen open. There was a little crust of damp sand where her forehead and cheek had rested against the red-leather upholstery. He noticed that, with some vague sense of wrongness at the back of his mind, when he disturbed the body in tucking the rug across it. But he had little time to notice anything else.

A voice from behind him called:

"Mr. Foster!"

And it was the voice of Commander Renwick.

13

The yellow eye of the moon on a ruffled sea, the white weatherboarded hotel with its two lighted windows, he himself holding a lighter-flame close to a crumpled rug which hid gruesome limbs: all these things entered into the category of what couldn't be happening.

It is to Dennis's credit that he did not jump or start guiltily when he heard that voice. All emotion had whittled down to a point of desperate coolness.

"Yes?" he called back.

He blew out the lighter-flame, closed the lid of the dickey with a soft slam, twisted the handle into place, and jumped down.

Commander Renwick's footsteps crunched on gravel.

Renwick was approaching round the side of the hotel, from the direction of the front. He moved at his somewhat clumsy walk, left shoulder higher than the other, as though the left leg had been affected in addition to his missing left arm.

As he passed the lighted windows, Dennis could see the faintly puzzled expression in the horizontal wrinkles that barred his forehead. A way look, a rather angry look: what was it? Yet there was a smile in

Renwick's beard, bunching up his cheeks.

"I—er—wished to have a word with you," he explained. But, at the same time, with a lift of the eyebrows like an interrogation-point, his eyes moved towards Daphne's car.

Dennis laughed.

"This," he said loudly, "is Miss Herbert's car."

"I was aware of that," said Commander Renwick.

"Mr. Egerton," again Dennis used the name Bruce had assumed, "asked me to get something out of the back seat. But apparently it isn't there."

"Ah!" Commander Renwick's eyes strayed to the dark stairway, and the dark windows above. "Mr. Egerton has returned, then?"

"Yes." (Was it all right to admit this?)

Commander Renwick took a deep breath.

"I wished to see you, first of all, about your accommodation."

"Accommodation?"

"Er—forgive me. You did wish to spend the night here?"

"Yes. Oh, yes! Of course!" Dennis's voice seemed to ring and thunder with false heartiness; he fancied a sharp glance at him.

"Your own accommodation, I fear, will be somewhat primitive. I must put you up in my office. But that," Commander Renwick made a slight gesture, "was not my main message." He paused for an instant. "Mr. Jonathan Herbert would like to see you in the lounge at once."

"Mr.—?"

"The matter is urgent," said Commander Renwick.

"But I can't . . . !"

"The matter is *very* urgent," insisted Commander Renwick, and fastened sinewy fingers round his sleeve.

All things seemed conspiring to drag him, to direct

156

him, to force him into the course that a predestined fate had determined. Dennis felt a momentary gust of anger. He shook off Commander Renwick's arm.

"Why is it urgent?"

"Mr. Herbert, Miss Herbert, and Miss West,"—his companion stepped back with a murmured word of apology—"are now in the lounge. Their voices are . . . somewhat loud. I could not help overhearing. Forgive me; but we *have* been making fools of ourselves."

"About what?"

"This man is not a murderer." To Dennis's astonishment, he saw that there was sweat on the Commander's forehead. "He is Bruce Ransom, the actor. He . . ."

The lights of a car, intolerably blazing into Dennis's eyes, swung into the yard as a small Hillman crunched on gravel and came inexpertly to a stop. Out of it crawled a stoutish figure, hatless, who hailed Renwick joyously and moved forward with a jaunty step.

Once before, Dennis realized as the newcomer passed the glow from the windows, he had seen that tall but pudgy body, the strands of brown hair brushed across the nearly-bald skull like the skeleton of a fish, the slightly pinkish face with the eternally pursed-up mouth and inquisitive blue eyes.

"My dear Renwick!" the newcomer began, greeting the Commander as though he were seeing him after an absence of six months. "My dear Renwick!"

Commander Renwick spoke in a clear, hard voice.

"Mr. Foster," he said, "may I present Mr. Horace Chittering?" He paused for a moment. "Mr. Foster is a friend of Bruce Egerton."

Again there was a pause. Mr. Chittering's eyes opened wide.

"My dear fellow!" he said to Dennis with great effusiveness, and shook Dennis's hand as though he were going to follow it with an embrace. "My dear

157

fellow! You really must come inside and have a drink with me. You really must! No, now, I insist!"

"But . . . !"

"Who else is with us to-night, Renwick?"

"The vicar's there . . ."

"Ah, the vicar!" cried Mr. Chittering, raising his hand as though himself offering a benediction. "A charming fellow! The Rev. Mr. Richard Berkeley. Not too proud, mind you, to drink his pint in a public-house just the same as the rest of us! No, indeed! Have you met the vicar, Mr. Foster?"

"No. I . . ."

"Ah, I'm glad you've met him. You'll be able to appreciate what a really fine fellow he is, in spite," Mr. Chittering lowered his voice, "of some unfortunate domestic trouble. But we won't discuss that. No, indeed! My dear Renwick! Have any others joined our festal club of the spirit?"

"Jonathan Herbert's in the lounge," replied Commander Renwick in that same harsh, clear voice. "He wants very much to speak to Mr. Foster."

"To speak to Mr. Foster?" repeated Mr. Chittering softly. "Ah, yes! Of course! About . . ."

Mr. Chittering's presence was like sticky fly-paper, clinging to you and fastening you round.

"Tell me, my dear fellow," he murmured to Dennis, "have you met the Herberts?"

"Look here! Let go the lapel of my coat! I've met—"

"A delightful couple!" said Mr. Chittering. "Clara," he lowered his voice, "made an unfortunate marriage years ago; some bounder whose name I forget. Daphne is the daughter of that marriage. But we won't discuss that. No, indeed! The point is, Herbert is as fond of that girl as though she were his own daughter. Fonder! He idolizes her. It would be very unfortunate if Daphne . . . if Daphne . . ."

158

And then a voice tore through that unreal air under the yellow moon.

"Stop it," said Commander Renwick.

He spoke as though with bursting veins and compressed chest. The dark-brown beard masked a good part of his face, all except the eyes and forehead. He was twisting, and twisting again, one of the leather-covered buttons on his jacket.

"My dear fellow!" protested Mr. Chittering in an injured voice.

"You were going to say,"—Renwick regained his suavity—"if Daphne fell in love with the wrong person?"

"Not yourself?" laughed Mr. Chittering.

Commander Renwick ignored this.

"I said, 'stop it'," he continued, "because we can stop worrying. I'm no gossip. I'm not at liberty to say anything more. But Bruce Egerton's not Bewlay. There's no murderer at all."

Mr. Chittering stared at him.

"No murderer?" he echoed.

It was as though you had taken a toy from a baby. In the light from the smoking-room windows Dennis could see his lower lip go down, and an expression of distress overspread his face.

"No _murderer?_" he repeated. "But, my dear fellow! The evidence! We agreed . . ."

"It's a hoax of some kind." Commander Renwick turned round sharply, left shoulder hunched high, to start towards the front of the hotel. As his face flashed past the light of the windows, Dennis noted furrowed forehead and gleam of teeth in beard. Then, just as abruptly, Renwick turned back again.

"Forgive me for being so insistent, Mr. Foster," he added. "But will you go in and see our friend Herbert? Or shall I ask him to come out and see you?"

159

If Daphne or her father were to come out here now, and get into that car . . .

Mentally, Dennis raved.

Where, he wondered, was Bruce now? Up in the dark bedroom, no doubt, gnawing his nails and cursing. Afer all, he and Bruce couldn't climb into Daphne's car in front of witnesses, and drive away without a word of explanation. On the other hand, Beryl couldn't detain Daphne and Mr. Herbert in the lounge for ever.

The gilt hands of the smoking-room clock, hypnotic now, stood at ten minutes past six. Sooner or later, Mr. Herbert at least would insist on going home. And if he did, before Bruce and Dennis could drive away . . .

"You spoke, Mr. Foster?" prompted Commander Renwick.

"I'll go in and see Mr. Herbert," said Dennis.

(Stall him! Stall them all, for a few minutes at least, until you can get up to Bruce's room and down again!)

Commander Renwick went on ahead, his humped shoulder and stiff leg giving an oddly deformed effect which was not noticeable when he stood in repose. Dennis followed, with Mr. Chittering gushing words at his elbow. Mr. Chittering was saying something about Renwick being all nerves because he had once had "an unpleasant experience with a murderer"; but Dennis did not take it in. Dennis was too occupied with wondering what yarn Beryl had spun, what she had told Daphne and Mr. Herbert, to keep them there for so long.

In a very few seconds he found out.

Snug and cosy, its dilapidation softened by artificial light, glowed the lounge of the Leather Boot when they entered by the front door. The wall-candles, augmented by an iron crown of electric candles from the ceiling, shone on white plaster and black beams. A bright fire crackled and popped in the fireplace on the side towards the smoking-room. The broad bar-hatch window, now rolled up and illuminated, showed inside a gaudy crowding of bottles presided over by a barman in a white coat.

Beside the bar counter stood a handsome, affable-looking man in a soft hat, a dark suit, and a clerical collar, with a pint of beer before him.

And in wicker chairs, at a little table over on the right, sat Daphne and Mr. Herbert and Beryl West.

Dennis had a terrible fear that Horace Chittering would plunge into the midst of this group. But Mr. Chittering, either out of elementary decency or because he needed a drink, bustled over to the bar-counter, effusively greeted the Rev. Mr. Richard Berkeley, and ordered a double whisky.

It was the two girls who were talking at the little table. Though their voices were low, Dennis caught every word as he approached.

"But why didn't Bruce *say* this?" Daphne was pleading.

"He tried to tell you, dear." Beryl's face was white and strained. Every word seemed to hurt her. "He tried to tell you only you wouldn't listen."

"But he didn't try to tell us!" protested Daphne. Lovely and naïve, she put her hand on Beryl's arm. The dark-fringed grey eyes were wide open. "He just—hinted. That's all! About some secret that even you didn't know. He just hinted! Why on earth didn't he tell us?"

"Dear, don't you see? He was playing a part."

"Playing a part?"

"Bruce," answered Beryl, with her hand at her throat, "has played the Great Detective on the stage so many times that he can't help himself. He's come to imagine stage-technique will apply to life. He's playing the Great Detective, who doesn't reveal anything till

161

the end! That's why he didn't say . . . didn't say . . ."

"One moment," interposed Jonathan Herbert, who had seen Dennis.

It was very warm in the lounge. The fire popped and spat with slaty coal. From the direction of the smoking-room drifted a click of billiard-balls on the Russian-billiard table, and a laugh. They heard a creak of footsteps as Commander Renwick went behind the reception-desk to open a ledger.

None of the wrath, none of the sick bitter expression, had left Mr. Herbert's face. Yet his eyes were full of doubt and wonder, as though he might have been doing somebody an injustice. He sat bolt upright, the palms of his hands flat on the table.

"Mr. Foster!" he said, and cleared his throat.

"Yes, sir?"

"Miss West," he nodded towards her, "has made certain statements. Not that they change anything, mind!" Tenderly, almost pleadingly, he turned to Daphne; and back again. "But they may perhaps . . ." He left the sentence unfinished, with a slight gesture.

"Will you, Mr. Foster, on your word of honour, confirm or deny those statements?"

"If I can. Yes."

Again Mr. Herbert turned to Daphne.

"You won't run away with this fellow, my dear? You promise me that, at least?"

"I promise."

"Good!" Mr. Herbert looked at Dennis. His grey hair gleamed under the dim wall-lights. "Our—our nimble friend upstairs is Bruce Ransom, the actor. Very well! I accept that. But Miss West goes farther."

Then, always with Daphne in mind, Mr. Herbert spoke softly.

"The madman Roger Bewlay lives in Aldebridge!" he said. *"And Mr. Ransom is here to trap him."*

162

In the lounge, dead silence.

It was as though, physically, all things had come suddenly to a stop. No click of billiard-balls issued from the smoking-room. The fire drew straight and steady, soundlessly. At the bar-counter Mr. Chittering, a glass halfway to his lips, stopped motionless with his eyes upraised. The man in the clerical collar seemed congealed into a figure of prayer. Behind the reception-desk Commander Renwick, who had been running his finger down a ledger, stopped but did not look up.

It may have been an illusion, a trick of heightened senses. It seemed improbable that Mr. Herbert's very soft tone could have carried to every corner of that chipped room.

Yet in this straining of silence, this immobility, Dennis sensed a presence of evil whose influence flowed round them. Something had been said which should not have been overheard. It was dangerous. It loosed forces. In the next moment stillness exploded; small noises crept back in the clink of a glass, the stir of a foot on bare boards; and Jonathan Herbert spoke again.

"Is this true, Mr. Foster?"

"Yes!"

"Then it wasn't—just a joke!" Daphne said quietly.

"No, Miss Herbert."

"It wasn't done to humiliate anybody," pursued Daphne, with her eyes shining and her elbows on the table. "It had a good purpose; an awfully decent purpose, really. That's different!"

"Daphne, for God's sake!" said her father. His fists were clenched on the table.

"You needn't worry about me," smiled Daphne, and shook her head with that look of tensity round eyes and mouth. "Something changed in me, up there, when I saw him. I don't know why. I don't know how. It had

163

nothing to do with this. I only know . . . sorry! What were you saying?"

"Evidence!" said Mr. Herbert, and threw out his hands. "We may—perhaps—have misjudged—I don't know! But where's Ransom's *evidence* of all this?"

"I say, son," interposed a new voice. "Do you mind if I answer that?"

And Sir Henry Merrivale, the Old Maestro himself, came lumbering in from the front door.

Dennis Foster could have shouted with relief at the sight of that homely, hearty, heartening presence. H. M., his spectacles pulled down on his broad nose and a glare of indescribable malignancy on his face, still wore the suit of tweed plus-fours. His unmentionable bowler hat was clutched under his left arm. He dragged out a wicker chair, sitting down with a thump that shook the creaky floor.

"Merrivale!" exclaimed Jonathan Herbert. Dennis remembered H. M. speaking as though he had been acquainted with Mr. Herbert. "Merrivale! I didn't know . . ."

"You didn't know I was here? Hey?"

"Not within a thousand miles of here!"

"Well . . . now." H. M. sounded apologetic. "I been keepin' it quiet, sort of. I'm at the Golden Pheasant in Aldebridge."

"We're in a mess, my boy," said Mr. Herbert.

"Oh, ah?"

"We're in a mess," repeated Mr. Herbert. His strong face now looked only tired and kindly and muddled. His voice sounded almost pitiful. "The fellow's Bruce Ransom. And Daphne's in love with him. And—what did you say you wanted to speak about?"

"About Roger Bewlay," replied H. M.

He did not trouble to lower his voice. Again that name had its electrifying effect on the whole lounge.

"Bewlay," continued H. M., "Bewlay, in his conceit, wrote a play about his own career and bunged it along to Bruce Ransom. He never intended to claim it as author, of course. And he tried to be awful crafty about seein' it could never be traced to him, in case it gave away too much. So he signed a fake name and a fake address, and posted it in London."

Beryl West sprang to her feet.

"Well?" she cried.

"And then," H. M. raised his voice, "the silly dummy went and wrapped it up, inside the brown paper, with a piece of paper that could be as easily identified as kiss-your-hand. Oh, my eye! It was a piece of thin wrappin'-paper with the pale green letters: 'Ye Olde Tea Shoppe, Aldebridge'."

And Dennis remembered.

He remembered that thin crumpled piece of wrapping-paper, with its lettering, carefully put away in the drawer of Bruce's writing-table along with those significant sheets of manuscript. It was evidence, a part of the design, and still more proof that Bruce had been telling the truth.

"Bruce Ransom," H. M. resumed, "didn't exactly have to be a mental giant to guess the author of the play lived in Aldebridge—or near it. He was right. Bewlay *is* here. And I'm mad. Burn me, I'm mad! I got a friend, an awful rat named Chief Inspector Masters. He's mad, too."

And now at last they caught the undercurrent in H. M.'s voice.

"Mad?" echoed Beryl. "Why?"

"Well, y'see," answered H. M., "we think he's committed another murder."

Across the lounge, somebody upset a glass.

It was the white-jacketed barman, who instantly retrieved it. No one else moved, while a click of billiard-balls and a laugh rose from the direction of the smoking-room.

Jonathan Herbert was looking sick. He put out his hand, instinctively, to protect Daphne.

"In Aldebridge?" he said, and cleared his throat. "This is frightful! This is . . . The murder couldn't have been . . . ?"

"Couldn't have been who?"

"Never mind! Who was murdered?"

"A gal by the name of Mildred Lyons. We think."

"Mildred Lyons?"

"Uh-huh. She was comin' down here to identify Bewlay. But she was crafty too. She wrote to the local police first; she said that, if she didn't phone 'em by five o'clock this afternoon, they'd better look out for something pretty sticky." H. M. paused for an instant. "Masters and I have just been to Aldebridge police-station."

"You don't *know* she's dead?"

"We haven't found her body, no. But then Bewlay's an artist of disposin' of bodies. It's goin' to be very, very unpleasant for anybody we do find in possession of that body."

Dennis's heart stood still.

He was conscious of many details in the damp heat of the lounge: of Daphne's eyes and mouth as she bent forward in a fervour of horrified fascination, of Commander Renwick leaning over a ledger, even of the initials which one of the military had carved in the black beam beside him. Yet every word H. M. spoke tended to prove Bruce's innocence, to clear away the last shred of doubt.

"H. M.," Dennis appealed suddenly, "listen!"

The sharp little eyes behind the big spectacles were fastened on him.

"Yes, son?"

166

"Bruce told us," Dennis moistened his lips, "that he knew all about your being down here, and that he'd talked to you. Is that true?"

"Quite true, son."

"Bruce *is* innocent, sir? And you know exactly what he's doing?"

H. M. hesitated for a second.

"Oh, yes, son. I know exactly what he's doin'."

"Then wait here," roared Dennis. "Wait here for just one moment!"

And, before anyone could comment or even speak, he raced towards the stairs.

Dennis, taking those carpeted steps two at a time as he hurried up towards Bruce's rooms, felt that for the first time his head was clear. What madness had impelled him to half-agree in "disposing" of that body, even snared by Bruce's stronger personality, he could not now imagine. But he shivered in retrospect at what they had avoided.

The police weren't suspicious of Bruce. They never had been suspicious of Bruce. It had all been an illusion of Beryl's. But if Bruce in his role of great detective had been allowed to take Mildred Lyons's body away from the hotel, and hide it heaven knew where, then both of them would have been involved in deadly serious trouble; perhaps as accessories after the fact. All he had to do, now, was tell Bruce! All he had to do . . .

Upstairs, the gutted shell of the hotel echoed to his running footsteps. He threw open the door of Bruce's sitting-room, and stopped short.

"Bruce!" he shouted.

The door to the bedroom, and beyond that the outer door to the stairway, now stood wide open. A strong draught poured through into the grey-and-blue sitting-room. It wildly fluttered the pages of the *New Yorker* and the *Radio Times*; it carried a drift of loose letters from the writing-table, and swirled them round in a cloud that scattered like Dennis's wits.

For the first time, the cover was off Bruce's portable typewriter. A sheet of paper, stuck upright in the carriage, fluttered beckoningly and attracted his attention. The word DENNIS in capital letters brought him running to read the message.

SORRY, OLD BOY; I COULDN'T WAIT ANY LONGER.
I'M HAVING A CUT AT IT MYSELF. BRUCE.

For what seemed endless minutes Dennis stared at it, while the loose papers whirled.

"Bruce!" he shouted again.

He was answered, from a distance, by a noise that made the teeth ache. It rose piercingly. It was a screaming of gear-meshes, a grinding and tearing to the bone, as though a metallic giant were having his own teeth pulled. A motor roared to its highest note in bottom gear.

"Look out, you damn fool!" yelled a distant voice.

Bruce, who couldn't drive a car but only "knew the motions." Bruce, who . . .

Dennis raced through the bedroom, and out on the little balcony under the rising, whitening moon. He was just in time to see the getaway.

Daphne's Ford V.8, with Bruce dimly to be seen at the wheel, plunged past the post supporting the arc-lamp, and shaved within a hair's breadth of another car reeling into the yard as the driver yanked his wheel over. Head-lamps flashed and crossed. The Ford V.8 slewed sideways into the main road, righted itself, and, with a metallic screaming as Bruce attempted to strangle it into second gear, lurched out of sight southwards in the direction away from Aldebridge.

Then there was no sound except that of the other motorist cursing.

Done. Finished. Sunk. And the police . . .

Dennis stood with his head down, gripping the railing of the little balcony, the dark bedroom behind him. A voice in his head said: To the devil with it. You've done all *you* can. Forget it. But they couldn't forget it; they couldn't forget any of this entangling mess, until the damnable figure of Roger Bewlay had been pushed into a corner at last.

That was where Dennis became aware that the bedroom behind him was no longer dark. A switch clicked; thin light flooded the balcony. Dennis turned round, and took two steps into the bedroom.

In the doorway to the sitting-room, smoking a black cigar, stood Sir Henry Merrivale.

"I say, son," observed H. M., taking the cigar out of his mouth. "Hadn't you better tell me what in holy blue blazes has been goin' on here?"

14

With great care Dennis closed the door to the balcony. In that sick, dispirited moment he hardly cared what happened. Yet he fought back.

"Going on?" he repeated. "I don't understand."

H. M. regarded him dismally.

"Oh, my son!" He nodded towards the hairpins still strewing the carpet of the bedroom. "Mildred Lyons was on her way to see Ransom. If the bogey-man caught her . . ."

Then his tone changed.

"I'm the old man," announced H. M., suddenly inflating his chest and assuming an air of aloof majesty which would have done credit to King Edward the Seventh having his portrait painted. "If there's any flum-diddling of the police to be done, I'm the man to do it." A spasm of ghoulish amusement crossed his face. Then his tone changed again.

"Seriously, son: if you think I'd breathe a word to the coppers that would get any friends of mine into trouble, you don't know what I feel about that reptile Masters. For the love of Esau, what *happened?*"

"Come into the next room," Dennis requested curtly.

They went into the sitting-room, and Dennis closed the door. Loose papers had ceased to scutter about the wainscot like pursued hens. Bruce's discarded dressing-gown, a sand-speckled handkerchief protruding from one pocket, had been flung down across the corner of the settee.

And Dennis told H. M. the whole story.

He began with the encounter on the golf links, and went on to every fact, every detail, even every sense of doubt and wrongness that had dogged his thoughts. H. M., glowering on the settee and smoking the vile cigar in short puffs like a railway engine getting up steam, listened with an expression of awe gradually overspreading his face.

"Cor!" he muttered.

"Yes. I quite agree."

"Ransom," demanded H. M., "has gone haring out of here in a car he can't drive? Liable to smack into the nearest lamp-post or be stopped by the first bobby he sees?"

"That's about the size of it."

"Is the feller scatty?"

"I've sometimes wondered."

"But where's he takin' her?"

"I don't know!" As a matter of fact, Dennis had the answer; but it had slipped through his mind and been forgotten. "All Bruce said," Dennis went on, "was that he could hide the body in a place where you couldn't see it even if you happened to be looking at it."

H. M. swore with some comprehensiveness.

And yet, behind this angry surface, Dennis had the distinct impression that the Old Maestro was pleased. H. M. had seen something. He had pounced on something. He was moving closer to some objective in his own mind; there was a kind of ghoulish voluptuousness about the way in which he puffed at his black cigar.

Very casually he impelled himself to his feet, and began to pace up and down the room. But all Dennis could see, in his own mind, was the large figure of Chief Inspector Masters bearing all the terrors of the law.

"You understand, sir," he burst out, "this all arose out of a misunderstanding!"

"So?" inquired H. M., with his eye on Bruce's writing-table.

"Beryl and I were afraid you believed Bruce was Roger Bewlay. We thought you'd told Masters . . ."

"Me?" said H. M., turning round abruptly and taking the cigar out of his mouth. *"Me?* Tell Masters? Oh, my son! I haven't told that weasel *anything."*

"Aren't you working with him?"

"Well. Now. That depends on your definition. For eleven years," H. M. said darkly, "he's been sayin' he didn't need my help in this business. All right! That's fair enough. But he can wait a little longer before I start to spill over with fetchin' secrets. Maybe you noticed I was a bit coy and enigmatic in speaking to Masters this afternoon?"

"Candidly, I did notice something of the sort."

"Kind of evasive and oyster-mouthed, hey?"

"You might call it that, yes."

"Yes," said H. M., nodding very vigorously. "That's one reason why I didn't tell the blighter what really happened in this case. The other reason why I didn't tell him what happened . . ."

"Well?"

H. M. peered round to make sure they were not overheard.

"Well," he confessed, "because I ain't quite sure myself."

"But you said—!"

"Listen, son!" H. M. held up his hand. He spoke very soberly and sincerely. "I know what happened to Mrs. X, the gal who was apparently Bewlay's fourth wife, the gal who disappeared at Torquay. I know how *she* disappeared. But what happened to the other three?" Then his big voice roared out. "Burn it all, what happened to the other three?"

"But is that important?"

"Is it important?" H. M. stared at him. "Oh, lord love a duck!"

"And how did you learn Roger Bewlay was really here after all? Was it because Bruce confided in you about that play?"

H. M. looked distressed.

"Partly that," he conceded, "and partly something I'd first seen for myself, that made the hair I haven't got practically stand on end. Y'see . . ."

Puffing smoke like a dragon, he lumbered over to the writing-table. Its drawer still stood wide open, as it had been open most of the evening. Putting down his cigar on the edge of the table, H. M. carefully lifted out the few typewritten sheets of the incriminating play, together with the wrapping-paper from the Aldebridge tea-shop. With the same care he placed them beside the typewriter.

Suddenly H. M.'s eyes moved to the piece of paper still stuck in the carriage of Bruce's typewriter. They remained riveted there for several seconds before they moved back again. Afterwards, his back now turned, H. M. stood motionless for so long a time that Dennis wondered whether he had fallen into a trance.

"H. M.!" he called.

"Hey, son? What's that?"

Dennis fashioned his syllables loudly and with rounded enunciation, as though he were speaking to a

174

deaf man.

"I'm not Masters, you know," he pointed out. "*I* never tried to do you down. *I* think your advice is the best possible advice on any occasion. But Beryl and Bruce and I, to say nothing of the Herbert family, have nearly gone out of our minds."

Then he asked the direct question.

"Who is Roger Bewlay, sir? And how did he dispose of that woman's body?"

H. M. regarded him steadily, and then nodded.

"Yes." H. M. drew a deep breath. "Yes, son, I think maybe it is time to put a few cards on the table. In fact, I think maybe you can help me."

Dennis felt his veins heating with that madness of curiosity which was eating him away.

"Well, sir?" he prompted.

"I told you at the beginning of this business," growled H. M., picking up his cigar from the edge of the table, "that you didn't know what your problem was. That's what set you all lookin' straight in the wrong direction. The line you should have taken, son, the clue you should have followed, was that . . ."

This was the point at which someone knocked briskly on the door to the corridor. Mr. Horace Chittering marched in, closely followed by the pleasant-looking clergyman with his hat in his hand.

Dennis Foster, that sedate young man, could have thrown the typewriter at them for intruding at this moment. Yet Chittering, his pink complexion heightened by a number of whiskies, his eye grown moist and even more affable, was not abashed. Two voices spoke together.

"We hope we don't—"

"We are sorry if—"

The voices clashed, Chittering's husky tenor against the vicar's strong baritone; and both stopped at once.

175

"My dear fellow!" urged Mr. Chittering. "Do go on!"

"No, no! You go on!"

"My dear fellow," said Mr. Chittering, clutching at his companion's arm, "I insist!"

The Rev. Mr. Richard Berkeley was one of those hearty, likable parsons whom people praise by saying that they are not at all like parsons. His handsome, rather flattish face, with the strong jaw, was surmounted by fair hair crisping and going dry at the temples. Dennis could not help liking him, the smile as well as the flash and frankness of the eye; but all this smoothed itself out now in a steady, deep concern.

He pressed his hat over his heart, and inclined his head a little.

"I believe," he said politely, "that I address Sir Henry Merrivale?"

"That's right, son. What can I do for you?"

"We wished,"—Mr. Berkeley looked H. M. straight in the eyes—"we wished to apologize for Mr. Ransom."

"So?"

"Murder is not a subject for jesting talk. I shall try to remember that in the future."

"But why should you want to apologize to Ransom?"

"Because we might have caused a serious tragedy by our . . . our academic discussions. Heaven help me, I have had to prevent one or two of my parishioners from coming out here and doing him physical violence."

This man, thought Dennis Foster, is a good man in the best sense of the word. It shone in his eyes. His conscience seemed to hurt him like a physical pain. He moistened dry lips, still keeping his hat pressed tightly over his heart.

"The extraordinary thing," Mr. Berkeley went on, "is that none of us recognized Bruce Ransom." Again he looked full at H. M., with grave dignity. "Sir, I have seen you before."

"Oh?" H. M.'s voice was sharp. "Where was that?"

"That," replied the vicar, "is another extraordinary thing."

"Why?"

"It was exactly a fortnight ago, in the lounge of the Golden Pheasant in Aldebridge. You were sitting in a corner, with a newspaper held up over your face. And a group of us were discussing—this same subject."

"Roger Bewlay, you mean?"

"No! No! No!"

The syllables seemed wrung from Mr. Berkeley, who tightened his stocky shoulders.

"I mean," he corrected himself, "that we were talking no slander or scandal. Chittering, if I remember correctly, said: 'Here's a little item in the paper that Bruce Ransom may do a play about Bewlay.' Herbert looked at the paper and said: 'He can't do a play if he hasn't got a manuscript.' And Chittering said: 'Well, here's the story; and here's his picture: look at it.'"

"That, sir," added the vicar, "was where I noticed you tip-toeing out with your own newspaper held over your face." A feeble smile choked and hopeful, flickered over his face. "Rather like Birnam Wood going to Dunsinane. It was what called my attention to you.

"But it is still more extraordinary," he went on, as though his courage was oozing, "in that Chittering's hobby is a study of the stage . . ."

"My dear fellow!" protested Mr. Chittering, with a moist and benevolent eye. "My dear fellow!"

"Surely I state the fact?"

"Of the old-time stage!" cried Mr. Chittering. "Of the days when giants walked the earth. Of the days before these cosy, intimate little theatres expressly designed so that the actors can hear the audience's lines. Of Irving and Tree, of Mansfield and Sothern, of Forbes-Robertson and Martin Harvey. *That* is my study."

Here Mr. Chittering got out a handkerchief and blew his nose. H. M., whose cigar had gone out, stared at him for a long time.

Slowly H. M. picked up the typewritten sheets, with the wrapping-paper, from the writing-table. He juggled them in his hand. The other two regarded them with such intensity that the room seemed to grow several degrees warmer.

"I understand, son," he said to Chittering, "I understand you're interested in writin' plays."

Mr. Chittering laughed very heartily.

"If you refer," he said, "to the little text-book I often carry with me, and which I have often loaned to my friends . . ."

"Uh-huh. That's just what I did refer to."

"If I wrote a play," said Mr. Chittering, "it should be a heroic drama in four acts. Of the sort Tennyson wrote for Irving in the nineties. Culture," said Mr. Chittering, who was perhaps a little tight, "is dead. Dead, dead, dead!"

And he waved his fingers in the air, as though over the grave of culture.

"As dead," said H. M., "as Mildred Lyons."

A sort of jerk went through the group. But Mr. Chittering paid no attention.

"Now I," he declared, "heartily approve of Ransom's masquerade. Yes, yes, yes! He trusted his instinct. You recall the anecdote of Irving, I think in Bram Stoker's biography? 'That fellow's a crook! I tell you, I've played too many criminals! I *know* that fellow's a crook'!"

178

Again Mr. Chittering laughed so loudly that he had to wipe his eyes.

"*I* approve. Yes. But Renwick, I fear, does *not* approve. Renwick thinks he deserves a thrashing. Poor, poor Renwick!"

"What's the matter with Renwick?"

"You—ah—may have observed that he has only one arm?"

"Now you call my attention to it, son, I may just have had a dim ghostly idea of that. Well?"

"He didn't lose it in the line of duty. No. He was attacked, in Port Said, by a drunken Portuguese. With a hatchet." Mr. Chittering made a gesture of one who chops. "He has nightmares, sometimes, about murderers. Renwick, I fear, is a trifle neurotic. His hobby is sailing-ships. He . . ."

Abruptly Mr. Chittering paused, putting a hand to his fleshy throat. He seemed to realize that he was babbling. The pink countenance, the moist protruding eyes, even the fishbone skeleton of hair across his perspiring head, proclaimed the need he announced next.

"Forgive me. I see Ransom isn't here. I feel the necessity for liquid sustenance, a small whisky perhaps, to uplift my soul and . . . and waft it into realms of Elysian bliss. Yes. Exactly. Excuse me."

After which he almost bolted out into the corridor.

"I also," observed the vicar, whose eyes were lowered, "must go. I'm late for dinner. My wife will worry. If you are dining here, gentlemen, you will fare very well. Renwick sets an excellent table. Excuse me."

And *he* was gone.

Dennis Foster stared at the closed door.

"The mere mention of Roger Bewlay," said Dennis, "scares those two as though you'd invoked the devil

179

in person!"

"Well, son," said H. M. very quietly, "it scares me too."

Dennis whirled round.

"What do you mean by that?"

"Bewlay's crazy." H. M. spoke flatly. "He's really gone off his rocker this time. Burn me, I should 'a' foreseen it!"

For the second time that day, H. M. was pale. Now this is a thing that very seldom happens to Sir Henry Merrivale, who has no nerves to speak of; and, had Dennis known it, he would have felt even colder than he felt now. H. M. stood there, his dead cigar in one hand and the typewritten sheets in the other, his face drained of emotion. He flung the cigar across at the empty grate. He dropped the sheets into the table drawer and closed it with a slam.

"If we don't nab that bounder, and nab him mighty quick, he's goin' to do somethin' much worse than he's ever done before. And his next victim . . ."

"Well?"

"Another woman," said H. M. "Probably Daphne Herbert."

"No!" cried Dennis.

"I'm tellin' you," H. M. said simply.

Downstairs underneath them, with a faint rumbling noise, the lounge and the smoking-room were filling up. For some time, at the back of their minds, they had been conscious of motor-cars grinding into the gravelled yard, of voices moving towards the front door. Now a burst of laughter floated up. Somebody began to strum a piano. Dennis hardly heard it.

"But why can't you nab Bewlay, sir? If you know who he is?"

H. M. lifted both fists.

180

"Oh, son! What's the good of nabbin' him if we haven't got a charge to convict him with? The Torquay business won't wash. *He's* seen to that."

"What about the murder of Mildred Lyons?"

"I dunno," muttered H. M., nervously rubbing his big chin. "He's made one howler there, which was more bad luck than anything else. But is it enough? Is it? I don't think so. As for Daphne Herbert . . ."

As though summoned there, as though hurrying in response to her name, the door opened and Daphne came in.

In the loosening of emotion all Daphne's shyness, all of what Bruce would have called her repressions, had melted away as Dennis's had. Though she was acquainted with Sir Henry Merrivale, it is significant that she ran straight across to Dennis and instinctively put out her hands. He took them; it had been a gesture of absolute trust.

"Mr. Foster,"—Daphne's eyes searched his face—"where's Bruce?"

He didn't know what to answer. His glance appealed to H. M., who made no response.

"Has he—has he borrowed my car?"

"What makes you think he's borrowed your car?"

"It's gone," replied Daphne, and swallowed hard. "Bruce can't drive a car. But Mr. Otis, who came into the bar a while ago, says some lunatic tried to run him down at the entrance to the parking-place; and he says he thinks it was Bruce. My father's phoning the police about a stolen car."

("That's torn it!" thought Dennis.)

"H. M.," he said aloud, "where's Masters?"

"Masters," returned H. M., with a hideous grimace, "will be here any minute. Looky here, my wench. You'd better nip downstairs and get your old man to countermand that order. Or else . . ."

"There'll be trouble?"

"There'll be all hell and Napoleon too."

"It's so utterly absurd!" Daphne started to laugh. "I think, in his heart of hearts, my father still believes Bruce *is* Roger Bewlay. And that's absurd!" She hesitated for an instant. "Isn't it?"

"It's entirely absurd," Dennis assured her. Now that Bruce had been cleared of all suspicion, he could put a real warmth and ring of conviction into his tone. Yet for some reason it hurt him. Daphne's fingers were cool; a current of vitality seemed to flow from them into his own.

"Bruce," he went on, "is no more Roger Bewlay than I am. You heard what Sir Henry said. That's one thing you can stop worrying about for good!"

"I'm—I'm glad," said Daphne, and pressed his hands in reply. "I'll go down and do what I can."

She turned away, hesitating as though she would say something else. Behind Daphne in the doorway appeared Beryl West, with the shadows of spiritual exhaustion under her eyes. Momentarily the two of them made a strong contrast: the light-haired girl in the tan coat, all solidity and innocence, with the dark-haired girl in the green frock, all dreams and imagination and nerves. As Daphne passed by, she leaned over suddenly and lightly kissed Beryl on the cheek.

"You know," observed Beryl, staring after her, "I'm just beginning to realize that girl does radiate sex-appeal. She couldn't act for toffee; you can tell that from the way she talks. But she does radiate sex-appeal."

Then Beryl's tone changed.

"My God, darling," she added, cradling her arms as though she were cold, "I'm the Roman sentinel who stood at his post while Vesuvius erupted. I kept 'em

182

there as long as I could. Really and truly I did! But it couldn't go on for ever." Her eyes flashed round the room. "Did Bruce really take that car?"

"Yes."

"The fool! He'll kill himself!"

"Probably. But what difference does it make? The fat's in the fire, Bewlay's out for murder, and unless H. M. gets an inspiration pretty quickly . . ."

"Shut the door," roared H. M.

Beryl, a little scared, did so.

"H. M.," Dennis said sharply, "is going to tell us all about Roger Bewlay."

"I didn't say that, son," returned the great man, with considerable weariness. "You've got such an ingenuous dial that if I told you the whole truth the cat would be out of the bag with a reverberatin' yowl. But I did say it was time to put some cards on the table. Because, burn me,"—he shook his fist in the air—"you may be able to help."

"I'll help you, Lord knows, in any way I can. What did you want to ask?"

"Well," said H. M., "do you play golf?"

"What's that?"

The question was so utterly unexpected, so apparently irrelevant, that for a second Dennis could not take it in.

"I said: do you play golf?"

"No, I'm afraid I don't. I had a stab at it once, long before the war, but I couldn't keep my temper any better than you can."

"What d'ye mean, I can't keep my temper?" bellowed H. M., with his eyes bulging behind the spectacles and a rich purple colour suffusing his face. "I'm known for the utter imperturbability of my temper on any and all occasions! I'm known . . ."

"All right! All right! Sorry!"

183

"I thought," H. M. said in despair, "all you solicitor-blokes did over the week-end was play golf and swindle rich clients. But it's no good! It's no good at all! Unless . . ."

He broke off, staring round him.

"My Scotchman!" he bellowed. "Where's my Scotchman?"

It was as though he had expected Mr. Donald Fergus MacFergus to materialize out of the fireplace or through the window. And, in a sense, this is precisely what happened. For Mr. MacFergus, unruffled but stern-eyed as an Inquisitor, calmly opened the door and appeared as once he had appeared from behind a tree.

"I'm still watchin' ye," he said.

"Where have you been? Hey?"

"I tookit your clubs back tae the hotel. I'd have ye know, ma mannie, that I'm no caddy tae fetch and carry."

"Sit down over there," said H. M., sternly pointing to the settee.

Mr. MacFergus obeyed. Yet he bristled like a terrier, as though longing for instructions which he could disobey. H. M. stood for a time ruffling his hands over his big bald head. Then he turned, in a kind of malevolent appeal, to Dennis.

"You understand, son, there may be nothing in this. It may be only a wool-gathering idea of mine. But I was sittin' and thinkin' about those first three murders, the first three wives who disappeared. If you remember the evidence, one of 'em was polished off at Crowborough. One at Denham. And one at Scarborough?"

"I remember. What about it?"

H. M. made a hideous face.

"The only thing I could think of as common to those three places," he said, "was a noble golf links. Burn it

184

all, Bewlay's cottage at Denham was actually *called* 'Fairway View.' So I just wondered."

Here he turned to Mr. MacFergus.

"I never asked you this before, son," he said seriously. "In fact, I'd given up asking you any questions at all. Because, d'ye see, all you ever do is say: 'Hoots!' and look at me as though I was somethin' that had just crawled out of the salad."

"Aye," said Mr. MacFergus, folding his arms with considerable satisfaction.

"But I'm askin' you a question now, short and sweet. And it's awful important, son, because lives may depend on it. It's this. Could you possibly hide a body on or under a golf links?"

"Hoots!" said Mr. MacFergus.

And then, as H. M. lifted both fists once more, Mr. MacFergus did what he had never done before and what Dennis perhaps imagined he could not do. He began to laugh.

"But why not?" yelled H. M. "What's so funny about it?"

"Ye were speakin', maybe, about buryin' a body?"

"Yes! Why not?"

Mr. MacFergus told them.

Those who considered Scotsmen as not being loquacious, Dennis thought, should have listened to this one. The ensuing lecture, delivered with gusto and with a richness of Doric speech which at times passed comprehension, was as exhaustive as a surgical treatise.

The one place you could *not* bury a human body without traces being noticed, he explained, was on a golf course. The greens? Unthinkable! On the fairways, even failure to replace a loose divot was noticed by the hoose-committee. As for the rough, that wiry jungle carefully arranged to be a rough, any displacement

185

there would be observed no matter how carefully put back, because it meant rending and tearing. Even the huge grassy humps of the bunkers received the same careful scrutiny. An all-seeing eye, Mr. MacFergus explained almost lyrically, was the jealous eye which kept a course in perfect condition. The thing was impossible.

And H. M. was beaten.

The Old Maestro, Dennis saw, was well and truly beaten. In utter despair H. M. stumped over to the fireplace, and stood there with his head down.

Below in the smoking-room, the piano was now banging loudly, with a vast shuffle and tap of feet following it, in an encouragement to Roll out the Barrel. Voices had become a droning hum. They scratched against the nerves like squeaky pencils on slate. But Donald MacFergus was enjoying himself.

"Ye cud hide a body, it may be," he was declaiming, "in the middle of Peecadilly Circus at broad noonday. Ye cud hide it, I'm not sayin' no, slap in the middle o' Prince's Street in Edinburgh. But the place ye cud not hide it, wi' no traces of digging or tearing or trampling or . . ."

"Stop it!" cried Beryl, who did not quite understand but had picked up the atmosphere. "We agree! But for heaven's sake stop it!"

"Uh-huh. We agree," said H. M.

Slowly he turned round.

"There's nothin' else for it," he added despondently. "Masters will just have to arrest the blighter now, to prevent further damage at the moment, and then turn him loose—an absolutely free man!—within a few weeks at most. As MacFergus says . . ."

Abruptly he paused, his mouth open, while the roll and tinkle of the piano acquired a new clarity against dead silence.

"H. M.!" cried Beryl. "What is it?"

For H. M. was staring, with a concentrated and murderous fixity of glance, at nothing more interesting than Bruce Ransom's blue-silk dressing-gown, which had been carelessly thrown down across the arm of the settee.

H. M.'s mouth fell still further open. His corporation, ornamented by the large gold watch-chain, moved in and out like a bellows. All the others followed the direction of his glance; they saw a silk dressing-gown, with its soft plaited cord tasselled at the ends, and nothing more.

What is it?" repeated Beryl.

"Wait a minute!" protested H. M., waving his hands in the air and then lowering them to shade his eyes. "Wait a minute, now! Lemme think!"

The minute really did become a minute, which can be a maddeningly long time while someone with an idea dancing in his head breathes noisily but does not speak. H. M., in a blind-bear kind of way, lumbered across the right-hand window of the two facing west. Rolling up the window, he stood looking out over a moonlit golf links and breathing deeply the cool moist air. Then he swung round.

"We've got him," said H. M. "By the six hours of Satan, I think we've got him!"

And he plunged towards the telephone.

187

15

Very faint and distant, the urgent voice clove through dreams.

"Dennis! Dennis! Dennis!" That was what it called out. And, phantom-like, a great ship sailed through a nebulous pinkish sea.

She was a full-rigged three-decker of Nelson's time, her hull brown-painted except for the scarlet squares round the gun-ports, her tall cloud of canvas, taut-curved by the following wind, rolling in stateliness from the wash past her bows to the peak of her topgallant-royals.

He could hear that murmurous wash rise at times to a boiling hiss, out of the pinkish sea. He could taste the wind on his lips. Yet, such is the fashion of dreams without any curiosity on the sleeper's part, even as sea hissed and tackle creaked Dennis could see through that ship to the events of the night before.

As in a distorting mirror, he could see them waiting endlessly for Bruce Ransom, who did not return. He could see them having dinner in the noisy, overcrowded dining-room at the Leather Boot. He could hear the bang of the piano. All this through the crash of sea-waves, pink as they billowed up, while the hundred-gun three-decker rolled to their motion.

Ten o'clock striking, and no Bruce. Eleven o'clock, and no Bruce. Midnight, and still . . .

"Dennis! Dennis! Dennis!"

A hand touched his shoulder. He was shocked awake.

The ship was a large ship-model of Nelson's *Victory*, placed on a shelf opposite the couch where his bed had been made up. The pink sea was the pink light of dawn, pouring in from two windows that faced the North Sea, pouring into a little oblong room with many other ship-models on shelves round the walls.

For a moment Dennis lay there in a daze. Then he saw the flat-topped desk, and got it. Commander Renwick's office, of course. His bed had been made up in Commander Renwick's office.

He heard, in reality, the boiling hiss of the tide up the beach, and felt its chill through open windows. Beside him, looking down with a very curious expression, stood Beryl West. She wore a quilted robe over her pyjamas, tightly tied at the waist; her feet were in mules and her hair was tumbled.

"I'm awfully sorry to wake you up, Dennis. But I had to."

Spectral was that dim pink light, tinged with a soap-bubble luminousness. It touched a ship-model of the *Royal George*, ill-fated in the eighteenth century. And the earlier *Sovereign of the Seas*, with her clumsy sprit-sail and her twinkling brass guns. And the *Golden Hind*, flaunting yellow canvas. It made these toys seem larger than life, throwing exaggerated shadows of spars and rigging on the panelled walls.

"What is it, Beryl?"

"I've seen Bruce."

Again the tide came seething up the beach. Dennis sat up, with sleep struck from his eyes.

190

"You've seen Bruce? When?"

"Not ten minutes ago."

"Where?"

"The—the idiot," stormed Beryl, trying to keep the tears back from her eyes, "climbed up to my bedroom window. Though there was no earthly reason why he shouldn't have walked up by the stairs. He woke me up and said . . ."

"Where is he now, Beryl?"

"He's—gone again."

Again there was silence, in that eerie deathly light among the crowding ship-models.

"Did you tell him," said Dennis, clutching at the bed-clothes, "that the whole county constabulary have been looking for that infernal car? That they don't suspect him of anything now; but, if he doesn't get back here very quickly, he's going to be in serious trouble and no mistake?"

"No, I didn't tell him," answered Beryl. "I didn't think of it. You see, he loves me."

Beryl sat down on the edge of the couch. She pressed her hands over her eyes. Against all the strength of her will she began to cry; not with sobs, which she could repress, but with painful tears that trickled through helpless fingers.

A compassion, a deep affection beyond words, touched the heart of Dennis Foster. He did not say anything. He merely put his hand on her shoulder, and kept it there while she wept, and wept, and fought so convulsively to keep back tears that her whole body trembled.

"It's all right, Beryl."

"It's not all right." She shook her head with violence. "But I had to tell you." Then, as though vehemently to change the subject, she glanced with smeary eyes over her shoulder and added: "'Red sky at morning, Sailors

191

take warning'."

"What did Bruce say to you, Beryl? Or is that an indiscreet question?"

"Of course it's not an indiscreet question. From you." She pressed her cheek against his hand. "He . . . he . . ."

"Go on, Beryl."

"He just grabbed me by the shoulders and said: 'You and I belong to each other. We're two of a kind. We speak the same language. I'll talk to you about it later.' Then he was gone, in that queer funny light just before dawn. I—I know it sounds silly; but it sort of flatters me that he climbed up by way of the window."

"But didn't he *say* anything, Beryl?"

"Say anything?"

"Where he'd been! What he'd been doing! Anything?"

"No. Oh!—except that he gave that queer kind of laugh: you remember? The kind of laugh that twisted him all up when we were talking to him about something being read backwards. I think he's still brooding about that."

Dennis felt a lump rising in his throat.

"What about . . . Daphne Herbert?"

"He was never in love with her," said Beryl, suddenly taking her hands away from her face and speaking with great intensity. "I *knew* he was never in love with her. I knew, and thought all along, he was only playing a part."

"Consciously?"

"Oh, Dennis! No! Bruce had got himself absolutely convinced he *was* this character in the play. So, of course, he imagined he fell head over heels for Daphne Herbert."

(Make-believe! thought Dennis. Make-believe! What is real?)

"And, to give the parson's daughter her due, she was

never in love with him either. She knows it, too. She was simply hypnotized by a mysterious stranger with a fascinating line of talk. She's not his kind for anything really serious; don't you see that?"

And, despite Beryl's curses that were like a prayer, the tears trickled between her fingers again.

"Easy, my dear! You're happy now, aren't you?"

"Yes. I'm utterly happy. That's why I k-keep on crying like this. But, oh, God, Dennis, I've been so miserable!"

"I know."

Beryl got to her feet. The surf seethed beyond the open windows; a cold wind struck in; the dim pink light broadened in tinges of purple and white, stirring into mimic illusion of movement the procession of ship-models with their bravery of gilt and guns and spider-web rigging.

"Do you remember last night, Dennis?" she asked. "When H. M. threw us all out of the room and wouldn't let us hear that telephone-call after he'd got his great inspiration? And then being involved in that party in the bar, when your friend Chittering got so dreadfully drunk?"

"Yes, I remember."

"I thought I was at the end of my string. I thought I couldn't take any more. And it's all different this morning. I—I'll get out of your room now, darling, in case we cause a scandal at the Leather Boot Hotel." Beryl tried to smile at him under reddened eyelids. "I just wanted to tell you that whatever happens now, whatever, ever, ever happens—I don't care. I don't care!"

There was something like a spiritual exaltation in her voice. She pressed her hands together. Then the door of the little office closed after her, with a click of the latch against the hush of that hotel.

193

Dennis put his head back on the pillows.

He thought he was wide awake. He thought there were new thorns to keep him awake: the problem of Bruce, uttering his wild laugh in the dusk before dawn, the problem of Daphne Herbert which he tried not to consider. Yet a great weight of exhaustion whirled him away into darkness before his head had touched the pillow for two minutes.

This time it was not pleasant.

This time all the ships got into his dreams, as pirate-ships of the Caribbean. Their images grew confused with his own experiences in the destroyer *Afreet*, off Crete. Bare-legged men with ear-rings, swarming up the ratlines, intermingled with diving Stukas that screamed and screamed again.

Out of an inferno the island of Crete became the island of Jamaica, where an adolescent Roger Bewlay in the stews of a sub-tropical climate learned crafts "from fighting with a knife to the art of practising Voodoo rites." Bewlay himself became a part of the noise and smoke, dodging and horribly menacing to Daphne Herbert. Once more the flash of a broadside from a two-decker became drowned in the whine of a diving Stuka . . .

Someone called Dennis's name, sharply and author-itatively.

He sat bolt upright, tearing himself free from dreams.

His first thought, in that sense of refreshment which tells us we have rested for a long time, was that he must have slept all through the day and into the evening. Outside open windows the sky was darkening, with little puffs of wind much too warm for Saturday the sixth of October.

"I don't like to disturb you," apologized the voice of Commander Renwick, who stood beside him. "But it's

194

past ten o'clock."

"In the morning?"

"Of course." Renwick smiled from under his hooded eyelids. "If you don't hurry, I'm afraid you'll get no breakfast."

Dennis shook his head to clear it.

"Oh! Yes! Of course! I was dreaming."

"You were talking in your sleep. I rather gathered . . . Forgive me: were you by any chance in the service?"

"Yes."

"Were you, by Jove! In what?"

"First in *Afreet*, before she was sunk off Crete. Afterwards in *Wraith*, and then in *Stiletto*."

"Destroyers, eh? Wickedest job in the service. Like it?"

"Not much. Especially when they dropped one slap down our forward funnel."

"Did it," Commander Renwick made a twirling gesture at his stomach, as one who indicates nerves, "mess you up?"

"I'm not sure. It all seems remote now. What I seem to remember best is the poker-dice."

The windows *were* darkening, drawing a veil across the ship-models. "Red sky at morning, Sailors take warning." Commander Renwick, who had regained much of his earlier suavity but who breathed in short hard gasps as though he had been running, kept his eyes fixed on Dennis in glittering scrutiny. He cleared his throat.

"Mr. Foster. When you've finished your breakfast, would you mind coming up to your friend Ransom's sitting-room at once?"

Dread struck Dennis again, as sharply as a dart in a board.

"Something else has happened," he stated rather than asked.

195

Then his voice rang out. "Some other damned thing has happened!"

"Yes," assented Commander Renwick. "Some other damned thing has happened."

"What is it?"

"Please! Have your breakfast first. We can—er—offer you bacon and egg. You'll find a place to wash there," he nodded towards a door in the wall behind Dennis's head, "if you haven't already found it. Then come upstairs."

He would say no more.

Dennis raced through shaving and dressing. The big dim lounge, when he emerged into it from Renwick's office, had been swept free from all traces of last night's party. A sultry wind blew through the empty hotel, which seemed to have more than the usual number of open windows and doors.

In the dining-room, opening out of the arched passage at the back of the lounge, many tables were laid with snowy cloths for the Commander's thriving transient-trade in meals. But Dennis was the only person there now. Served by a frostily disapproving waiter, he bolted down a breakfast which seemed to have no taste, and waited only long enough to drink off four cups of very strong tea before he hurried upstairs.

The door of Bruce's sitting-room was locked. That gave him a new qualm. He hammered on it.

"Who's there?" Renwick's voice demanded, from inside.

Dennis shouted something back, and the door was unlocked and opened.

"Look round, Mr. Foster," grimly invited Renwick, "and tell me whether this situation hasn't become really intolerable."

Commander Renwick and Beryl West, in a peach-coloured dress with more costume jewellery, stood amid a scene of ruin.

It was not merely that Bruce's sitting-room had been ransacked. It was as though it had been attacked, in a physical sense, by someone not quite in his right mind. The grey-and-blue-coloured settee, the grey-and-blue overstuffed chairs, had been slashed and stabbed with a sharp knife. Most of Bruce's golf-clubs, from the bag in one corner, were splintered as though across someone's knee. The writing-table was overturned, spilling a drift of letters and papers that covered a good deal of the carpet. The typewriter, now only twisted scrap-metal, had been chopped at with some object like a hatchet. Even the little telephone-table, at one side of a blue-marble mantelpiece, hung sagging and cloven in two.

But Beryl—her face glowing, in her eyes an ecstatic dream, looking even handsomer than Dennis had ever seen her—did not seem unduly disturbed. In fact, she scarcely seemed to notice.

"After all, Mr. Renwick," she pointed out consolingly, "it might have been much worse."

"One could, of course, have set fire to the hotel," said Commander Renwick, with powerful restraint. "It might have been much worse! Indeed!"

"I mean, when you first told me about it, I was afraid someone might have been . . . well! Hurt."

"So was I," confessed Dennis.

"But *why?*" demanded Renwick, spreading out his fingers towards the ruin. *"Why?"*

"Oh, my dear!" Beryl spoke soothingly, wanting to help him, yet the dream in her eyes would not let her concentrate on mundane matters. "Manuscript!"

"I beg your pardon?"

Beryl stepped softly over the papers on the carpet, so exalted and full of energy that it was as though she must keep herself from running. She approached the overturned writing-table, bent down, and pulled out the drawer sideways. The drawer was empty.

"Please, dear," she urged Commander Renwick,

"don't say you don't understand! Everybody in the lounge was jabbering about it last night. Bruce had some manuscript, a part of a play, that proved somebody knew too much about Roger Bewlay. And now it's gone. Look!"

Renwick smoothed at his moustache with long, broad fingers that trembled, and then moved down to tug at his thick close-cropped brown beard.

"Mr. Ransom," he said, "kept the manuscript in that drawer?"

"Yes!"

"I see. Who knew he kept it in that drawer?"

Dennis started to laugh.

"The matter, Mr. Foster," Commander Renwick spoke with polished courtesy, "no doubt has its amusing side. Wanton destruction is always funny. That is a part of our English sense of humour." His hand moved over, briefly, and touched his empty left sleeve.

"I beg your pardon!" Dennis said hastily. "All I meant was that the one who definitely did know the manuscript was there, because Sir Henry Merrivale stood juggling it in front of him, is the one person I can't possibly associate in any way with this business. Mr. Chittering."

"Horace Chittering?" crowed Beryl. "I think he's absolutely *marvellous.*"

"Indeed, Miss West?" inquired Commander Renwick. "It struck me last night that he was a trifle . . . a trifle . . ."

"Tight?" supplied Beryl. "Oh, my dear! He was stinko-paralytico! But I didn't mind that, even when he tried to paw me. And he told me some anecdotes about the Restoration stage that are absolutely priceless, though of course they're unprintable." She whooped with delight. "I can't *wait* to get back to London and tell them to Judy Lester and Nick Farren and Sam

198

Andrews. I . . ."

"Beryl," Dennis said softly.

Beryl stopped dead, her finger-tips at her cheeks. "I will stop burbling!" she seemed to be saying to herself, "I will stop burbling!" And this despite the dreamy smile of excitement that curved her lips, and the sense if not the actuality that she was standing on tiptoe, utterly in love with life.

"You see, Commander Renwick," Dennis hastened on, "Mr. Chittering's certainly harmless enough. But I don't understand his psychology."

"No?"

"No! When you first told him this was all a hoax, and no murder existed, he was as disappointed as though you'd taken a toy from a baby. Then he learned Bewlay was very much here. And he was so upset he had to keep downing double whiskies all evening."

"Can't you understand it?" Renwick asked harshly. "*I* can. Fancies!"

"How do you mean?"

"It was all very well for Chittering—for a lot of them!—when they saw Bewlay as a romantic figure who might have killed women in the musty remote past. But throw a dead body at their feet," his rather ghoulish gesture emphasized it, "let the mud splash their own coats, and it becomes very different. It always is, when death comes close and looks you in the eyes."

Commander Renwick paused.

"Chittering's all right, Mr. Foster. He is only ageing, and foolish, and lonely. Who can tell what goes on in the heart of a lonely man?"

After a curious silence, during which nobody knew quite what to say, Renwick walked across the drift of papers to the right-hand window, still wide open as it had been left last night, and stood staring out at the darkening golf links.

"I'm awfully sorry!" Beryl burst out.

"For what?" asked Renwick, without turning round.

"I—I don't know." Beryl spoke helplessly. "Except that you mustn't pay too much attention to what I say to-day. I'm happy, you see. I'm terribly happy. So perhaps I don't make too much sense. Bruce . . ."

The belling-out of grey curtains at the open window, whisking in a strong draught, was their first intimation that the door to the corridor was open. Jonathan Herbert, with Clara Herbert his wife on his arm, had taken a few steps into the room. They stood listening, perhaps praying.

Dennis sensed tragedy before a word had been spoken.

Mr. Herbert's countenance was calm and dispassionate, as though at a resolve taken. But Mrs. Herbert, whom Dennis had seen only briefly on the train, looked mute and stricken. Seen close at hand, she was a tall blonde woman in her late forties, whose face, in that moment at least, looked older than her grey-haired husband's. They stood there like a pair of children; and Mr. Herbert, with an oddly touching gesture, put his arm round his wife's waist.

"Jonathan!" whispered Clara Herbert.

Mr. Herbert moistened his lips.

"We hoped," he said, "you might be able to give us a bit of help."

Commander Renwick came to life then, in a rush of human sympathy of which Dennis would not have believed him capable.

"What is it, old chap?" he demanded, and lurched towards them on his stiffish leg so that he almost tripped across the overturned writing-table. "What is it? What's wrong?"

Again Mr. Herbert moistened his lips.

"Daphne," he said, "has eloped with Bruce Ransom."

200

16

It was Dennis who cried out: "I don't believe it!"

Afterwards Dennis did not look at Beryl. He dared not.

"Show them, my dear," Mr. Herbert requested. "This story is everybody's story now."

Clara Herbert was far too heavily made-up. The lipstick, the rouge, only dissipated a very genuine prettiness which remained, with a suggestion of Daphne round the forehead and chin. Eagerly, as though wanting something to do, she opened her handbag and fumbled inside it. She produced a little sheet of folded grey notepaper—and then held it out vaguely, her eyes moving from one side to the other of them, not knowing to whom she should give it.

Mr. Herbert took it from her, and handed it to Dennis. It was a brief scribbled note under a stamped letterhead that read, *The Old Hall, Aldebridge*. Dennis read it aloud.

DEAR MOTHER AND DADDY:

I'M GOING AWAY WITH BRUCE. I LOVE HIM. IT'S PERFECTLY ALL RIGHT; I'LL EXPLAIN LATER.

DAPHNE.

Clara Herbert woke up.

"Our maid," she said, "saw them going away together across the lawn. Mr. Eg—Mr. Ransom, it now seems he is, and heaven knows who else besides, was carrying Daphne's suitcase. They got into the car, the one that's been missing all night, and drove away."

Dennis's throat felt dry. He twisted the note in his fingers.

"Do you mind telling me when this was?"

"About—about an hour after daylight. Wasn't that what Molly said, Jonathan?"

"Yes. I think so."

"Mr.—Mr. Whoever-he-is," continued Clara Herbert, with an effort, "propped a ladder up against the window, for Daphne to climb down by. Just like a story-book or something. He . . ."

About an hour after daylight.

Dennis's feelings about Bruce Ransom, as he heard those words, are not fully to be described.

Why, he thought in a light-headed blaze of fury, did Bruce have to go and see Beryl just before that? Better to have killed Beryl outright! Better to have stabbed her to the heart and had done with it, then to mouth all that grotesque claptrap and then have Beryl hear the other details, car and suitcase and ladder, in cold sickliness a few hours later! For a time, in that light-headed blaze of fury, Dennis quite literally couldn't see.

He was roused by a choking from Clara Herbert.

"I did the same thing once myself," said Mrs. Herbert. "God help me. It's all my fault. Daphne's a *child*. She's got no judgment. She . . ."

"Don't worry, my dear," said her husband quite gently. "I'll see to it."

Through this welter of emotion struck the heavy, common-sense voice of Commander Renwick, in a tone of desperate whimsicality.

"Herbert, old chap! Look here! Listen to me!"

Mr. Herbert's eyes moved sideways.

"Yes?"

"For a minute, you know," Commander Renwick essayed a deep-throated laugh, "I was afraid something serious might have happened. But, as Miss West observed about the wreck of this room, it might be very much worse."

"Might it?"

"Of course it might! Look here!"

"I'm looking."

"Ransom, after all, is a well-known figure who must make a very great deal of money. If he and Daphne are serious about this, and mean to get married, where the devil is the harm? Even if you don't like Ransom, and I don't like him myself, what have you got against him?"

"He's Roger Bewlay," said Mr. Herbert.

"What's that?"

"He's Roger Bewlay."

"Nonsense!" scoffed Commander Renwick, pulling down the corners of his mouth so that moustache and beard followed it. Yet he was excited: the horizontal wrinkles in his forehead, and those radiating round his eyes, seemed to deepen as he made a face of mockery. "You're behind the times, surely? That's all finished. Sir Henry Merrivale . . ."

"Stop throwing Merrivale in my teeth! Merrivale's been wrong before, and he can be wrong again. In any case—"

Absentmindedly patting his wife's arm, Jonathan Herbert studied a corner of the ceiling.

"I told Ransom what I was going to do," Mr. Herbert said agreeably, "if he tried to see Daphne again. Apparently he thought I wasn't serious. He'll find out."

Dead silence.

"My dear," continued Jonathan Herbert, leading his wife forward, "this is Mr. Foster. He's a friend of Ransom's. But not like Ransom!" he added hastily. "Not like him! No, no, no! Young man," he looked at Dennis, "I appeal to you! As the business partner of an old acquaintance of mine, James Mackintosh, you must . . . that is . . . I appeal to you for the help I need."

"Help in what?"

"Where have those two gone?"

"I don't know, Mr. Herbert! How should I know?"

"Haven't you any idea?"

"None at all!"

"London, probably." Mr. Herbert pondered. "That's the most logical thing. London. But why an elopement at this time? Why an elopement at this particular *time?*" Again he looked up. "Had Ransom any reason of his own that would take him to London to-day?"

"Not that I know of."

"Any engagement, any business appointment, anything of that sort?"

"The only thing I remember," said Dennis, "is that long ago, close on a month ago, he said he had a broadcasting engagement in October. But . . ."

"Broadcasting," said Mr. Herbert.

Immediately afterwards Dennis could have bitten his tongue out. For Jonathan Herbert's gaze, vaguely puzzled at the wild disorder of the room but dismissing it as of no importance, wandered round and with a sort of pounce found the copy of the *Radio Times* lying among scattered papers on the floor.

"Please! Let me!" interposed Beryl West.

And then, to Dennis's stupefaction, Beryl hurried forward in a fever to help. She showed little sign of what she must be feeling except quick, hard breathing,

204

and the uncanny shining of her eyes. She smiled at them. Scooping up the *Radio Times*, she began to flick over its pages.

The air of that sitting-room was too warm, and thick with a piled weight of thunder which had not yet broken. The storm was moving in from the east. Already, outside these western windows, smoky damp-looking clouds were shifting into such deeper twilight that Beryl had to move closer to the windows.

Beryl found the item she wanted. Her voice, quick-breathing, rang out in a way that jarred Dennis's nerves.

"'Saturday Night Theatre'," she read aloud. "'Nine-fifteen to ten-thirty. Bruce Ransom in *Captain Cutthroat* by Willis Harmar. Adapted for broadcasting by . . .'"

And, with a bright smile, she handed the magazine to Dennis.

"To-night!" murmured Mr. Herbert. "That's got it."

Clara Herbert clutched at his arm.

"Your time-table!" she said. "Jonathan! You always carry one. Where's the time-table?"

"Listen, my dear." He tilted up her chin. "You may go with me to London, of course. But you must promise not to interfere."

"Jonathan, you *won't* do anything foolish?"

"That, my dear, as Dr. Joad would say, depends on what you mean by foolish. I'll treat Bewlay as Bewlay should be treated."

"Daphne mustn't make the same mistake I made! She mustn't!"

"I know, Clara. Will you leave this to my judgment?" Mr. Herbert turned to the others. "Thank you so much," he added courteously.

Again with his arm round his wife's waist, he led her towards the door. Both of them looked half-blind, in that sheer hysteria of domestic upheaval which for the time can seem worse than the blackest of tragedies. Dennis, Beryl, and Commander Renwick did not move. They heard Clara Herbert stumble in the hall.

It was some seconds before Dennis spoke.

"Beryl, for the love of God!"

"Is anything wrong, darling?" she asked coolly.

"That man," he stabbed his finger towards the door, "really believes Bruce is Roger Bewlay. He really believes it. He's going to . . ."

"Darling, I understand perfectly." Beryl contemplated him with the same bright, fixed smile. "Do you know anything about broadcasting?"

"Very little. Why?"

"For a long show like Saturday Night Theatre, they always have two days' rehearsal at the very least. Bruce was here all day yesterday; wasn't he?"

"Yes! You mean—?"

"Oh, Dennis! It means Bruce has rung up to say he can't do the show, and they've put somebody in his place too late for the billing. That's all."

"But suppose Bruce wants to swank it in front of Daphne, and goes and plays the part after all?"

"They'll have booked somebody else by this time. Bruce couldn't do it even if he wanted to." Beryl's voice rose. "If the Herbert family insist, let 'em go and kick up a row at Broadcasting House. It's the one place in London they won't find Bruce."

Dennis stared at her.

"Then, in spite of everything, you still . . . ?"

"Still what?" Beryl asked sharply.

"Nothing."

He dropped the *Radio Times* on the floor. In his other hand he was gripping Daphne's note, crumpled now into a wad. Dennis smoothed it out and read it once more. As a man will keep perversely touching his

206

tongue at an aching tooth, torturing it, he read the note again and again.

DEAR MOTHER AND DADDY:
 I'M GOING AWAY WITH BRUCE. I LOVE HIM. IT'S PERFECTLY ALL RIGHT; I'LL EXPLAIN LATER.
                                         DAPHNE.

As for his own feelings . . .

Well! That didn't matter. A girl he had seen for so brief a time, with whom he had exchanged so few words, could hardly be expected to have noticed him at all, let alone given him a thought in the midst of her overmastering passion for Bruce Ransom. What Daphne said about waking up, about being cured of an infatuation, had obviously been spoken only in one of those outbursts which any sensible person should have expected.

What was the difference, anyway?

The memory of twenty-four hours can easily be sponged from a man's life, as he forgets bereavement or physical danger or any other unpleasantness. Yet the image of Daphne's face, as she had looked at him last night, returned and swallowed up logic.

"Don't you see, Dennis?" cried Beryl, at the end of some words he did not catch.

"See what?"

"Those two silly old people are really sensible, when you come down to it. All Mr. Herbert needs is time to cool off. And I've provided that time. He can't possibly find Bruce now!"

"No," retorted Dennis, "and neither can anybody else find Bruce. Do you suppose they've really gone to London? Bruce and Daphne?"

"I expect so. He'll take the parson's daughter to his flat. It's an awfully nice flat. I've been there myself."

"Where is it?"

"St. John's Wood. But the number's not listed in the phone-book, so the old man can't possibly find it."

Dennis lowered his defences.

"Beryl," he said, "Bruce can't be such a swine as all that."

"My dear," Beryl said airily, echoing his own thoughts, "what difference does it make? Who cares? There's undoubtedly some explanation; and Bruce is the noblest of all created creatures I-don't-think; but who cares?"

"What's more," Dennis added suddenly, "there's something damned funny in all this."

"Why do you say that?" interposed Commander Renwick. Renwick had been standing there so quietly, a tall deformed figure in the dusky light, that both of them had forgotten him.

"For one thing, doesn't it strike you as odd that Bruce had been careering round the country in that car, with the police on the lookout for him, and yet not one of them seems to have seen him? It's almost as though the police were deliberately trying to . . ."

On its broken table by the fireplace, the telephone began to ring shrilly.

Commander Renwick, waving them back, moved over and picked it up. It had spoken to him only for a few seconds before he replaced it with a jarring click on the cradle.

"Sir Henry Merrivale," he told them, "is downstairs in the smoking-room. He would like you both to join him. It's very important."

"H. M.!" breathed Beryl, as one who sees hope in a desperate country.

Their exit from that room was hasty and somewhat impolite, though Renwick did not even seem to notice. He remained motionless, thoughtfully, with his hand still on the telephone.

This was the first time Dennis had ever been inside the smoking-room downstairs. Like the lounge it was a trifle battered-looking by daylight; its tables and wicker chairs with their bright cretonne cushions, its dart-board and Russian-billiard table and cigarette-burned piano, had an air of a somnolence now.

At first glance it appeared deserted, because its two occupants were sitting in a very broad, very deep embrasure of the east wall, rather like a room itself. Tall windows of many lights, joined together in a line, faced towards terrace and beach and sea. Out of twilight over a foaming sea, great breakers drove in to crash and explode beyond the terrace in a ghostly mane of spray.

The two occupants were Sir Henry Merrivale and Chief Inspector Masters. At the first words he heard from H. M., Dennis laid hold of Beryl's wrist and yanked her to one side of the embrasure; they could hear what was being said, though they could neither see nor be seen.

For H. M.'s first words had been:

". . . pretty plain, hey, why Chittering got drunk last night?"

"Oh, ah," Masters acknowledged. "I'm bound to say it's a good point."

"With the history of the stage at his finger-tips! And something that happened in the spring of '88! Irving was away from the Lyceum that season. Ah, me!" sighed the great man, with a sentimental melancholy. "Those were the days, Masters!"

"Just so, Sir Henry. But . . ."

"Did I ever tell you, son, how I gave an amateur rendition of Shylock in front of Irving himself? With my hands in my sleeves, like this; and an elegant black beard two feet long; and a bowler hat pushed down

209

over my ears, see, to give the realistic touch?" H. M.'s voice then began intoning on a strange, high-falutin note. "'Three thousand ducats; well!' I say, Masters: would you like me to deliver the opening lines now?"

"Hurrum!" said Masters hastily. "Some other time, maybe. Some other time! What I was asking you—"

"And the greatest actor of 'em all, Masters, said to me: 'My dear fellow,' he said, 'that was the finest . . .'"

"He smacking well never did!" said Masters. "I heard the inside story of that when we were mixed up in the Pineham case. He said . . ."

"Looky here, son," interrupted H. M. very sternly. "Are you goin' to shut up and let me get on with my exposition about Bewlay? Or are you goin' to keep dragging in irrelevant matters like my theatrical history?"

A strangled noise issued from Masters, above the crash of breakers.

"Has it ever occurred to you, Sir Henry," he asked with restraint, "that *you* might get murdered?"

"Me?" repeated H. M., in utter amazement.

"Yes, you!"

"I honestly dunno what you're talking about, Masters. I'm a friend of all the human race, I am. I exude the milk of human kindness like the fountains spoutin' at Versailles."

"Practically perfect, eh?"

"Well . . . now!" H. M. gave a deprecating cough. "I'm a modest man. I wouldn't like to say that much, no."

"Then will you stop being so blasted superior about one thing? I won't say, mind!" Masters sounded as though he wished to be fair, "I won't say, mind, but what those points you gave yesterday may not have been as unhelpful, or as much gibberish, as they sounded first off."

"Thank'ee, son."

"But will you take the lordly sneer off your face when you say that, once we've rumbled it Bewlay's in Aldebridge or near it, there are plain traces of where to look for him and what character he's assumed."

"As plain as a cat walkin' over fresh paint."

"How so? That stage-play about Bewlay . . ."

"Listen, Masters. We've heard a lot about that stage-play, which is supposed to be a reconstruction of his career after he'd left off killin' women. But that's only fiction. You can bet your shirt that Bewlay, the author, won't write down what really happened to him. That'd be too risky, even for a play under a fake name."

H. M.'s big voice assumed a note of anguish.

"But nobody seems to have wondered, Masters, what a feller of that particular and peculiar character *would* have done. Now, suppose you're Roger Bewlay."

"All right," said Masters, "I tell you straight, sir: I've had so much trouble over this I could imagine I was anybody."

"It's eleven years ago, and you've just committed what we'll call your fourth murder. Got that?"

"All right; well?"

"You've been a long time growin' up . . ."

Masters's voice sharpened, above the noise of the sea.

"Stop a bit, sir! I don't quite follow you there."

"Oh, my son! As a young lad you suffered from an awful inferiority complex about women. It's only in your middle twenties, in London, when you're broke and an exile without means of livelihood, that you slowly begin to realize something different. That's not unusual, Masters; the most thorough-paced Don Juan I ever knew never had an affair till he was twenty-six. But gradually you begin to realize, with delight, that women are your natural prey. You've only got to shake

211

the tree and they'll fall off like ripe apples.

"And then, Masters?"

"Joy and hosannah! Means of income! Self-confidence too, growing and strengthening every day. *That's* where you begin to show your teeth, Masters. *That's* why you can indulge in the sheer pleasure of stranglin' gals like Andrée Cooper, to show your power over the whole ruddy sex."

H. M. paused.

In the sultry, draughty gloom of the smoking-room, Dennis Foster glanced at Beryl.

A character was being built up for them, line upon line, colour and gesture and the evil mechanism of the brain. The trouble was, maddeningly, that the character lacked a face. Beryl, her mouth uncertain, was about to whisper something; Dennis shushed her as H. M. continued.

"That's how you see yourself, Masters. As a great intellect, unappreciated, that'll fool both confidin' females and the stupid police. But that gets too dangerous. And it's not really necessary. So, after one last flum-diddling of the police for a very good reason, you vanish into this sceptred isle and aren't seen again till you kill Mildred Lyons. Now I ask you, Masters: what in the name of Esau WOULD you do?"

There was a sound as though Masters had drawn a deep breath.

"Aha!" pounced H. M. "You already know the facts, son. D'ye see now the *interpretation* of the facts?"

"I do," breathed Masters. "By George, I do!" His voice rose and grew ferociously tender. "And as for Mr. Ruddy Bewlay, who now goes under the name of . . ."

This was the point, as breakers crashed and spray-drops whipped the glass of the windows, at which an inhuman countenance was thrust out of the alcove.

It was that of Sir Henry Merrivale, who had undoubtedly heard the scrape of a shoe or some

212

incautious movement. It appeared suddenly, like a bald head stuck round the side of a Punch-and-Judy show. Its gaze was fixed on the two eavesdroppers.

"Oi!" said H. M. sternly.

"Well, sir?"

"Have you two been listening to this little gabfest?"

"Yes," said Dennis, "we have. Without a great deal of enlightenment."

"Come here," said H. M.

They moved into the embrasure, where Chief Inspector Masters, his expression non-committal again, sat in a wicker chair with his notebook open on his knee. He merely nodded to the two newcomers, and continued to make quick shorthand notes. But H. M. glared at them, his fists on his hips.

"If you won't tell us anything," Dennis said despairingly, "you won't tell us anything. But it might interest you to hear, H. M., that Daphne's eloped with Bruce Ransom."

"Uh-huh. I knew it," said H. M. with a wooden face.

"What's more," cried Beryl, "somebody got in last night and practically tore Bruce's sitting-room to pieces."

"I know that too."

"But you haven't been up there!"

"I know it," answered H. M., "all the same."

"The point is," persisted Beryl, "that if you hope to prove anything by those manuscript sheets out of the original play—well, you won't. They're gone. Somebody stole 'em."

"Oh, no, he didn't," said H. M. Reaching into his inside breast-pocket, he produced a bundle of sheets folded lengthwise and flapped them in the air. "*I* got 'em, my wench, before I left last night. At least," he adjusted his spectacles and blinked at the papers, "I got most of 'em. I dropped one sheet on the floor, and I think it's still there; in fact, I'm dead sure it's still there, along with a little note Bruce Ransom wrote. All the same—!"

He stuffed the papers back into his pocket.

"These," H. M. added, tapping the pocket, "are only contributory evidence. They won't convict Bewlay of murder. That's why I asked you two to come down here. To ask you whether . . ."

The window-frames rattled. Abruptly Chief Inspector Masters closed his notebook.

"I wouldn't do it, sir!" he warned. "I told you before, I wouldn't do it!"

"Shut up, Masters."

"Miss West and Mr. Foster have no concern in this."

"Haven't they?" inquired H. M. "Ho! Haven't they!"

"I tell you straight: it's too dangerous."

"Sure," agreed H. M., with the windows night-black and foam-white behind him. "And Daphne Herbert's in danger too. She's in bigger danger than she's ever likely to be in her life. But there you are."

He turned back to the others.

"You've had a lot of heart-burnin' over this," H. M. went on, with a subdued roar of embarrassment. "And I don't want to keep on torturing you as though . . . as though . . ." He put up a hand to shade his eyes.

"Y'see, it's like this. I'm goin' on a little expedition this afternoon, me all by myself. I want to know whether you two would like to go along. But parts of what happens may be very unpleasant."

Dennis glanced at Beryl, who was terrified but resolute.

"Unpleasant—why?"

"Because," replied H. M., "there's goin' to be hell and high water when Roger Bewlay's cornered. He won't take it smiling, I warn you of that. Well? Do you want to go along?"

For the first time, in the distance, thunder rumbled.

214

17

The hands of the little illuminated clock, on the
dashboard of the police-car, stood at twenty-five
minutes past two.

Dennis noted this, over H. M.'s shoulder, just before
his eyes blinked shut to the white blaze of lightning.
Thunder followed close on it, a splitting shock. And
loud thunder is disquieting nowadays, not because it
suggests the natural menace of the elements, but
because it sounds exactly like those barrages which
tore the sky over London only a few years ago.

This wasn't London. But Dennis couldn't tell where
it was.

The rain, sweeping and sluicing in needle-gusts
against the windscreen, had been pouring down for
only a short time. The storm, in fact, broke over them
just as they were leaving the hotel after lunch. But it
now formed a whirling mist, wind-spun, in whose
darkness Dennis had lost all sense of direction.

H. M. was at the wheel of the car, a big but very old
relic with isinglass-windowed side-curtains, and Beryl
and Dennis were in the back seat. And H. M., if the
truth must be told, is a notoriously bad driver with an
absent-minded habit of leaving the handbrake on, or of

215

sitting and thinking about something else while the car bears straight towards a stone wall.

"Darling! Please!" Beryl begged.

"Wouldn't it," Dennis suggested, "be better if I . . . ?"

"No!" said H. M.

It had been all very well when they drove for several miles on the broad paved road, southwards from the hotel, along an open coast where rain-gusts flew at them with harpy violence and even the sea on their left showed as no more than an edge of foaming white. But afterwards, when H. M. turned off the main road on a road-surface that was bad and presently became vile . . .

Dennis dislodged one of the side-curtains to peer out.

As the lightning lifted again, picking out details with momentary clarity, he saw that they were approaching heavily wooded country through which the road ran. He thought he could discern, on either side of the road, a tall stone gatepost. No wall, no boundary, only those gateposts with a carved gargoyle atop each. And far ahead, over the sodden trees, he caught one glimpse of something he had never before seen in the English countryside.

It was a tower, a tall gaunt tower, built of roughly hewn logs.

Darkness descended. Thunder crashed out at them, its reverberations prickling along his nerves and making him doubt his own eyesight. The car jolted sickeningly, so that Beryl had to clutch at him for support; there was a hissing slur as one wheel spun against mud; then it righted itself.

H. M., glancing often at the clock on the dashboard, did not move or speak.

"Dennis! What is it? Did you see anything?"

"Nothing of importance, no."

216

Beryl spoke in a whisper against his ear.

"Where's the man taking us? Have you any idea?"

"Not the slightest."

A sense of unreality had invaded his mind. The damp, musty atmosphere of the closed-in car, the smell of the raincoats and goloshes they had borrowed at the hotel, the ticking windscreen-wiper, H. M.'s motionless figure in bowler hat and oilskins, all this added to it. They were among thick trees, since the force of the wind had dropped; but they might have been out of this world.

H. M. swung the car off on another road to the right. Five minutes later they were again unprotected by trees. There was a great whine of wind across open fields, and the rain came at them like a seven-thonged whip. Dennis faintly glimpsed those open fields, just as . . .

"Beryl. Did you see it?"

"See what?"

"Another of those infernal towers. I picked it up by the head-lights. And there seem to be roads running in every direction."

They still spoke in whispers. It was as though neither of them dared to address H. M., who swung the car again. Dampness had got into their nostrils and their very lungs. It was only when Dennis began to fear the ride would go on for ever, a journey into time, that there suddenly appeared in front of them a little corrugated-iron shed, once painted brownish-green, its doors open.

H. M. shot the car in, dangerously; he bore down on brake and clutch, yanked the handbrake over, and instantly switched off every light. Then there was nothing, except the drumming and thumping of rain on an iron roof.

"Now listen, my wench," said H. M.'s voice out of

the darkness.

"Yes?" answered Beryl. She added, a little wildly: "Where are you?"

"Just where I've been sittin' all along. Will you follow very carefully what I'm goin' to say?"

"Yes, of course!"

"Maybe in a very few minutes, now, you'll encounter a whole series of rummy incidents you won't understand at all. But there's nothing that can possibly hurt you. Got that?"

"Yes! Only what . . . ?"

"Now I want you to promise me that there'll be no screaming, or jumping, or anything like that. I'm dead serious, my wench. If you can't promise that, you stop here till we get back. What about it?"

"I promise. Truly!"

"All right. Got your raincoats and goloshes? Then climb out of this rattletrap and follow me."

The wind had fallen a little, though it was still difficult to keep your eyes open against whirling rain. A soaked world, a glutinous world, with just enough light in the sky to show them the deeply rutted road along which H. M. was lumbering. Dennis, wondering what was so vaguely suggestive about the very broad ruts, found himself conscious of another atmosphere in this place. That was its utter desolation.

Not mere loneliness, which can be felt by anyone in a country cottage. But desolation in the sense that a bombed area is desolate, a gutted city is desolate: that earth once populous has been stricken lifeless along with the thoughts and emotions and human feelings that made it live.

As a shock of thunder rolled out over their heads and split in tumbling echoes down the sky, Dennis realized that for miles in every direction that countryside was dead.

Dead.

He heard Beryl's step splash in a rut, and he caught her under the elbow as she stumbled. Yet the word rang in his mind—dead!—as distinct as thunder, as vivid as the image of those gaunt empty towers, or the gateposts without walls.

"Here!" called H. M. softly.

H. M. had turned off to the left, and was pointing. They found themselves staring at nothing more alarming than an ordinary English farmhouse.

Or, rather, what had been a farmhouse. It was set back some fifty yards from the road, behind a low stone wall and a flat stretch of churned ground. It was built of stone once white-washed, but now a dirty grey. Two windows, all glass smashed, were on either side of the front door, and more windows above. The roof-tiles gaped open. On each side of the front door stood a ragged laurel-bush.

It was dead too, like the dead fields that had once been its farm. Behind it they could see a walled yard, with a farm-wagon and an upturned hay-cart.

"That's where we're goin'," said H. M.

Beryl, shading her eyes with wet hands against the rain, bit very hard at her under-lip. The scarf she had bound round her head was now sodden.

"Who's in there?" she demanded.

"Nobody," said H. M., "yet. Or at least I hope not."

"You know," Beryl observed suddenly, "that place is sort of—I know! Haunted!"

H. M. swung round.

"How d'ye mean?"

"Some strong and violent emotion." She spoke a little incoherently. "Over and over! Scaring people! In there! I'm not trying to be psychic. I tell you I *know.*"

"You're right, my wench," agreed H. M. "You're quite right."

Dennis, as an outlet for his own violent feelings, strode on ahead. He was some ten yards from the house when his foot, in a golosh clogged with mire, kicked a smallish cardboard box so sodden that it hardly moved. He glanced at it, and then bent over it. It was an ammunition-box.

His eye, close to the ground, caught the shape of something else: a brass cartridge-case, half buried. Then another, among dancing spatters of rain. Then, a few feet farther along, still another.

Dennis glanced at the house. Two flickers of lightning, one short and the other illuminating the whole sky with deathly pallor, kindled a sight which pitched Dennis Foster headlong into the realm of nightmare.

He had been wrong about the dead house. Something *was* alive there.

Something stirred behind the ragged laurel-bush to the left of the front door. Something moved. Something jumped up, as though pulled on strings, and moved sideways to look at him. It was the figure of a man in uniform, with a rifle, and the man was wearing a German helmet.

This he saw, or thought he saw, until the second blaze of lightning painted grey the dripping stone façade of the house, and the lurching front door, and the windows retaining only ragged teeth of glass, and the torn laurel-bush; and it showed him that there was nothing there.

God Almighty! Was he awake or asleep?

Dennis scarcely heard the ear-splitting assault of the thunder. Yet he could distinguish the fact that Beryl was saying something a few paces behind him, and H. M. answering. These two had noticed nothing. With a twinge of doubt about the reality of the world, with a horrible sense of dead men springing from dead soil, Dennis heard the rain thump on his hat-brim and splash down the front of the house.

H. M., silent again, moved past them. He went up one stone step, pushed wide the broken-hinged door, and beckoned. With his fingers round Beryl's arm, keeping her a little behind him, Dennis followed.

They were in a darkish passage, damp and heavy with the smell of broken mortar and plaster-dust. From somewhere upstairs, through holes in the roof, rain scurried like a noise of rats. H. M. indicated a door on the right, at the front.

Dennis hesitated. But the gesture was peremptory. Dennis opened the door—it moved quite easily—and entered with Beryl still a little behind him, H. M. followed, closing the door.

They were in a square room, its floor bare-boarded and creaky, with two windows at the front and one at the side. By the eerie light which filtered through these openings, Dennis could make out that the room contained only two or three wooden chairs, one of them overturned, together with a table near the side window.

And a German officer, with a revolver in his hand, rose to his feet from behind that table.

The flare of the lightning, springing as though from the ground rather than the sky, outlined that officer's figure in black silhouette against the window. It showed the hump of the shoulder, the crook of the elbow, the hooded menace of the helmet. It also showed the bullet-holes in the officer's stomach, so that you could see lightning through them.

This time it was a near thing.

Dennis clapped his hand over Beryl's mouth to prevent an outcry, holding her tightly as an enormous crash of thunder burst into several lesser peals and slowly vibrated away.

"Looky here," said H. M.'s voice out of the twilight. The voice sounded very strained. "There's nothing to be afraid of. But . . ."

"But what?"

"This isn't my doin', y' know. So help me, I'm not guilty! Somebody's working the mechanism. And I don't like it."

"Working the mechanism?"

Dennis glanced across at the side window. The German officer was gone.

"Those figures," said H. M., "are only made of plywood on ropes and pulleys. The house is full of 'em. You're goin' to see things far worse. Burn it all, don't you realize where we are?"

"No! I can't say I do."

H. M. came a step closer, heavily.

"This whole area," he swept out his arm, "about five miles by three, was once a battle-school for the Army. This house is a unit of it."

"Battle-school!" exclaimed Dennis. He released Beryl, whose whole body was trembling. "Battle-school! Bruce Ransom did mention . . ."

"He did, did he?" rumbled H. M., with a sort of whispered roar. "And you forgot it? Hey?"

"Yes. I forgot it."

"This school," said H. M., "was used for trainin'-courses to toughen up the troops. And, oh, my eye, did it toughen 'em! You noticed those rummy-lookin' towers; they were built by the Sappers for observation o' combat. You missed the sand-pits, full of barbed wire, that the blokes had to jump across carryin' full kit. But this house, the fellers'll tell you who've been through it, was the worst nerve-test of the whole lot." He broke off. "Are you all right, my wench?"

"Perfectly all right," answered Beryl. "*I* saw that ghastly thing by the door, Dennis. Don't you think I didn't! But I'd promised to be good, and I was going to *be* good."

Slowly, with a creak now discernible, the German officer again got to his feet behind the table. They saw him against the window. Even knowing what he was, in that dusk of rain and lightning, you did not find him pleasant company.

H. M., barrel-shaped in rustling oilskins, stared for a moment at that plywood figure. H. M. turned round, hurried to the door, and opened it. He peered up and down the passage, apparently without seeing anything. Then he returned, wiping his sleeve across his forehead.

"Listen!" he growled. "I want to show you how this Crazy House worked for the troops, because it's got an awful important bearing on why we're here.

"Each feller, you understand, had to go through it to show how he could keep his wits about him. Outside,"— H. M. pointed—"he was briefed by an officer, who handed him two live hand-grenades and a Tommy-gun loaded with exactly fifteen bullets.

"'*Now*,' says the officer, '*there are fifteen Jerries inside that house. You've got to clean 'em out with fifteen bullets. An instructor will go just behind you, whispering advice in your ear. But, mind! Don't shoot at anybody you see except Jerries.*'

"Got it?

"The feller starts at a run for this house. Up pops a Jerry behind that bush. One gone! In here, and up pops the officer. Two gone! No sooner out in the hall, than another Jerry pokes his face through a back window. Cleanin' out the downstairs rooms, seeing those faces everywhere; then upstairs, with the instructor hissin' over your shoulder like Satan and only confusing you as he's meant to.

"You grab hold of a door-knob, to open it—and the door sticks.

"'*Aya!*' says the instructor, '*you've given yourself away. They've spotted you. What do you do now, you silly so-and-so? Chuck in your grenades, you this-and-that, and then go in and finish 'em with bullets.*'

"*Bam* go the grenades, gougin' the walls to blazes and not very pleasant when you have to dodge back from 'em yourself. In you go, and get two more. Then the cellar. Down to the cellar! That's what the instructor shouts at you now: you've forgotten the cellar!

"Down you go haring, and tread on a loose board just at the head of the cellar stairs. And a machine-gun cuts loose at you with live ammunition, just missing the top of your head and spraying you with plaster-chips. But this time, if you got any nerves in your body at all, the blast of that machine-gun has got 'em jumpin' under your skin like grease in a hot frying-pan. But bang down the cellar stairs you go, by this time not even rememberin' how many bullets you've got left in your Tommy-gun. And in the cellar . . ."

H. M. paused, his fists on his hips.

The plywood German officer, with the pattern of bullet-holes in his body, swung and swayed behind the table. Dennis, his eyes growing accustomed to this grey light, made out that the walls were pitted with bullet-gouges where neophytes in this House of Nerves had fired wildly.

All the emotion they must have felt, whipped on by illusion and goading speech into a game that became momentarily as vivid as battle, flowed in this room. To Dennis Foster it was as real as the pressure of his own soaked raincoat and dripping hat. He hadn't been through it. But he knew.

Beryl's voice roused him from his dream.

"And in the cellar?" she asked. "What do you find?"

"Come on," said H. M., with a wheezy sigh. "We're

224

goin' down there and see."

"There isn't—?"

"Isn't a machine-gun up over the cellar door? Oh, no, my wench. That's gone long ago."

All the same, as they stumbled out into that darkish passage which was as gritty as sand underfoot, Dennis wondered.

"Somebody's been working the mechanism."

That was what H. M. had said. The chill of the passage made Dennis shiver, and he half expected to see one of those plywood figures thrust its face through a gaping window at the far end. He envisaged a house full of such figures: draggled, sagging now on their useless ropes, yet all in some fashion connected with the uglier figure of Roger Bewlay.

But how? In the name of sanity, *how?* How could Bewlay, or the capturing of Bewlay, have anything to do with a deserted farmhouse rigged for terror? On the other hand . . .

"Easy!" H. M. called softly.

The cellar door was at the rear of the passage, under the stairs, facing the back of the house. It was no door at all, being merely an oblong open space that led down into a black hole. That, Dennis thought, would be no very good place to meet Bewlay now.

Despite his reassuring words, H. M. trod very carefully, and trod again, on every board at the top of the stairs. One of those boards, presumably, had controlled the once-hidden machine-gun. But nothing happened. Only the rain roared. H. M., his bowler hat dented, fished an electric torch out of the pocket of his oilskin water-proof.

"Let's have some warning," Dennis said suddenly. "What are we going to see?"

"A dummy," answered H. M.

"You mean another of these infernal Germans?"

225

"No!" returned H. M., with a wicked look behind the big spectacles. "This time it's a three-dimensional dummy, stuffed with straw and wearin' clothes. I want you to see it, son, so you'll both get used to it later."

"Later? Are we going to be here long?"

"Maybe."

Lightning and thunder flooded the farmhouse. H. M. switched on the small electric torch. Its beam explored heavy wooden steps, worn black, between stone walls stained with dark trickling patches where the rain had leaked through. H. M. led the way down, to a dark doorway that opened at right-angles on the left.

Dennis was still on the lowest step, and Beryl on the step above, when H. M. abruptly swung round.

"Now," he went on, "imagine again that you're the bloke who's makin' a spooks' tour of this house. I want to emphasize that you're in no calm, soothed frame of mind. Your heart's got a thump like a steam-hammer. The instructor's cursin' just behind your ear. Your trigger-finger's on the itch. You plunge into this room after Jerries, and . . ."

The beam of H. M.'s electrical torch swung through the doorway on the left. The other two crowded round him.

They were looking into a low-ceilinged room of rough-stone walls. Barred windows, high up, would have admitted light had there been much to admit. A door opposite evidently led into a smaller room, with a stairway up to the outer air. But that was not what they noticed.

A human figure was hanging, hanging by the neck, from a thin rope attached to a ceiling-beam. That was all Dennis caught, the wry-necked weight with its back turned, before H. M.'s light instantly went out.

"You plunge in here wild-eyed. That hangin' figure

jumps up at you, and you let loose a shot at it. Over you go, racin', to that smaller room. And, as a climax to all this, a German officer—a real, breathin', living man—steps straight out in your path. You press the trigger, almost convinced you're goin' loony; but there's only a click. Your ammunition's gone.

"*'Now, you half-witted so-and-so,'* bawls the instructor, *'you've lost the game. You've used up your last bullet. If this man had really been a Jerry you'd have been dead by now.*

"*'You were told not to fire at anybody but Jerries. If you'd looked for two seconds at that other figure, you'd have seen it was a civilian the Jerries hanged for partisan work. But, oh, no. You fired without thinking; you wasted your last bullet; and now you're dead.'*

"Uh-huh. Nice work. End of test."

H. M. paused, sniffing. He did not turn on the light again.

"Wait a minute!" said Dennis. His voice boomed back at him in that ill-smelling, close-pressing cellar.

"Yes, son?"

"Did you say a real person stepped out in front of this soldier with the Tommy-gun?"

"Uh-huh."

"But suppose the fellow hadn't fired his last shot?"

"The instructor knew how many shots had been fired. The instructor would 'a' signalled. All the same, son," H. M. spoke with awe, "it's not a job *I'd* want to take on in a hurry. Oh, lord love a duck!"

"And who worked the plywood figures upstairs?"

"The instructor himself. From a bell-pull knob inside the door of each room, that you're too excited to notice. All except the Jerry outside; he's worked from the back of the house. Y'see . . ."

"Put on that light," said Beryl, in a voice that rose up piercingly. "Please, for God's sake, put on that light!"

227

"I was goin' to, my wench. Take another look at the hangin' dummy."

Again the beam of the electric torch probed into that room.

Sordid and bedraggled it hung there, the dummy of a woman in a long, dirty gingham dress cut by bullet-holes. A dusty woven shawl was draped over its head like an executioner's hood. It hung with its back to them, swaying a little as wind crept in. Knitted mittens were on its hands. Dennis, staring at that dummy as the light slowly moved over it, suddenly took a step forward.

Dummies, however well made, do not wear tan stockings with seams carefully arranged down the back of the legs. They do not wear polished brown shoes, one loose so that you can see the dummy's heel. They do not . . .

Abruptly Beryl West turned her back. She pressed her fist to her mouth and bit, very hard, at the middle joints of the fingers.

"Oh, yes," said Sir Henry Merrivale. "It's Mildred Lyons's body."

18

"Come upstairs," said H. M., after a pause. His big voice was subdued, more than a little uncertain. "I had to show it to you. Burn me, I had to! But come away from it now."

Beryl did not comment. She marched ahead of him, in her thudding goloshes, while H. M.'s light pointed the way. It was a relief to get out of that evil-smelling cellar, with its gurgle and drip of water, even into the grotesque rooms above.

H. M.'s fierce gesture indicated the room at the front of the house, the room into which they had first gone. The German officer still stood behind the table, moving as rain-gusts blew in at the window behind him. Once more H. M. followed Beryl and Dennis in there, and closed the door.

"I know," H. M. surveyed them from under his dented bowler, "Masters told me not to bring you people out here. Maybe he was right. There are times," he hesitated, "when even the old man gets a bit of a queasy feeling. Because it's not as though there'd been any unpleasantness yet. The unpleasantness hasn't even started."

"What exactly," asked Dennis, "do you call unpleasantness?"

"I'm ignorin'," said H. M., looking him up and down, "the essence of a smart crack hidden in that Old-School-Navy manner. What I call unpleasantness, son, is what's goin' to happen."

"If you're thinking about me," observed Beryl, "please forget it."

As though to show her contempt for bogles, she went over leisurely and sat down on the edge of the table, with the bullet-riddled figure looming up over her shoulder. She crossed her legs in the same casual way. But her voice betrayed her.

"It was Bruce," she cried out, "who hung that body down there in place of the dummy?"

"Uh-huh. That's right."

"Innocently, of course?"

H. M. kept one eye fixed on a corner of the floor. "Oh, sure. Cloth-headed but innocent. Just like all Ransom's actions. Wouldn't you say that?"

With a ferocious scowl, without giving Beryl time to answer, he went on to Dennis.

"And in general, son, it was perfectly true when Ransom said he was hiding the body in a place where you couldn't see it even if you happened to be looking at it. He knows, as everybody hereabouts knows, all about this Crazy House.

"This whole area, d'ye see, is far from being a very popular place. It's got a funny feel about it. People don't come here much, even kids. I think," H. M. lowered his voice, imparting a deep secret, "I think they're a bit skeered of it. Anybody who ventured into that cellar would see just what he expected to see: a grubby-looking dummy with a shawl over its head. You wouldn't 'a' seen anything yourselves if I hadn't pointed a light at the shoes and stockings."

He held up the electric torch, with a leer like a thoughtful ogre, and then dropped it into his pocket.

"But why did Bruce have to do that?" pleaded Beryl. "Why?"

"Well . . . now. That's a bit of a story. I'll have to tell you about Roger Bewlay."

"Wait a minute!" snapped Dennis Foster.

"What's that, son?"

"I can't stand," roared Dennis, "any more of this intellectual cat-and-mouse. More hints? More innuendoes?"

"Oh, no!" said H. M., in a voice as sharp as his own. "It's past the time for hints or innuendoes now. I'm goin' to tell you the whole ruddy story."

The thunder seemed to be dying; there was only a faint growl of it in the distance, though the rain fell no less heavily, in silver vagueness outside the windows. A damp steam, an exhalation of mortar-and-plaster dust, rose up from the floor at the continued splash through those empty windows.

H. M. picked up one of the wooden chairs, inspected it to see that its legs were reliable, and sat down. His cigar-case appeared fumblingly from inside the oilskin waterproof. He took out a black cigar, stuck it into his mouth, and snapped on a pocket-lighter.

As the little core of flame was reflected in H. M.'s spectacles, Dennis had a sudden memory of him, a month ago, sitting just like that by the table in the back room at Alf's public-house.

"Wrong problem!" H. M. said abruptly.

"What's that?"

"Wrong problem!" growled H. M., blowing out the lighter with extraordinary violence. The end of the cigar pulsed and glowed.

"This morning," he went on, "when you two were deliberately eavesdroppin' on a private conversation— which the same," said H. M. with a lordly sneer, "which the same I would scorn to do myself—you

231

heard me give a little character-sketch of Bewlay.

"You heard how this feller, broke and slung out of his own homeland, gradually discovered in the happy huntin'-ground of London that women were his natural game. How it went to his head and gave him a crazy self-confidence. How he reared back and showed his teeth over the rich pleasure of murdering Andrée Cooper.

"That was where the police got after him.

"The police knew he'd picked up with this palmist's assistant, brimmin' over with sex-appeal. They knew he'd bought her clothes. They knew he'd taken her north, to Scarborough in Yorkshire, and to a cottage he'd rented under the name of Richard Barclay—"

Beryl interrupted uncontrollably.

"Berkeley?" she exclaimed. "But that's the same name as . . ."

"Barclay," said H. M. "B-a-r-c-l-a-y." He took a few violent puffs at the cigar. "Are you goin' to shut up and let me get on with this?"

"All right. I was only thinking something."

"There," said H. M., with a curious look at Beryl, "he killed her. And her boy-friend complained. And the hunt was up.

"Now lemme repeat something I said yesterday. The police, with all due respect to 'em, have got a one-track mind. When X disappears after last being seen in Y's company at a certain house, they're dead sure the body's hidden in the house or the grounds. They come to depend on it. You heard Masters admit that. And in practically every case they're right.

"Cor, what activity then!

"They'll dig up the garden for hundreds of yards round, rememberin' Dougal of the Moat Farm and Thorne of the chicken-run. They'll break open concrete floors or hearth-stone, always suspect since Deeming disposed of two wives and three children. They'll excavate the cellar, a favourite choice from the Mannings to Dr. Crippen. They'll rake out stoves and furnaces, in memory of Landru. They'll grab for trunks and boxes, which have had a nasty look about 'em since Crossman covered his wife with concrete and put her in a tin trunk under the stairs.

"They'll tear down brick walls, pry up the floor-joists, measure partitions between rooms. Oh, my eye! They're as thorough as the Prefect G. in Edgar Allan Poe. And they won't start looking farther afield until they're convinced the body's not in the house."

H. M. paused.

Dennis and Beryl looked at each other. It was as though, in that rain-dripping house among the dummies, they could hear Bewlay laughing.

H. M. pushed his dented bowler to the back of his head, and bent forward with hideous earnestness.

"Now, mind you, all this was in the Press. It was published that the police were 'anxious to interview' (that term always makes me shiver) a man called Roger Bewlay or Roger Bowdoin or Richard Barclay. It was known that they were 'investigating' houses, in Bucks and Sussex as well as Yorkshire.

"But what does Bewlay do?

"Blatantly, as R. Benedict, he goes down to Torquay with a new wife. He takes a furnished place of just the same sort. After a few days he *knows*—Masters admitted it—he *knows* there's a night-watch on the bungalow. He knows it's there when he strangles his wife. There's a gapin' peep-hole in the curtains of the room where the murder's done. On the following morning, he walks out of there in a hat and raincoat on a fine day, as though to underline the suggestion that he's goin' to do a bunk."

H. M. pointed with the glowing cigar, sighting one

233

eye along it.

"Now, we all agree Bewlay's got a bit of a leaky belfry. Sure! But nobody's ever suggested that he's ten times madder than a March hare about wanting to be caught. In fact, this coyness of his about being caught has been givin' Masters blood-pressure for the last decade.

"That conduct of Bewlay's, obligingly makin' the police think he's killed this woman and disposed of her remains inside the house, makes the brain reel. It's just plain incredible. Unless . . .

"Cor! Wait a minute! Unless . . . ?"

Here H. M. paused again, arching up his eyebrows very high as though ghoulishly inviting suggestions.

Dennis exchanged a glance with Beryl, who lifted her shoulders in a helpless shrug.

"Unless—what?" Dennis demanded.

"Unless," said H. M., "that's just exactly what he wants the police to think."

Dennis stared at him.

"Hold on, now! Bewlay *wants* the police to think he's committed another murder?"

"Uh-huh. That's right."

"He wants 'em to think he's disposed of the body again?"

"Yes."

"But why?"

"Because, for once in his sweet life," returned H. M., "Bewlay hasn't committed any murder and hasn't disposed of any woman's body."

Beryl, jerking backwards and bumping into the German officer, was for an instant so startled by the plywood figure that she almost cried out. The roaring twilight of the rain pressed against Dennis's wits.

"H. M., what in hell's name are you suggesting?"

"A fake murder," said H. M.

234

After a pause, during which he smoked with ogreish concentration, H. M. went on.

"Now suppose that Bewlay—with perfect safety to himself, mind!—can apparently commit a murder under just those circumstances? What'll happen?

"I'll tell you, son. Just what did happen. Such a breeze went up the police's shirt-tails as hasn't been known for fifty years. They now thought they'd got their problem defined in clear, hard terms. They were utterly convinced, as they'd believed all along, that in some way Bewlay had polished off another one and disposed of her inside the house. Got that? *Inside the house.*

"And now, my cloth-heads, you see the key to the whole business?

"Bewlay wanted 'em to think that about the real victims, Angela and Elizabeth and Andrée, because in fact he hadn't done anything of the kind. He'd hidden their bodies—somewhere away from the house. But, sooner or later, the police would stop grubbin' in cottages and look just a little farther afield. Then God help him. He might be done for. Yet, just as long as the police were certain about his fool-proof method of indoor extermination, he was as safe as though he'd already been acquitted.

"He was, in a literal sense, safe as houses. Got it now?"

The rain was slackening. A little more faint daylight crept into the room, smudgily grey, showing up bullet-pocks in the walls and the rivulets that ran across the floor. Dennis, who had tortured himself for so long with this same problem, could not help bursting out with the question uppermost in his mind.

"How did Bewlay dispose of the bodies, actually?"

"Aha!" gloated H. M., putting the cigar back in his mouth and rubbing his hands together. "There we got a

235

neat problem too. But let's not think about that for a minute. Let's concentrate on this other matter.

"If we're goin' to suppose Bewlay's fourth murder was a fake murder, have we got any contributory evidence to support us?

"Well, yes.

"There's 'Mrs. Bewlay,' the most intangible character that ever floated out of a spirit-cabinet. Mrs. Bewlay, as we know, kept 'aloof' from everybody. Even the watchin' policemen never saw her except at a long distance, because they'd had orders to keep away from Bewlay. She hadn't any friends. She hadn't been married anywhere. She didn't even have a name. As I told Masters, all I could find was a great big X; and that's what she was.

"Bewlay, naturally, had to have a female accomplice to help him. This accomplice, who played the part of 'Mrs. Bewlay,' was somebody else altogether in real life. Of course you've guessed who the accomplice was?"

Beryl made a noise like a seething kettle.

"You know perfectly well we haven't!" she cried. "Who was the accomplice?"

"Mildred Lyons," said H. M.

"Mildred Lyons?" screamed Beryl.

"Sh-h!" howled H. M., taking the cigar out of his mouth and quickly peering right and left. "For the love of Esau keep your voice down!"

"But—Mildred Lyons?"

"Uh-huh."

"But she was . . ." said Beryl.

"The witness for the prosecution, who . . ." amplified Dennis.

"Who," said H. M., "couldn't possibly have convicted Bewlay of murder or anything else. Maybe," suggested H. M., with a sort of meek ingenuous leer, "the idea strikes you as a little bit surprising?"

"You might call it that," said Dennis.

"But think again, son. If you postulate Bewlay's 'murder' as a trick to save himself, then Mildred Lyons had to be an accomplice. Even aside from the lurid and terrible tale of the View Through A Curtain, she was the one solitary person who ever professed to see 'Mrs. Bewlay' close at hand or speak to her.

"And if you want evidence, I'll give you evidence. Do you remember one night, about a month ago, when we were all in Alf Partridge's pub beside the Granada Theatre?"

Beryl drew a breath of deep feeling.

"We remember," she said.

"Up to now, y'see," pursued H. M., "the ideas I've been giving you were only the ghosty ideas I had when Masters, years ago, sent me that big file on Roger Bewlay.

"Cor!" breathed H. M., his wrath slowly and terrifyingly mounting as he remembered the past. "After sayin' he doesn't need my help, that weasel has the unspeakable, star-gazin' crust to send me a file on Bewlay and say would I read it, please, and give my comments?

"I really am a meek sort of feller, my wench. Honest. I'm a man of mild language. I never use profanity, God damn it. Otherwise, so help me! I'd have told him to take his ruddy file and stick it . . .

"What I mean is," coughed H. M., suddenly remembering his high-mindedness and assuming an air of piety, "that it wasn't a very nice thing to do; now was it? And me, in spite of that, I did look through the file."

"That was awfully Christian of you," conceded Beryl, who was torn between bewilderment and fear and a wild desire to laugh in the Old Maestro's face. "But what exactly—?"

"Am I gettin' at?"

"Yes!"

"That night in the pub, Masters says they've got new evidence. 'Some unknown author wrote a play about Bewlay; and this author knows too much.' Meaning, of course, that the author may be Bewlay himself: which subsequently turned out to be true. 'He knows the witness was a woman,' says Masters, 'where she looked and what she saw; every smacking thing that's supposed to be known only by the police, by you, and by the Lyons girl herself.'"

"And I stopped lightin' my cigar," added H. M. "I felt as though I'd just got a conk over the onion with a golf-club."

"But why?"

"Well, my wench," said H. M., "you've had a lot of heart-burning over askin' yourself who knew these facts, and why. But how did *Bewlay* know 'em?"

There was a silence, while the rain splashed.

"This point," emphasized H. M., "becomes still more strikin' if you examine some manuscript sheets of the original stage-play, carefully preserved by Bruce Ransom. Has either of you see 'em?"

"Yes!" Beryl nodded. "Bruce showed them to me last night."

"He showed 'em to me," said H. M., "when I first came to Aldebridge a fortnight ago. Did you notice anything, my wench?"

"Darling, I'm afraid I was so horribly flustered that I . . . I . . . !"

"Bewlay, the author of that play,"—H. M. spaced his words with care—"knows the woman witness was 'red-haired.' He knows she went out to see him that night about a bad ten-bob note. He even knows (oh, crikey!) she went out there *on a bicycle*. How does he know all that?"

238

"He couldn't have!" cried Dennis Foster. "It's impossible! Unless . . ."

"Unless," agreed H. M., "Bewlay and Mildred Lyons were working as accomplices to flum-diddle the police."

Dennis Foster took two steps across the room, and two steps back.

"Make-believe!" said Dennis.

"What's that, son?"

"Nothing, sir. Go on."

"Would it have been possible, says I to myself, for Mildred Lyons to have played both her own part and the part of Mrs. Bewlay?

"Answer: easily. The Lyons gal, we learn, had no assistant in her typist's office; she could come and go unobserved. The police, we also know, kept watch on that bungalow only at night. She could have gone out there by a back way through those wooded hills (the bungalow was built against 'em) without bein' seen. Even before any coppers kept watch, she had days to establish herself as 'Mrs. Bewlay' in the eyes of casual passers-by, of the postman and the butcher's boy and so on.

"In any kind of wig over that notable hair, loaded with conspicuous fake jewellery provided by Bewlay, she would be seen—always at a distance!—takin' tea with him in the garden, 'very lover-like,' or in a deck-chair on the lawn. Once that was established, she needn't ever go near the place till the crucial afternoon of July 6th.

"You follow it then?

"On that afternoon she sets out openly, as Mildred Lyons, on her bike, with a typewriter. Of course no letters were ever dictated. She goes into the house, comes out as Mrs. Bewlay, has tea for the last time with her 'husband,' and goes away as Lyons in the late afternoon.

"That night, the fireworks! There never was a bad banknote either: that whole transaction was simply an inspired bit of eye-wash, to explain, first, why she went out there in the afternoon, and, second, why she came back at night. She did come back on her bicycle, peeped through the window-curtains at nothing except Bewlay himself, and hared away. And the thing was done."

H. M. shook his head. He took one brief draw at a cigar that had almost gone out. His voice swelled up on something like a note of admiration.

"The beauty of that scheme, d'ye see, was that it couldn't fail either way. Suppose, at any point along the line, those two had slipped up? Suppose somebody tumbled to it? Suppose, in that tickling moment when Bewlay made his getaway in the morning, the waverin' constable had said 'Oi!'

"Well! There was still no harm done. Nobody'd been killed. Bewlay, with his famous smile, could say to the coppers: 'You've been hounding me (an innocent man!) with your detestable suspicions which you know you can't prove. Can you blame me for wanting to make you squirm a little with a bit of flum-diddlery? In any case, what in blazes do you propose to do about it?'

"On the other hand, if the scheme succeeded . . .

"Oh, Lord love a duck!

"D'ye mind my repeating that Bewlay would be *safe?* Safe for good and all, in whatever character he wanted to assume next? The police would never find out what he really did with his victim. Because they'd be lookin' straight in the wrong direction: in an eternal search of harmless houses for corpses that weren't there.

"Who would suspect Mildred Lyons, the witness for the prosecution, the gal who could bring Bewlay into the shadow of the gallows, of actually bein' his

240

accomplice? I think Bewlay, in his chilly little soul, must 'a' howled with joy over that. He'd coached her, coached her with care, in everything she had to say when they questioned her.

"It couldn't have been easy, either. I'm pretty sure Mildred Lyons's hysterics, in front of the police, were real hysterics. She was scared, scared out of her wits. But he was sure she'd do it; she'd do anything on the broad earth for him; because she was his adorin' Mildred."

After a pause H. M. added:

"I say. Did I mention that Bewlay's clever?"

A deeper chill seemed to have settled in that room. The face of Mildred Lyons, before it turned blind and dumb with sand in the eyes and mouth, arose in Dennis's imagination and looked at him.

"His—adoring—Mildred," repeated Beryl. And she shivered.

"Uh-huh."

"Another of Bewlay's mistresses?"

"That's right. With a difference."

"Yesterday," Beryl began, and stopped because of the lump in her throat. Her fingers were now gripping the edges of the table on either side of her. Dennis could see her silhouetted against the window, the wet hair and the wet scarf bound round it, with the German officer leaning forward as though in close attention.

"Yesterday," Beryl went on, "when you were talking to Mr. Masters beside the golf course, you said that these mass-murderers always have one woman they go back to. One woman they live with between murders."

H. M. nodded.

"Usually," he avoided Beryl's eye, "it's a colourless woman with no looks at all. The Bewlays of this world seem to find it a comfort."

"'Smith,'" Beryl quoted in a thin voice, "'had his

241

Edith Pegler. Landru had his Fernande Segret. And Roger Bewlay—.' Had his Mildred Lyons? Is that it?"

"Uh-huh."

"I nearly fainted," said Beryl, suddenly pressing her hands together and wringing them. "I was afraid you meant me." Again her voice went up. "But it's the one woman, you said, that they *don't* kill."

"That, my wench, was where *I* made an awful mistake." H. M. closed his eyes for an instant. "Bewlay did kill her. He did something that Smith never did and Landru never did. But then he had to."

"Had to kill her? Why?"

"Because he deserted her completely," answered H. M. "For eleven years he never saw her, or wrote a line to tell her where he was. When a woman's been through the flames of hell for your sake, that's one thing you mustn't do."

The flames of hell . . .

Very distinctly now Dennis Foster saw in his imagination, as it had come back to him several times before, a picture whose meaning had always just eluded him. He saw the expression on Mildred Lyons's face as she slipped out by the stage-door of the Granada Theatre: the furtiveness and excitement, the mingling of fear and triumph, the glitter of the blue eyes as they moved right and left. He had the answer now.

It was an expression of hatred. Sheer hatred.

Mildred Lyons lived, lived and breathed for him in that picture: the freckled girl grown into a gaunt raging woman. Her image filled this rain-darkened room. Dennis stared across at Beryl, who was saying something to H. M., until something else riveted his attention and startled him to alertness.

There were now two German officers standing at Beryl's shoulder.

Dennis blinked, and blinked again.

242

Was there, in this House of Nerves, the House of Dummies, another booby-trap springing up at them? Outlined against the window, a dark blur, hung this second figure a little to the left of the first. But its helmet was not quite so bulbous. There were no bullet-holes in its chest and stomach. On the contrary, its hand moved stealthily along the window-sill . . .

"H. M.!" shouted Dennis. And he plunged at the window.

His left hand encountered the lapel of a wet overcoat. His right hand, grotesquely but instinctively, fastened on somebody's necktie and twined it round his fingers like a dog-lead. He yanked forward, so that the figure uttered a disconcerted bleat.

Sir Henry Merrivale stood up, cursing. The beam of H. M.'s electric torch flickered across the room, and rested on the face of the man standing outside the window.

Peering at them with mouth open, a startled and reproachful look on his pink face, was Horace Chittering.

19

H. M.'s voice, low-pitched in wrath, was nevertheless so full of astonishment that Dennis realized he had not expected this.

"What in holy blue blazes," breathed H. M., switching off the torch, "are *you* doin' here?"

To laugh lightly, to adopt a manner of airy inconsequence while you stand rocking on an upended wooden box with someone's hand entangled in your necktie, is a matter of some difficulty. Mr. Chittering, in a dark-blue overcoat and bowler hat, merely uttered as much of a cough as the strangle-hold would permit.

"Not to put too fine a point on it," he said, his chin up like Vitellius's with the sword under it, "and due to a concatenation of circumstances which candour as well as expediency compel me to admit, I was—er—listening."

H. M.'s face turned purple.

"You were, were you?"

"I fear so. My dear fellow, please let go my necktie!"

Dennis glanced at H. M. and H. M. nodded. Dennis released the prisoner, who coughed again.

"Come on, son! Climb in through that window!"

Mr. Chittering eyed the jagged edges of glass in the

lower frame.

"I greatly fear . . . !"

"All right, then. Sneak round to the front door. Only for the love of Esau don't let anybody see you!"

Beryl had slid off the table to her feet. They all looked at each other until Mr. Chittering entered, nervously, from the passage. Even in that gloom his face, with its small button-nose and bulging eyes, showed as pink-mottled. He removed his hat, emptied the rainwater from its brim with a trembling hand, and replaced it.

"How long," inquired H. M., replacing the torch in his pocket, "have you been here?"

"In point of fact . . ."

"Looky here, son. We ain't got time for any eighteenth-century prose now. How long have you been here?"

"About three quarters of an hour."

"Was it you,"—H. M. pointed to the plywood German—"who was making those jumpin'-jacks work for us? Was that your idea of a screamingly funny joke?"

"No!" the other assured him, with jowl-shaken sincerity. "No! That is," he amended, "at the back of this farmhouse I found what looked like a bell-pull. I used it. I crept (forgive me; that is the word) into the passage, I heard voices in here, and I saw (mysteriously) a bell-pull beside every door. I tried one, and nothing seemed to happen. I crept back, and tried it again, and crept away."

"You hadn't got any other object?"

"My dear sir! None at all!"

"Sure of that?"

"I am," Mr. Chittering confessed, "of a somewhat inquiring turn of mind. My impulse is to pull a bell and see what happens."

246

"My impulse," said H. M., "is to pull a nose and see what happens. What made you come here to-day?"

"The fact is," replied Mr. Chittering, patting his readjusted tie and moving his neck curiously, as though he felt the pressure of a rope, "in the High Street at Aldebridge I happened to overhear an amazing conversation. It was between Inspector Parks, that excellent man, and . . ."

"That's enough!" H. M. said sharply.

H. M., moving as softly as his big feet and the majestic figurehead of his corporation would allow, went over to one of the front windows and peered round outside. His cigar had long ago gone dead, and he hurled it into the rain. Heavy thunder rumbled while they waited for him to speak. The storm, which for a time had slackened, was now wheeling back in full gust.

At length H. M. faced round again.

"I dunno!" he muttered, as he surveyed the newcomer very thoughtfully. "You might be a bit useful to us, at that. How much did you hear of what I was sayin'?"

"Sir," answered Mr. Chittering, "everything."

"So!"

"I don't like this place." Mr. Chittering spoke not without a certain dignity. "I didn't want to come. But I could not help myself. Curiosity was stronger than fear. When I heard your voice and made sure it was your voice, I remained very close to your party. I—I don't really wish to meet murderers in real life. I only wish to meet them in books and plays."

"Speakin' of plays," H. M. said sharply, "I'd like you to hear a few words, in front of these two," he nodded towards Dennis and Beryl, "about a play written by Roger Bewlay."

"I am at your service," said Chittering. But his tall, pudgy body stiffened.

"The play!" quavered Beryl. "That awful, unspeak-

247

able, entangling, sticky play that's caused all the trouble!" She appealed to H. M. "Darling, did you know that for a while Dennis and I were afraid we'd got inside the play and were living it?"

"That's not so surprisin', is it? Since the play was written about people that really existed?"

"No. I suppose not. But, thank God, at least we've scotched the ending!"

H. M.'s eyes narrowed.

"How d'ye mean, my wench?"

"Don't you remember? The old doting father, in the play, thinks the central character really *is* Bewlay, and . . . Anyway, we've stopped that. Mr. and Mrs. Herbert have gone on a wild-goose chase; and it can't happen. It can't!"

Then Beryl's tone changed.

"H. M.," she added, "when we were at Alf's pub that night, why did you write Bewlay's initials on the table?"

"Because I guessed," said H. M., "what Bruce Ransom's game really was. And why he was goin' to Aldebridge."

There was a slight stir through the group, a tensing of muscles; none of them could have said why.

"You," H. M. glowered at Dennis, "had told us the whole story about the play and Ransom's proposed expedition to Aldebridge. It confirmed my notion, as I was sayin' a while ago, that the play had probably been written by Bewlay himself. It confirmed my notion that the 'murder' at Torquay was a bit of hoo-ha managed by Bewlay and Mildred Lyons.

"A few days afterwards, when Masters sent me the stuff about Bewlay's early life—the twisty legal tricks!—I was convinced. Meantime, we'd got nothing except the discouragin' news that the only copy of the play-script had been pinched. So I decided, after some more sittin' and thinkin', I'd better go to Aldebridge and take a hand.

"There was already a strong indication of where to look for Bewlay. And something I heard in a pub made me dead sure. But, even presumin' I could prove his identity, what could I do about it? That was where the exquisiteness of this swine's plans stuck me in the seat of the pants like Patrick Cairns's harpoon. The only act I could possibly prove against him was the murder he hadn't committed."

H. M. sniffed, dismally.

He lumbered forward and clamped his hands round the back of the chair, blinking down at it.

"It wouldn't do, y'see. Unless I could think of one more thing—one more thing, as I told Masters!—it was all n.b.g. Somehow, *somehow,* I'd got to think of how he disposed of his real victims' bodies."

"And for the second time, sir," urged Dennis, "how did Bewlay dispose of 'em?"

H. M. raised a strained face.

"It's a funny thing, son. His trick there was almost as ingenious as the fake murder. He had a system."

"A system?"

"Sure. Always the same way. Mass-murderers usually have a system. It was my only hope."

"Another point, if you don't want all of us to go crazy! What did you learn by looking at Bruce's dressing-gown?"

"I learned," H. M. answered carefully, "how Bewlay disposed of the bodies."

"You learned that," asked Beryl, "just from looking at Bruce's dressing-gown?"

"Uh-huh."

Beryl and Dennis exchanged a wild glance. Mr. Chittering, motionless, remained blandly smiling at nothing in particular. H. M. was silent for a time, his head lowered, staring at the chair.

"Meanwhile," he went on, "I'd had a conference with Bruce Ransom. I learned he'd save some appallin'ly revealing pages from the original manuscript, together with the tea-shop wrapping-paper that he said made him suspect Bewlay was in Aldebridge. He told me his side of the business.

"Ransom said he was just about ready to throw in his hand. It was the end of September; he hadn't got any change out of anybody; and people were ready to lynch him. He said the only thing to do now— which he said he'd been too proud to do before, rather fancyin' himself as a detective—was to write to Mildred Lyons and ask her to come down there and identify Bewlay."

Here H. M. raised his head, glanced briefly at Beryl, and looked down again.

"I didn't tell him I could identify Bewlay already. I didn't tell him I thought it was an awful waste of time to get Mildred Lyons: because she was an accomplice of Bewlay and wouldn't give the blighter away. And I was wrong. Burn my soul and body," roared H. M., and shook his fist in the air, "I was so wrong it makes me sick in the stummick to think of it!

"I didn't guess the bitter, burnin', flamin' hatred she had for Bewlay. Oh, no. Trust the old man. I forgot Mildred Lyons. Until it was too late."

And he dropped his hand.

Beryl spoke softly.

"Of course," she said in an offhand tone, "it was on Bruce that Mildred Lyons went to call that night at the Granada. Bruce admits that much himself."

H. M. nodded without answering.

"Mildred Lyons," Beryl rushed on in growing excitement, "worked at that typewriting office in Bedford Street. She was given the play to copy. Even— even after the alterations Bruce made, it reeked of Bewlay because it was written by Bewlay. So she went

250

to Bruce to find out if he knew the author. I knew it! I guessed it! I told Dennis so in the train yesterday!"

Again H. M. nodded.

"I wonder," Beryl said slowly, "whether I was right about anything else?"

"I wonder too," said H. M. He looked up. "Bruce Ransom, as I was tellin' you, wanted to get the Lyons girl to Aldebridge. So he sat down then and there, in my room at the Golden Pheasant Inn, and dashed off a letter to her. Maybe it's sort of significant,"—here H. M. looked very steadily at Horace Chittering— "that he didn't use a typewriter?"

"Is it?" inquired Mr. Chittering. "I really don't follow you."

"Anyway," Dennis interposed, flinging this aside, "Bruce did write to her. She said she'd be here yesterday. Bewlay caught her, and wrung her neck and smothered her to death on the beach . . ."

"Oh, no!" said H. M. very sharply.

From under the roof in this room—sudden, loud, preemptory—issued two heavy knocks.

Dennis, whose nerves were not as steady as he had imagined, nearly jumped out of a crawling skin. They were not alone. It was as though the dead woman herself were claiming their attention. Mr. Chittering was so pale that the reddish patches stood out on his face like a rash.

"That's done it." H. M. spoke in a wooden tone. "It's time we all got downstairs to the cellar."

"For what?"

"Maybe for nothing at all," said H. M. "Maybe for flat failure. On the other hand . . ." His eyes fixed on them. "We'll stand where we stood before: just outside the door of that cellar room. None of you is to move or speak whatever you see or hear. Is that understood?" His listeners were dumb. *"Is that understood?"*

251

They all nodded.

The two knocks were repeated, insistently. H. M. strode towards the door, where he swung around.

"I say. There's just one thing I'd better mention. I haven't mentioned it before, d'ye see."

"Yes?" (Dennis could not afterwards remember who said that.)

"Your friend Ransom," H. M. told them, "is somebody else beside the person you think he is."

And he opened the door, and went out into the dim passage.

Lightning touched the passage, briefly, a pale whip-flick. The storm tore down in one of those deluging bursts which seem to have punctured the sky and opened it like a tank. Stopping by the doorway to the cellar, H. M. faced the others again. But it was not necessary for him to point downwards, or to caution silence.

In the larger of the two cellar rooms there was now a light. It penetrated out, faint and yellow as they looked down, and touched the foot of the stairs between those stone walls. Worst of all, they clearly heard voices.

One was the voice of Bruce Ransom.

The other was the voice of Daphne Herbert. Daphne's voice rose up to them on a note of anguish or entreaty.

"Don't! Don't! Don't!"

"Look at her, Daphne," they heard Bruce's disembodied voice. "That's Mildred Lyons. Let me take the shawl off her head, and you can see the sand in her eyes. That's what happens to women who . . ."

"Don't! Please don't!"

"H. M., you lied to us," said Beryl West.

Dennis felt his knees shaking under him. Beryl's voice was only a whisper. But it was so passionate a whisper, so fiercely articulated, that its clarity pierced

252

out like a cry. Beryl stood with her back to the cellar door, her hands gripping the posts as though she would bar the way down.

"You lied to us," the whisper went on. The lightning through the back window made her lips look black, her eyes as though outlined with mascara. "You deliberately led us in the wrong direction. Bruce *is* Roger Bewlay. He *is* Roger Bewlay. He . . ."

"Get out of the way," whispered H. M.

Beryl jerked away from him, took a step backwards, and nearly pitched down the cellar stairs. H. M.'s big hand caught and held her. They stood in a huddled group, hard-breathing, before H. M. led the way down and the others followed him.

Two seconds later, and from the foot of the stairs they were looking into the larger of the two cellar rooms.

A paraffin lantern, burning with a clear strong flame, stood on a wooden box beside the opposite door to the smaller room. It illuminated, among tall shadows, the low-ceilinged room whose darkened stone walls were scored with whitish bullet-nicks.

The yellow flame of the lantern, too, picked out other details not noticeable before. Scattered straw on the floor, a broken spade and a discarded wagonwheel. A shimmer of rain dancing at the semi-underground windows, dripping with shining sluices down the walls and crawling across a gritty floor.

What should have been a dummy, and still looked like a dummy in grimy gingham, swayed a little as it hung by the neck from the beam in the middle of the room. Its heels were some two feet off the floor.

Bruce Ransom, hatless, in a brown suit, immaculate except for his mud-clogged shoes, stood on one side of that hanging figure with his back to the watchers at the door.

On the other side of the hanging figure—peering past it, her hands behind her back as though she were hiding something—stood Daphne Herbert. They could see her face clearly, the soft line of the cheek and the strange, waiting, listening look of her eyes. Daphne's whole body seemed poised. She wore, open over a flowered summer frock, the same fleecy tan coat she had worn last night.

Two voices went echoing up inside that stone room.

"Come here!"

"I won't!"

Bruce took a step forward, and Daphne a step backward. You could hear the footsteps rasp on a gritty floor. It was then that something, perhaps a flash at the corner of the eye, caught their attention and made them stop. Both swung round towards the opposite door, which led to the small cellar room beyond.

In the doorway, chalk-white but smiling agreeably, stood Jonathan Herbert.

Nobody spoke, not even Mr. Herbert.

He was strongly illuminated by the light of the lantern on its box beside the door. His hands were thrust into the pockets of his Burberry, whose collar was turned up. His eyes, normally pleasant, gleamed from under the down-turned brim of a sodden hat as they moved first to Daphne, then to Bruce, then slowly round the room.

On a pile of straw near the box where the lantern stood, he saw a discarded raincoat which was presumably Bruce's. In a leisurely way—with exaggerated leisureliness, as though he were at his club—Mr. Herbert removed the Burberry, let it drop in straight folds, and threw it on top of the other coat. His hat followed.

Afterwards he walked forwards quickly, his hand

moving to his hip-pocket.

It was Daphne who broke the silence.

"Daddy!" she said. She ran towards him, one hand extended. "Daddy! They're trying to tell me . . ."

Then occurred a shock of transformation.

Mr. Herbert was not even looking at Daphne. He was looking at Bruce. His powerful right hand and arm went out and back with a sweeping viciousness as though he would clear some obstacle from his way. It caught Daphne under the chin; it flung her backwards with a startled cry rising to her lips. But Daphne never uttered that cry, because her head struck a crag of the stone wall. She went down sideways in the dirt and water, and rolled over; they saw her eyes just before she fell.

Mr. Herbert took another step forward, smiling, and kept his eyes fixed on Bruce.

"*You fool!*" said Jonathan Herbert with great distinctness. "*I am Roger Bewlay.*"

20

So the two men stood there, with the wry-necked corpse hanging between them.

A crash of thunder, exploding over the house and shaking it as though with physical attack, made even cellar walls vibrate. It drowned out a few words that were spoken next. But Dennis Foster, with H. M.'s fingers digging into his shoulder to keep him from moving, would not have heard in any case.

Nor would he have moved.

Perhaps, he has admitted afterwards, in the light of so much he had seen and heard but did not understand, he should not have been so dumbfounded. But so it was. Twenty feet ahead of him, moving sideways so as to get a better view of Bruce, stood the man they sought.

Bewlay, a little sleek and fattened by years of good living, a little overlaid by sanctity as squire and J.P. Bewlay, his thumbs hooked in the waistcoat-pockets of his sober grey suit. Bewlay, with his strong face and cleft chin, the engaging eyes under dark eyebrows and grey hair, the ingratiating smile, the manner that inspired confidence and respect.

And Bewlay, just now, with a youthful zest creeping

back into those eyes.

His voice became sharp.

"Did you hear what I said?" he asked, and the pride in his voice was the pride of achievement. "I am Roger Bewlay."

"Yes," said Bruce, without moving. "I know you are."

"What's that?"

"I said I know you are," returned Bruce. "I've known it ever since last night."

"*You* knew," said the other. "*You* knew!"

His voice was so full of utter contempt that it twitched on the edge of laughter.

"Let's face it, Ransom," he said, pleasantly enough. "You and I have hated each other's guts from the first minute we met. We have a number of things to settle between us. Don't you think we ought to settle them?"

"By God, I do!"

"Here and now?"

"Here and now," said Bruce. And, in fact, the hatred between those two men was a palpable force which could be felt. Bruce took a step forward, raising his voice a little. "Have you any idea who *I* am?"

"I'm afraid I haven't. Should I have?"

They couldn't see Bruce's face; only the back of the brown suit and dark hair. Bruce spoke in the same slow, repressed monotone.

"I don't suppose you remember," he said, "a woman named Elizabeth Mosnar. She was one of your victims. Take time off, and spell 'Mosnar' backwards."

"Why should I?"

"All right," said Bruce, "I'll do it for you. 'Mosnar' spelled backwards reads like this. It reads: R-a-n-s-o . . ."

Lightning, a white dazzle, blinded the two little windows, momentarily dimming the lantern-light.

Thunder blotted out the final letter of the name as Bruce spoke. But it was not necessary for anyone to hear.

"Yes," nodded Bruce. "Mosnar is my real name."

"Silly sort of name," said Roger Bewlay, and laughed.

"I quite agree," said Bruce. "Wouldn't look well in lights."

Without any change of tone Bruce went on.

"You thought it was uproariously funny of her to be 'artistic.' You thought it was funny if she cried when she listened to music. Maybe you even thought it was funny to kill her, and put her—where you did put her—when you'd got what pitiful little money she had. She was my sister."

Bruce paused.

"I don't claim to be any great shakes as a brother. Oh, no! I was much too concerned with my own career, making my own way, to bother two hoots about poor old Bet. Even when the police, back in '34, asked me to come down to that Denham cottage they were searching: a little journey from the West Country, mind!"—suddenly Bruce lifted both fists and beat them against his own forehead, as though he would batter out his brains—"I put 'em off, I put 'em off for a week, because I had the lead in some potty little repertory show.

"But I'm older now," Bruce said. "I get the horrors sometimes."

Roger Bewlay, alias Jonathan Herbert, was really fascinated.

His quick, watchful, absorbed gaze never left Bruce's face; his dark eyebrows were raised; the smile was still on his mouth.

Bruce broke out in a fury: "When you sent me your play . . ."

"Ah!"

"I knew it was you. I knew it from the account of the second murder. My sister's murder."

"Ah!"

"I was going to get you. So help me God, I was going to get you. My first idea was to come here and investigate. Then Beryl West gave me a better idea: to pretend to *be* you, and make you betray yourself."

"Which you didn't," said Bewlay, not without complacence. Again he hooked his thumbs in his waistcoat pockets, the very picture of a solid and successful business man. "Which you didn't. And neither did the police."

"You so-and-so," shouted Bruce, using a term seldom heard in society either polite or impolite, "don't you realize Sir Henry Merrivale had you taped to start with?"

Bewlay merely smiled and looked interested. But his eyes were growing congested; he had not liked that term.

"Go on, my dear chap," he suggested.

"Old H. M. knew where to look for you, even before he got here. He asked me once, as I expect he's asked others, what Bewlay WOULD do when Bewlay'd stopped killing women for their money eleven years ago. I didn't see then. But I see now, after he told me the whole story late last night.

"You'd had your fling of murder. The police were after you. You'd killed a girl named Andrée Cooper . . ."

"Andrée!" repeated Bewlay, and he rubbed his hands together and his eyes moved slowly round the room. "You're bringing back old memories."

"Am I?"

"I haven't thought of Andrée in years. No, that's not true. Say months. Say months!"

And his eyes flickered over his shoulder, briefly, at

260

Daphne lying huddled beside the wall.

Bruce sprang forward.

"Let her alone," Bewlay said. "My dear girl isn't really hurt. She's better out of this, until you and I have settled matters." His eyes grew greedy. "Go on, my dear chap. Tell me more about myself!"

"You'd just discovered, after being afraid of women half your life," as Bruce said this, Bewlay's eyes did change, "that any woman—any particularly silly woman, that is—was yours for the asking. You didn't need to kill 'em, did you, for a potty couple of hundred quid? It wasn't shrewd. It wasn't thrifty, and you might get hanged. What would you do? Why, you'd *marry money*.

"And that's what you did. I remember telling my friends you were only a footling J.P. and would-be country squire; it was your wife who had all the money. You got the Old Hall, and thousands of acres, and a doting wife. But look at you!"

Bewlay cast a glance down over himself, again with considerable complacency. He smiled.

"You like to pretend you're middle-aged," snarled Bruce. "That's a part of the gag. That's because your hair went grey very early. But anybody who sees you beside your wife—sees you for a minute!—ought to notice your face is far younger than hers, even when she's only forty-eight.

"And you overdid it—God, how you over did it!—in something else. Whenever you talked about me, you instinctively couldn't keep away from references to actors or the stage. If I'd been a better psychologist, I'd have seen it myself. What's more, after I'd given a little lecture on how easy it was to strangle people, you went rushing about telling everybody it was the most devilish thing since you saw Richard Mansfield play *Jekyll and Hyde*.

"Mansfield did that show at the Lyceum in '88. A baby couldn't think you were seventy years old. But I, the damn fool, *I* swallowed it.

"You slipped again, badly, on the very first night Sir Henry Merrivale got to Aldebridge. In the bar at the Golden Pheasant: remember? Chittering said he'd seen an item in the paper that Bruce Ransom might do a play about Bewlay. You said: 'He can't do a play if he hasn't got a manuscript.'

"I can testify, and so can Dennis Foster, the theft of that script from the typewriting office was a dead secret. Not a word in the Press; everybody concerned sworn to keep quiet. But Bewlay knew about it,"— Bruce flung the words out—"because I'd written to the author and said there might have to be changes, but I was sending the script to Ethel Whitman's to be copied.

"Bewlay knew about it. Bewlay got scared. Bewlay broke into that office, and thought he got the whole script. Whereas . . ."

Both men were moving now, on their toes. The lantern-light threw huge, distorted shadows on them swaying across walls and floor.

"*I* didn't learn any of this," Bruce said.

"How very unfortunate," said Roger Bewlay.

"Because I was the outcast. I was the pariah they threw stones at. I didn't even know Daphne wasn't your real daughter, though Chittering or any of the gossips could have told me. I kow-towed to you. I humbled myself in front of you. I even let you hit me in the face . . ."

"A pleasure, I assure you."

Hatred was now flaming brighter than the lantern, thicker than the tumult of the storm round the house. It hissed like the raindrops inside the windows.

"It is funny, isn't it?" asked Bruce. "It *is* funny. All the time I was trying to get the goods on you, everybody

262

thought you were trying to get the goods on me."

"I have a knack," said Bewlay with perfect seriousness, "of arranging things like that."

"Have you?"

"Yes."

"Did you arrange it, for instance, that Daphne should steal your portable typewriter—I told my friends so last night—and lend it to me? *That the very typewriter on which that play was written has been in my room the whole time?*"

There was no reply.

"As for Daphne . . ."

"Well?"

"Did you arrange it," asked Bruce, "for Daphne to fall in love with me?"

At last, at long last, Bruce had said something which transformed his smiling companion: which made the fingers twitch, and altered the face and the eyes as a pattern is altered.

"*I* couldn't guess," said Bruce, "why you hung over Daphne like that. Why you kept pressing her hands and breathing down her neck. Why *my* turning up on the scene did so much to you.

"You married Daphne's mother ten years ago. You watched Daphne grow up—into what she is. You want her; she's got into your vitals. You can't forget your old habits. You daren't touch her. You daren't treat her as anything except a daugther, because you might endanger a cushy life. But you want her. You want her. You want her."

A heavier gust drove at the grated windows, scattering raindrops wide. It made the body of Mildred Lyons, with dusty shawl-covered head and gingham dress, swing back and forth amid grotesque, flying shadows across walls and ceiling.

"I ought to know," Bruce said.

"*You* know?" Bewlay repeated huskily. His chest rose and fell. He had to clear his throat. His eyes, glittering, were fixed unwaveringly on Bruce.

"What scares me," said Bruce in a kind of horror, "is that deep down inside I'm a damned egotist like you. I never killed anybody. I never even wanted to *hurt* anybody, though that's what I'm always doing to the people who like me. I mean well, and never get anywhere with it. But I can understand what's going on in that crazy brain of yours."

"Crazy, did you say?"

"You want her. You want her. You want her . . ."

"Stop that!"

"Then you'd kill her, as you killed Andrée Cooper."

"As a matter of fact," said Bewlay, "you're quite right."

And his right hand moved to his hip-pocket.

It came away again, and stretched out so as to show the neat cuff concealing something in the palm and partly in the sleeve. It was a thin half of handle, the handle of a very large clasp-knife. He touched a button, and the blade clicked open.

"About that settlement of ours . . . ?" he suggested.

"Come on," said Bruce.

"Don't you mind the knife?"

"Come *on*," shouted Bruce.

Bruce was frantic with rage, his judgment beclouded. The watchers could tell that from the very way he moved his shoulders and hands. Bewlay began to edge sideways—but very, very slowly, his boot-soles scraping on grit—as though he were circling. On the floor near the opposite door, Daphne Herbert suddenly writhed and moaned.

If Daphne got up at this moment . . .

Dennis Foster jumped forward. H. M.'s heavy hand clamped on his shoulder; and, startlingly, Beryl seized his other arm. Dennis, at a quick glance, would never have recognized the imaginative, fastidious Beryl. All her soul, as she twisted her body from side to side, seemed to be concentrated on sending a telepathic message to Bruce.

"Get him," it seemed to be saying. "Get him! Get him! Get him!"

Bewlay's voice struck out of that stone jug.

"When I was a young lad," he said, edging a few inches sideways, "I used to be pretty good at handling one of these." He held the knife loosely; its blade flashed by lantern-light. "I want to see if I've forgotten."

"Come *on,*" said Bruce. "What's delaying you?"

"Plenty of time," said Bewlay, with the breath whistling in his nostrils. He edged a few inches farther. "Tell me some more about myself."

"What the hell are you talking about?"

"Do you have any idea you were ever a danger to *me?*"

"I gave you some pretty unpleasant moments, didn't I?"

"Not that I'm aware of."

"You knew I was Bruce Ransom. You guessed I was there after Bewlay. You didn't think I knew you were the man who sent the play, but you couldn't be sure. I couldn't prove you were guilty of murder with that play; but I could upset your cushy life. It worried you when you went to the police about me, and they only laughed: it might all be a police-trap against you. But your conceit held up very well. The first time you got into a flat spin was yesterday evening."

"Why yesterday evening?"

(Bewlay was edging forward now.)

"When you and Mrs. Herbert and Daphne got back from London in the afternoon . . . do you remember?"

"Perhaps I do. Tell me!"

(Still farther forward.)

"Daphne ran out to the Leather Boot to see me. You followed her in Daphne's car. It was the first time you'd ever been in my sitting-room. You heard my impersonation of Bewlay was apparently all a gag, and realized I hadn't got any suspicions of you. You were so relieved, sheer relieved, that you went crackers and swung one at my face. But a few minutes later it all changed. Because, on my table, you saw your own portable typewriter, *with your name-tag attached.*

"That wasn't all you saw, either. The table drawer was wide open. Inside were those typewritten pages from the original script. You were so petrified that Daphne had to speak to you twice before you woke up."

"Clever of you!" said Bewlay.

(Still farther forward.)

"It wasn't clever."

"No?"

"I only saw it when the old geezer with the spectacles put it together for me. I hadn't even taken the cover off that typewriter, as yet. The only two letters I've written while I've been here, one to Beryl West and one to Mildred Lyons, were both written by hand. But all I had to do was type out a couple of lines on that machine, and compare 'em with the sheets in the drawer, and I couldn't help knowing who wrote the play.

"That made you sick enough. But you were sick already. Because, on the way to the Leather Boot, you killed Mildred Lyons . . ."

"Look out!" Somebody's voice screamed it, piercing and shrill. And Bruce himself woke up just as Bewlay jumped.

Bruce had undoubtedly been expecting an overarm stab, a lift and flash. What followed nearly finished him. The five-inch blade, whetted to a hair-edge of sharpness, jerked upwards in an underarm slash that should have laid open his stomach.

The watchers in the doorway couldn't see what happened. Some eye-movement must have telegraphed the direction of the knife. They heard heavy cloth rip in the same instant that Bruce jumped backwards, shifted his weight, and let drive with his left fist.

The blow was a staggerer, full shoulder-weight behind it. It caught Roger Bewlay between the eyes. It flung him backwards, six-broken-kneed paces, to bump into the hanging figure and set that figure swinging wildly as Bewlay lurched past it.

Bruce was after him in the same flash. Yet not for a second did Bewlay lose his footing. He was waiting, smiling and alert, a red patch spreading in ruin underneath the skin round the eyes and up the forehead. His knife-hand moved, slippery and incalculable. Bruce made the mistake of trying to grab that wrist as the knife came up again. His fingers slipped; Bruce himself reeled as he had to leap back again, and his vicious right-cross missed Bewlay's head by inches.

Bewlay laughed.

Then both of them backed away, panting. They began to shuffle, with short gritty-sounding footsteps, and circle round that swaying figure. Bewlay took a step to the left, Bruce took a step to the left as well. Bewlay to the left, Bruce to the left.

Five seconds, ten seconds, fifteen seconds . . .

The watchers could see Bruce's face now, his eyes glazed. There was a grotesque vertical slit in his waistcoat, from abdomen to breast-bone, through which the shirt bulged. Bruce's hand closed over it as though it were an open wound.

His voice went high.

"Are you some kind of damn Dago, or what are you? Can't you throw away that knife, and . . ."

"Ah! So you're afraid! I thought you would be."

"Come *on,*" said Bruce. "No, stop a bit. I think I'll come in and get *you.*"

It was now Bruce who moved forward, among huge circling shadows. He moved his head to the left, and moved it to the right. His elbows were crooked, his open fingers like tentacles.

"You were saying," panted Bewlay, "something about Mildred Lyons."

"What are you trying to do? Get me off guard again?"

"As though I could!—E-easy! Don't run in on it!"

"I'm not going to."

"Mildred Lyons?"

"This is Mildred Lyons," answered Bruce. He stopped by the hooded corpse, touched one leg, and steadied it. "She was your stooge, and you killed her. The police know all about that fake murder at Torquay."

Bewlay stopped motionless.

"That's a lie!"

"Is it? Then how did *I* happen to hear about it?"

"Mildred Lyons . . ."

"She read the play too. She saw me at the Granada Theatre, and admitted she'd once known you. She came down here yesterday, to see me and identify you, in the same train with Dennis Foster and Beryl West. But she lagged behind 'em at Seacrest Halt. She was in pretty much of a flap herself, and didn't want to be seen or talk to anybody. Have I got something that interests you *now?*"

"No. I don't think so."

But the knife-blade had ceased to draw little glittering patterns in the air. Bruce saw it.

"My friends began talking to some other blokes, Sir Henry Merrivale, and Chief Inspector Masters,"—here the blade made a savage flash—"and a golf pro named MacFergus. They seemed planted there for ever. So Mildred Lyons sneaked along the road towards Aldebridge, far along to a place where she could cross the golf links to the Leather Boot without being noticed.

"In the meantime, at Aldebridge, you'd got into Daphne's car . . ."

"That's a lie!"

"You told us so yourself."

"What if I did?"

"And," said Bruce, with his eyes and voice growing more hypnotic, "you drove out along the road that runs past the Leather Boot. On the way there, just as it was getting dark, you saw Mildred Lyons crossing the golf course.

"You were all alone there, you two. You stopped the car and got out. You waited for her. You caught her," Bruce's vulturish pounce of a gesture described it, "and you caught her *where?*

"Not on the beach, as I thought. That beach is shingle: coarse gravel and pebbles. There'd be some rough sand on the beach, but not the fine white sand that was on her face: yes, and on my handkerchief after I wiped off her face! That fine white stuff is found where? In the sand-hazard of a bunker on a golf course. Look here at the eyes!"

And he reached up and twitched the shawl off the dead woman's head.

It was when Bruce started to swing this dead woman round that Beryl uttered a little whimpering cry. Dennis Foster put her face against his chest and held her head down. Horace Chittering, behind them both, was beyond speech.

"You put her body," Bruce's voice went on, "in the dickey-seat of the car. You drove to the Leather Boot. And you planted the poor devil—on me; where else? I'd gone swimming and you could see me on the beach. But you made one bad howler. Or was it only bad luck?"

"Luck," said Bewlay. "Luck!"

(Bruce, his hand behind his back, was edging forward.)

"Her face was all over dampish sand: remember?"

"Do I?"

"I wiped it off. I can swear, and so can Dennis, this woman's face was perfectly clean when we put her . . . where?"

(Still farther forward. But the knife was moving again.)

"Tell me about myself! Tell me about myself! Tell me about myself!"

"In the same blasted car that had been used to bring her there. But that's what did for you."

"Is it?"

"I noticed, in a dumb-Jane kind of way, and the Old Maestro says Dennis noticed there was a crust of sand on the red-leather upholstery in an outline of Mildred Lyons's forehead and cheek. It couldn't have come there—*then*. It came there when you drove the car to the hotel with her body inside."

(Still farther forward.)

Out of the corner of his eye Dennis saw a movement of a flowered cloth and a draggled coat. Daphne, looking dazed-eyed and very sick, had crawled to her knees in the grit and water; she was trying to get to her feet by clutching at the rough stone wall.

She did not even notice Roger Bewlay or Bruce Ransom, any more than they noticed her. Their voices now sounded with inhuman loudness; and that, the watchers realized, was because the storm had begun to die away. Inside that stone jug, words themselves leaped like attackers.

"You did kill 'em, didn't you?" Bruce demanded.

"Kill who?"

"My sister. And those other women. Or are you too afraid of me to admit it?"

"Afraid of *you?*" said Bewlay. "Yes, I killed them! And what about it? You'll never prove it, because you don't know what I did with them."

"Oh, don't we?" yelled Bruce. "That's why it's poetic justice. They're hidden in . . ."

Then Bruce was upon him.

Bruce's hand darted out from behind his back, whirling up something that rose like a black shadow in lantern-light. It was the dusty, close-woven shawl that had hooded a dead woman; and Bruce flung it straight at Bewlay's head and face.

He might as well have tried to snare a rearing cobra. It gained only a split-second's grace. Bewlay's left hand flung away the shawl. With his right he stabbed sideways for Bruce's ribs. Bruce's left arm went straight down, rigid as iron, and caught the driving arm between wrist and elbow like a fencer's parry.

Then there were three separate sounds as Bruce upreared at close quarters: right to the point of the chin, left low to the body, and right again, shatteringly, to the point of the chin.

"Got him!" Bruce panted. "Got him!"

But he hadn't.

Somebody—it may have been Mr. Chittering— uttered a despairing curse. Roger Bewlay slithered backwards, fell heavily and very nearly on the point of his own knife, kicked out, gave one gasp, and bounced to his feet like an India-rubber cat. The knife still moved. Even gasping, Bewlay laughed.

This was the point at which Sir Henry Merrivale,

tapping Dennis on the shoulder and nodding, stepped out into the room. Dennis followed him.

"That'll be enough, son," H. M. said to Bewlay. "You'd better put that knife down, or the three of us will have to sit on your head."

Bruce Ransom turned a frantic face.

"Keep back!" he was raving. "This is my job. Keep back! Won't *anything* put the swine down?"

"No," said Bewlay.

He had retreated, circling, until he was standing with his back to the door of the smaller room. He smiled with difficulty, after those jaw-punches; his chin was cut like Bruce's knuckles; strange colours, as the yellow lantern-light fell strongly on his face, bloomed round eyes and forehead like the effect of a mask.

He was within three feet of Daphne Herbert. But he did not see her.

"Put *me* down?" he said.

"Want to go on with it?" Bruce suggested softly.

"By all means."

"Get back!" howled H. M. "I tell you there's . . ."

"Sorry, Maestro. This is a personal issue."

"This time," said Bewlay, "I'm going for your face. I warn you."

The knife gleamed. Bewlay glanced sideways—and saw Daphne.

All movement, even the movement of breathing, seemed to stop inside that room. H. M. and Dennis, who had been moving forward one on each side of Bruce, halted where they stood. With the tumult of the storm drained away to a splashing trickle, it was a silence that could be felt.

"My dear!" said Roger Bewlay.

His expression, as he addressed a terror-stricken Daphne, was ineffably tender and touching. He even seemed to grow taller. Out of the indulgent father, as

272

you may see one image take form through another, emerged briefly the old, ingratiating, all-conquering Bewlay of a dozen years before.

"I've decided," he confided, "to go away. I'd decided it even before I came up here this afternoon. New places, new roles, what shall I say: new pleasure? Of course you'll go with me?"

"Go with you?" exclaimed a staring Bruce. "Go with you? Why, she was the one who set this police-trap to start with!"

"Quiet!" said Sir Henry Merrivale.

But the damage was done.

"What's . . . that?"

Daphne, her brown-gold hair tumbled, her dress and coat black-stained, stood flat against that wall as though she were trying to press back through it. The grey eyes were still dazed, but her breast rose and fell convulsively. Roger Bewlay had taken one of her hands; with infinite soothing gentleness, he was stroking it with the hand whose thumb gripped the knife.

"Listen, my murdering friend," said Bruce Ransom, completely blind with rage. "Daphne was never in love with me, though she didn't know it herself and I didn't know how *I* felt until . . . Anyway, you're ready for Broadmoor. Daphne was afraid to have her mother spend another day in the house with you. That 'I love you' note she wrote me was only a part of the gag to get you here. Do you understand now?"

"I understand," said Bewlay.

His knife flashed for the last time.

It was for the last time because, even before he spoke, an arm emerged from the dark doorway behind him and fastened in almost leisurely fashion round his neck. Another had expertly brought Bewlay's wrist round behind his back, bending up the arm in a way that

273

distorted Roger Bewlay's mouth and sent the knife rattling down on stone.

Bewlay was carried backwards through the door, not gently, by two police-constables. Chief Inspector Masters pushed past, followed by a burly man in the uniform of an inspector.

"Hurrum!" said Masters, whose colour was far from ruddy and who avoided H. M.'s eye. "I'm afraid we're—hurrum!—a bit late."

"So," breathed Sir Henry Merrivale in a shivering kind of voice. "You're afraid you're a bit late, hey? You're afraid you're a bit late?"

"Now don't go and fly off the handle, sir!" roared Masters, himself infected by the general madness. "We got bogged. This storm's swept away half the roads. I never did like this fool stunt anyway; and it's not necessary now." He paused. "We've had a phone-call from Crowborough."

H. M.'s hands dropped to his sides.

"Crowborough," he repeated. "So! Angela Phipps?"

"Yes, sir. At least, it's only a—" Masters glanced quickly at Daphne, and coughed. "Anyway, we'll get the Home Office Pathologist to see what's left."

"Where I said?"

"Oh, ah. Just where you said."

H. M. drew a deep breath, and turned away. He removed his dented bowler. Across his malignant face passed a shadow of relief which would presently become vocal in such an outburst of vituperation, such a torrent of profanity and vile obscenities, as could not have been matched by half a dozen loud-speakers. But not yet. Not yet!

He touched Dennis's arm.

"Son," H. M. said gently, "this afternoon you kept hammerin' at me with a certain question. And I couldn't tell you (burn me, I couldn't!) because it might

274

only 'a been a wool-gathering notion. The question being: what was so almighty interestin' about Ransom's dressing-gown?"

"Yes?" said Dennis.

Bruce began to laugh, rather shakily, and checked himself. Beryl West came softly into the room and went to Bruce's side.

"Do you remember," asked H. M., "where the dressing-gown was?"

"Where was it? It was lying across a corner of the settee, where Bruce threw it down!"

"Uh-huh. And what was projectin', very plain to be seen, out of the pocket of that dressing-gown?"

"It was a handkerchief!" Beryl cried out, before Dennis could answer. "Bruce's handkerchief. Speckled all over with fine white sand."

H. M. nodded.

Again he drew a deep breath.

"That's right. Donald MacFergus had just finished givin' us a lecture to show there was no possible place you could hide a body on a golf course without any traces of diggin' or tearin' or tramplin'. It was that word trampling that did it. Because there *is* a place.

"You can bury a body in the earth, three or four feet down, underneath the thick layer of sand in the sand-trap of a bunker. And ten thousand golfers can trample that sand to blazes, because it's there to be trampled, and yet swear not a single thing on the whole course had been disturbed. And nobody will ever know."

From the dark little room next to them, where a certain person was being held by two police-constables, issued a single, unearthly, terrifying scream. Roger Bewlay was no longer smiling.

EPILOGUE

A clear sky, luminous and pearl-coloured, showed outside the windows of the House of Nerves as twilight drew in. The air, after that storm, would have had a clean freshness if it had not been for the omnipresence of mud, the atmosphere of mud, the exhalation of mud breathing up from miles of ground like the steam from a mud-bath.

In the ground-floor room, to the right of the front door, three persons waited for the word to go back to their hotel.

Bullet-riddled, infinitely dreary in that soft clear light, the room seemed to have imposed its mood on two of the occupants. Bruce Ransom heavy-eyed, sat in one of the wooden chairs and gloomily contemplated the floor. Dennis Foster, unnoticed, like a piece of furniture, except when his help was needed for some practical matter, stood there with the blackest of thoughts.

But all this had no effect on Beryl, in a borrowed raincoat much too large for her. Beryl was utterly happy. Her voice rang out tenderly.

"Bruce, you great gawk!"

"All right, all right!"

"You're an absolute *fool!*"

"Angel-face, how many times in my life have I got to admit that?"

"You might have been killed!"

Bruce's response to this was not very romantic.

"You're telling me?" he inquired, pointing to the ragged slash in his waistcoat through which shirt-bulges protruded. "That swine nearly opened me like a tin of sardines. There's a walloping great cut in the shirt, and I think the under-vest too." He felt at it. Quick interest gleamed in his eyes. "By hell, I wonder if it got through and nicked the skin? Let's see."

And, hastily unbuttoning his waistcoat, he began hauling his shirt out of his trousers.

"Bruce, for heaven's sake stop undressing!"

"But I was only . . . oh, all right!" Bruce complied, and again glowered at the floor. With the stone-bruise at his temple, the graze across the cheek, the dried blood on his knuckles, he would have been sufficiently startling if at that moment he had walked into the Savoy Grill or the Ivy. "I say! Beryl!"

"Yes?"

"Look here, angel. What I mean is . . . can't you give us a kiss?"

Dennis Foster, very weary but trying to do what he believed was the tactful thing, turned towards the door. Bruce's embarrassed voice stopped him.

"Oi! Dennis! Wait a minute!"

"What is it?"

"Look here, old boy. I expect you still don't understand why I wanted to hoick that body out of the hotel last night and hide it?"

"No, I'm hanged if I do!"

"Well," acknowledged Bruce moodily, "maybe my original idea wasn't very good. And," he avoided Dennis's eye, "I played a filthy trick on you to get you

278

to help me. I mean, suggesting that you . . . I mean, about Daphne . . ."

"That's all right. Forget it."

"No, but look!" Bruce seized Beryl's hand. "I want to tell you both what happened, because it's got such an important bearing on the whole business when—when things changed.

"I was all worked up then. I still hadn't got any idea who Bewlay was. I was determined to prove to Daphne and her father . . . her father; think of that! . . . to prove I could nab Bewlay. That's even aside from—the other reason."

"Bruce." Beryl spoke softly, her head averted. "I don't like to talk about it. But why couldn't you have *told* us one of those women was your sister? Wasn't it carrying the great detective's silence too far?"

Bruce's nostrils dilated.

"That wasn't the reason," he said. "I didn't want anybody to know I'd acted like such a hound when Bet disappeared.

"Anyway," he flung this aside, "I knew I was beaten unless I could get Bewlay within the next twenty-four hours. I could only do it by a trick. My idea was for Dennis and me pinch Daphne's car and come out here. Everybody would know, later, the car had been taken. It'd get about (it always does) we'd been driving towards the battle-school. But nobody would wonder *except the murderer*.

"The murderer had planted that body on me. He'd get the wind up when it wasn't found in my bedroom. He'd wonder what I did with it. This is a very big area; but there's only one of these trick houses. Nobody *except the murderer* would think to connect a body with a stuffed dummy, or notice a body even if he happened to be looking at it. But the murderer would come out here. And I'd be waiting. We did a play once,

279

called *The Green Shadow* . . ."

"A play!" groaned Dennis. "A play!"

"What's wrong with that, old boy?"

"Never mind; go on."

"So I hared off on my own when you held up. I did it.
Only I'd forgotten something. It's all very well to say
you'll sit, with folded arms, in the spookiest place on
earth, for a night and a day and maybe a night again.
But—"

"But what?" asked Beryl.

"I hadn't got any food," Bruce answered simply,
"and I hadn't got any cigarettes."

"So you decided to come back to the hotel?"

"Yes. I walked back. I'd got that car out here without
breaking my own or anybody else's neck, God knows
how; but I couldn't risk it again. It's a good thing I
didn't, because by then the rozzers were after me.

"By the time I got back to the hotel it was well past
ten o'clock. There was a party in full blast downstairs.
Nobody heard me when I sneaked up the outside stairs.
And I found my sitting-room looking as though the
German army had been through it. You understand
what had happened?"

Dennis nodded. He saw only too clearly.

"Jonathan Herbert," Dennis said bitterly, "Jonathan
Herbert, let's call him that, knew he had to get rid of the
manuscript-sheets and his own typewriter. He couldn't
just take the typewriter away; that would call attention
to it. So he smashed it to scrap-metal, letters un-
recognizable, with a hatchet. He had to wreck the
rest of the room to conceal that."

Bruce Ransom pressed his hands to his temples.

"Dennis," Bruce said, after a pause, "do you
remember a note I typed for you, just before I hared
away in the car? 'Sorry; can't wait.' And stuck it in the
carriage of the typewriter?"

"Do I remember!"

Bruce shivered.

"I didn't notice anything at the time. I was too excited. It was the first time I'd ever touched that typewriter. But afterwards, when I came back . . ."

"Well?"

"On the floor, in the wreckage, was that note I wrote you. And beside it was the one sheet from the script of the play."

"But, Bruce!" Beryl's fingers had tightened on his shoulder. "How could it have been there? Herbert, or Bewlay, didn't get the typewritten pages, because they weren't there! H. M. had taken 'em away beforehand!"

"Not all of 'em," said Dennis, staring at the past. "Don't you remember, Beryl? H. M. told us this morning he'd dropped one sheet on the floor. And— wait a minute: I've got it! There was a strong draught through those rooms when Bruce ran out and left the door open; the floor was scattered with papers anyway. When Herbert got there, and found the drawer empty, he thought the rest of the papers were letters. You were saying, Bruce?"

"I found those two pieces of paper," Bruce said, "side by side."

He swallowed hard, his eye wild and uncertain.

"I didn't have to be an expert. I'd pored over Bewlay's script till I knew every crankiness of the machine that wrote it: the 'w' above the line, the 'o' with too much dirt in it, the whole bag of tricks. So I just stood there, in that wreckage, and laughed and laughed and laughed like a maniac myself.

"Mind you, I *couldn't* believe that Old Man Herbert, the dirty swine, was—! But all sorts of funny bits began to come back to me. Especially his conduct towards Daphne. So I tore out of there. I phoned H. M. at the Golden Pheasant in Aldebridge. He told me to come straight there. And in his room, in front of that fellow Masters, H. M. told me the whole story."

Dennis wanted to turn his eyes away; wanted, in sheer embarrassment, to get away from there. Bruce Ransom was horribly shaken by a very real emotion.

"Look here," Bruce began, and stopped.

"I suppose," Bruce went on, "there's a time in every man's life when he gets the power that the giftie gie'd us. He sees himself, and his own soul, for sixpennyworth of God-help-us.

"I'd never been in love with Daphne. I was playing a part. Once the whole show was shot to blazes like a glass flower-vase, with the news that her jealous stepfather was Roger Bewlay, I felt half-sick.

"Listen, Beryl. All the time H. M. was talking, every second of the time, the only thing I could think about was you. Of you. And our past. Of what we felt. Of what we'd done and hadn't done. And I knew . . ."

"Bruce! Please!"

"I knew," said Bruce, "there was only one person for me. Or ever would be. Would you like me to get down on my knees?"

Beryl looked at him.

"Oh, Bruce, you—you—!" She broke out in a kind of fury, as though seeking the worst possible epithet. Then, abruptly, Beryl turned her back to them and walked to the window.

"Sorry," muttered Bruce.

"G-go on," Beryl said unsteadily, without turning round.

"In H. M.'s hotel-room, you see, Old Sleuth and Masters and I planned the campaign."

"You mean to nab Jonathan Herbert?" Dennis asked.

"Yes. H. M., in my sitting-room hours before—he

says you were there, Dennis—had compared that typewriter with the manuscript-sheets. You'd told him 'Herbert' had been there, with the table drawer wide open to show 'em. That's when H. M. realized this blighter was up the pole, a lunatic with designs on Daphne; and what the devil could we do about it?"

"H. M. had got his inspiration about the sand-hazards on a golf course, yes. But it might be wrong, or it might take weeks to prove. What's-his-name, Chittering, suspected there was something funny . . ."

"Chittering?" exclaimed Beryl.

"Well, Chittering knew from the very first I was Bruce Ransom. Trust him! He even kidded 'em about it in the bar at the Golden Pheasant. But he thought it was a grand joke, an excellent joke, to pretend there was a murderer here, until . . ."

"Until," supplied Dennis, "it came out publicly—in the lounge of the Leather Boot last night—that Bewlay really *was here?*"

Bruce nodded.

"That Bewlay was here, yes, and had written a play. Crikey!" said Bruce. "Enter Caesar, in nightgown. Chittering remembered 'Herbert' had told a lot of whoppers about plays he couldn't have seen. Chittering remembered 'Herbert' had borrowed that famous book on writing plays. He remembered 'Herbert' had been pouring poison into everybody's ear about me, not forgetting the ear of Commander Renwick: who's a decent bloke, really, only with a Thing about murderers ever since he was attacked with a hatchet in Port Said. Old Daddy Chittering was so scared he downed half the booze at the Leather Boot. But he couldn't *help* us, don't you see?

"So it was suggested, in fact . . . well, *I* suggested, that I could make 'Herbert' give himself away. But we

283

had to have Daphne as bait."

"That came out of a play too, I suppose?" inquired Dennis.

"No, old boy! I swear it was my own idea! But it was the hardest part of the whole business. I climbed in to Daphne's window in the middle of the night—"

"You've got a habit of doing that," observed Beryl.

"Well, how else could I get to her without that swine knowing? I was afraid she'd scream the place down. But I persuaded her to put on something, and slip out of the back door to the summer-house, for a talk with Chief Inspector Masters and Old Sexton Blake himself.

"She took a lot of convincing," said Bruce in an awed voice. "But I'll say this for the kid. She's a game chicken."

"You never thought," asked Dennis, "how *she'd* feel about it? After thinking you were in l—"

"I'm sorry, old boy! Only . . ."

"Never mind! Go on!"

"There's not much else. Beryl nearly dished us—"

"*I* did?"

"By trying to send 'Herbert' to London for that broadcast. Of course he never intended to take his wife along; that was only more of the old domestic hypocrisy, for which curse his soul to fire. Fortunately, there wasn't a train until three o'clock in the afternoon.

"We were giving him time, you see, to get really worked up to a pitch where his judgment went to pieces. Inspector Parks, the local man (and an old friend of 'Herbert's', if you've ever heard him say so?) stopped him in the High Street with some very, very confidential information.

"The police had learned that *I* had hidden a dead woman's body here in this house: which was true.

They'd learned, Parks said, I was hiding here with Daphne, waiting for dark to clear out. Just before dark, Parks said, they were coming up here to get me.

"You could bet, as sure as guns, Bewlay would be here before 'em. Daphne and I were to be at a vantage-point along the road up here. As soon as we saw the swine coming, we were to slip into this house by the outside cellar stairs—through that other room—knock twice with a broom-handle on the ceiling of a coal-cellar at the front, and put on an act for his benefit."

Bruce Ransom got to his feet.

"We couldn't tell you!" he burst out. "You were both too what-is-it, emotionally concerned. You'd have given the show away. Look, Beryl! Even when I climbed up to *your* window before daylight . . ."

"Who cares?" said Beryl, turning round from the window. "Who cares?" And she held out her hands to him.

Presently Beryl said: "Dennis! Where are *you* going?"

"Only out to where the cars are parked. I'll see you later."

"Dennis." Beryl hesitated, her eyes shining oddly. "Where's Daphne?"

"Daphne,"—he spread out his fingers and examined them—"is with H. M. She's undoubtedly had a bad shock. I don't think this is quite the time to intrude. I'll see you later."

"Dennis!" she called after him.

But he left Beryl, and Bruce, and the plywood German officer who still leaned crookedly behind the table. He went into the gutted passage, and then out the front door into a sea of mud under soft, clear light that was darkening with purple tinges towards the east.

Go your ways, he was thinking. Go your ways,

stuffed shirt! Go your ways—what was Beryl's term for him, once at the Granada Theatre?—'sludgy slow-coach'! And that was true; there could be no denying it. He would never be anything else. Go your ways, sludgy slow-coach, on a road of mud like this!

Not that it mattered, of course. To-morrow was Sunday: he would have to make sure of the trains, so as to be early at the office on Monday morning. The Parfitter case was coming up, and those tricky title-deeds of Bob Engel's. There was nothing like work. And yet (the thought wormed through with angry, foolish pain) if only Providence had given him the power, as it had given Bruce Ransom the power, to charm a certain girl as Bruce had charmed her . . .

"Hello," said Daphne Herbert. She was walking beside him, her eyes fixed on the ground.

"Hello," said Dennis, trying to show no signs of the violent start that had brought his heart into his throat. He looked straight ahead as they walked.

"I'm not, you know," observed Daphne.

"Not—?"

"Upset. About their catching him."

"Oh. Yes. I see."

"I never was at all upset," said Daphne. "It was a relief, rather. I've always been a bit frightened of him, though I couldn't have told why. Everything that's happened," she added slowly, "has been a relief."

They walked a few more steps in silence.

"H. M.," continued Daphne, still with her gaze concentrated on the ground, "said I was to be sure to tell you that. He—he said you probably wouldn't recognize it, if somebody didn't."

"H. M.?" Dennis repeated blankly.

Daphne gestured ahead.

In the broad tank-rutted road, curving past what had once been the front garden of the farmhouse, stood the large and very ancient motor-car in which Dennis had travelled there. Its top was now down, its side-curtains gone.

At the wheel, in awful majesty, disdainfully above all human emotion, sat a barrel-shaped figure in an oilskin waterproof and a dented bowler hat. As perhaps a concession to less than Olympian aloofness, this figure was smoking a black cigar.

"He says," faltered the girl, "that, since he's got nothing better to do, he might as well drive us back." Then Daphne rushed on, as though to blot out what had already been said. "He says he's an awfully good driver, the best in the world. He says he won the Grand Prix motor-car race in 1903; and could show me the medal, too, only a goat ate it. He says . . ."

Daphne paused. Dennis Foster, that sedate young man, had suddenly swung round and gripped her by the shoulders.

"You're real," said Dennis, tightening his grip. "You're *real*."

"Yes, I'm real," smiled Daphne. The grey eyes looked up at him steadily, as they had looked once before. "And I think I understand why you say that. Will you tell me why, please?"

Still holding her shoulders, Dennis glanced behind him. He saw the farmhouse, stone-built and yet ghostlike, looking against a purple-tinged evening sky. He saw the laurel-bush that concealed its plywood dummy. He saw other such dummies, faintly glimpsed through the windows; and it grew confused, somehow, with an image of the Granada Theatre. It was a long time before Dennis answered.

"Make-believe!" he said.

THE BESTSELLING NOVELS
BEHIND THE BLOCKBUSTER MOVIES —
ZEBRA'S MOVIE MYSTERY GREATS!

HIGH SIERRA   (2059, $3.50)
by W.R. Burnett
A dangerous criminal on the lam is trapped in a terrifying web of circumstance. The tension-packed novel that inspired the 1955 film classic starring Humphrey Bogart and directed by John Houston.

MR. ARKADIN   (2145, $3.50)
by Orson Welles
A playboy's search to uncover the secrets of financier Gregory Arkadin's hidden past exposes a worldwide intrigue of big money, corruption — and murder. Orson Welles's only novel, and the basis for the acclaimed film written by, directed by, and starring himself.

NOBODY LIVES FOREVER   (2217, $3.50)
by W.R. Burnett
Jim Farrar's con game backfires when his beautiful victim lures him into a dangerous deception that could only end in death. A 1946 cinema classic starring John Garfield and Geraldine Fitzgerald. (AVAILABLE IN FEBRUARY 1988)

BUILD MY GALLOWS HIGH   (2341, $3.50)
by Geoffrey Homes
When Red Bailey's former lover Mumsie McGonigle lured him from the Nevada hills back to the deadly hustle of New York City, the last thing the ex-detective expected was to be set up as a patsy and framed for a murder he didn't commit. The novel that inspired the screen gem OUT OF THE PAST, starring Robert Mitchum and Kirk Douglas. (AVAILABLE IN APRIL 1988)

Available wherever paperbacks are sold, or order direct from the Publisher. Send cover price plus 50¢ per copy for mailing and handling to Zebra Books, Dept. 2384, 475 Park Avenue South, New York, N.Y. 10016. Residents of New York, New Jersey and Pennsylvania must include sales tax. DO NOT SEND CASH.